DOORS

## Other writings by Eugene A. Kelly

For What It's Worth: A Guide For New Stockbrokers (1985)
For What It's Worth: A Guide For New Financial Advisors (2001)
The Pendulum Letters (1990 – 2019)


## Under The Name E. Aly

107 Secrets To Success For The Graduate (2019)
For What It's Worth Essay Blog (2019 - )
Change Happens But Will They Understand (2021)
Three Questions (2021)
19 Rules for Getting Rich and Staying Rich Despite Wall Street (2022)
A Third Option (2022)

E. Aly

Marshwinds
Press Company

ISBN: 978-1-7341170-8-0   (Hardback)
ISBN: 978-1-7341170-9-7   (Paperback)
ISBN: 979-8-9936432-0-5   (Ebook)
ISBN: 979-8-9936432-1-2   (Audible)

Library of Congress Control Number: 2025923228

Category: Fiction

Book Club virtual readings and Q&A sessions are available by contacting:

Marshwinds Press Company
P. O. Box 21099
St. Simons Island, Ga 31522
646-283-1115
or go to www.uniquereads.com

Cover and Interior Design:  Glen Edelstein, Hudson Valley Book Design

*For Judy,*
*Who makes it all possible.*

# DOORS

# CHAPTER 1

Today was the day, and David J. Hopkins-Wilson knew it. Bonuses would be distributed and new managing directors named. He wore his tailored pinstripe navy suit, a white silk French-cuff shirt, and his one and only Hermes tie with its gold background and small red diamond pattern, the one Meg gave him when they got married. David knew his bonus would be in six figures, and he might be promoted. He sat in his cubicle on the firm's expansive customer office floor, sipping coffee with the *Wall Street Journal* spread open. He started on page one and was now on page five, scanning, and speed-reading any article that might offer a clue to the fate of the markets and companies his clients owned. He liked being the only person in the office before seven. When he arrived each morning and saw the numerous cubicles and the few private offices along the outer wall of windows, he vowed to himself that he would have one of those offices soon—as a stepping stone to the executive floor. It was his early-bird-gets-the-worm attitude and determination that got him through four years of undergrad at Princeton and his Harvard MBA classes.

He was startled when his email chimed. Looking up, his surprise turned to delight as he read:

*David,*
*Please come up to my office as soon as possible.*
*Earl Stoddard*

His anticipation turned to glee. He may get a promotion, an office, and the bonus. There could be no other reason behind this summons to the rarefied world of the executive floor, with its paneled walls, oriental carpets, private dining room, and hushed atmosphere. For more than a month, he had spent his expected bonus over and over in his head. He and Meg would take a celebratory week in St. Bart's. They would begin looking for an apartment they could own instead of rent. They would get a two-bedroom unit so they could share the extra room as an office. He'd have bookcases on two walls and let Meg place her desk in front of the window. His thoughts turned to a potential promotion and a higher base salary. Meg would be ecstatic. He straightened his tie and put on his suitcoat.

"Come in, David," said Earl Stoddard III, executive vice president of Murray, Davidson, and Stoddard, known on the Street as MD&S and by some competitors as Mad Dogs & Schmucks. Stoddard motioned to a chair in front of his desk.

"Good morning, Earl," David responded, sticking with the firm's culture of always using first names. His heart raced from the excitement of being in a partner's office. Four years ago, starting as a business development officer, he had set his sights on making it to this executive floor within ten years. When he became a relationship officer three years ago, he knew he was on the fast track. Sure, he had inherited some accounts, but he had opened others and skillfully communicated with his clients, helping them see the merits of the investments the firm's bankers crafted. The market had been good over the last four years, and he was now responsible for over a billion dollars in client assets. He had a little over five years to go to achieve his goal, and Stoddard recognizing him was proof that his path to the executive floor was clear.

There was a light knock at the office door. "Come in," Earl called out. Turning to David, he said, "I've asked Robert Exeter to sit in on our meeting."

Exeter slid into the room, nodded at Stoddard and David, and sat in a chair off to the side. David didn't know Exeter or what he did, but from the way he carried himself, he figured he was a senior executive.

As Exeter was making his way to the chair, David took a moment to look around the office. It looked just the way he would have his future office. The chairs and sofa were covered in money-green tufted leather. The oriental rugs were old and looked expensive. The partner's desk was massive. The bookcases were full of books—some sets, but mostly newer titles covering all aspects of business. There were no glaring overhead lights. Illumination came from five crystal lamps. The end tables and coffee table were antiques. Every aspect evoked power and wealth. Yes, this was what David wanted, and he would do what it took to get it. As he'd already done uncountable times, David committed himself to being an important person in the firm of MD&S. He turned his attention to Stoddard, who started reading from a paper Exeter handed him.

"David Hopkins-Wilson, due to your inappropriate and negligent placing of unsuitable securities in your clients' accounts, you are summarily dismissed from Murray, Davidson, & Stoddard. Your U5 regulatory form will corroborate this finding. It is our agreement with the SEC that this termination will take place immediately." Stoddard put down the paper and looked at David.

David's breath caught in his chest. The silence was deafening. Unable to speak, he began hyperventilating. Tears rolled down his face. Finally, he broke the silence. "There must be some mistake. I never placed any investment in a client's account that the client didn't agree with. You're wrong. What are you talking about?"

Stoddard looked at Exeter.

Exeter coughed once and said, "Is Elinor Jacobson one of your accounts?"

"Yes, of course."

"Is Ms. Jacobson in her eighties?"

"Yes."

"Last October, did you place $250,000 of her inherited IRA portfolio in the Ivanhoe LBO LP?"

David's stomach convulsed in rhythm with the staccato questioning by Exeter. When the bile reached his throat, he put his hand to his mouth and clenched his jaw. Stoddard saw David's face go pale, grabbed the trash can sitting next to his desk, and almost made it to David as the vomit spewed from his mouth.

After a couple more retches, David mumbled, "I'm sorry." Sitting back in his chair, with his fingers white as he gripped the chair's armrests, he continued. "Please, there has to be a mistake. You can't do this to me. I didn't do anything wrong. I don't understand." He pleadingly looked at Stoddard with perspiration and tears rolling down his face and dropping on his coat and shirt. Spittle on his chin followed the path of the vomit and sweat.

"Did you place $250,000 of the Ivanhoe LBO LP in Mrs. Jacobson's inherited IRA last October?" Exeter asked again.

"Yes, but she asked for the investment. *She* called *me*. Said her friends were investing and she wanted to invest."

"What friends?"

"She didn't say."

"Mrs. Jacobson says you coerced her to make the investment. She said it was your idea, that you told her she would make a lot of money."

"That's not true," David insisted. "Look at the accredited investor form and the trade ticket. Both are marked 'unsolicited.' She requested the investment."

"She has testified that she knew nothing about the investment. You told her it was safe, and she only signed papers you said were necessary to make the money."

David stared past Stoddard and tried to remember everything about the phone conversation with Mrs. Jacobson. She had called him. She did ask for the investment. He thought it was an odd choice since her investments were all bonds and stock mutual funds. He'd asked her why she wanted the Ivanhoe, and she did say that her friends were investing, and she wanted to do so as well. She picked the amount. He, David, didn't argue with her. The investment helped him meet his goal, and she had called him. She wanted the investment. He didn't sell her the partnership.

David was about to respond when Exeter pulled out a sheet of paper from his folio and handed it to him. It was his own tally sheet about the Ivanhoe investment, showing each client who invested and the amount. He'd wondered where the worksheet went, and now he knew. Anger began rising. He was being railroaded by that bitch.

"Is that your handwriting and your list?" Exeter asked.

"Yeah, it's mine." David noticed that Exhibit A was stamped across the top.

"It shows a goal across the top of $3 million, then a list of accounts with amounts alongside each name and a total at the bottom of $2.75 million. Below that total is the name Jacobson, the number $250 thousand, and the word 'bingo.'" Stoddard half-smiled and sat back in his chair. The smile turned into a smirk.

"Please, I can explain." The air in the office was now putrid with vomit and fear. "Please listen. She called me. When the call was over, I wrote that last line. It was her idea to make the investment. She called me."

Stoddard sat forward and snarled. "That's not her story. But even if it were, she's a widow in her eighties with two million in an inherited

IRA account, and she needs regular withdrawals. You put 12.5% of those assets in a high-risk, long-term private placement that can't be readily sold. What were you thinking? I'll tell you what: you were thinking of yourself, not the client or the firm."

"Charles said the investment was good for anyone with a million in their account. He said it was safe and should do well." David rubbed his face vigorously with both hands and wiped them on his suit coat. He loosened his tie without thinking, then immediately tightened it back up. His mind raced from one thought to another. He knew the Ivanhoe investment had started going bad almost immediately, but he'd trusted that the firm's investment bankers had done their due diligence and were not stupid. They would make it work out because so many of the firm's best clients were involved.

"So now you're saying your boss told you to stick little eighty-year-old ladies in this security? Have you gone brain dead? Did you forget about fiduciary duty and suitability? I thought you would be a man about this. Mr. Exeter has some papers for you to sign. If you sign and leave quietly, you will get to keep your deferred comp and 401(k), and you'll have COBRA healthcare for eighteen months or until you're covered elsewhere."

David's anxiety and fear were receding and his anger rising. "And if I don't?" David asked.

"We'll move to sue you for your 401(k) account and deferred comp, cut off your medical benefits, and seek a final judgment that will put you in bankruptcy." Stoddard smiled.

"What about the bonus I'm due for last year's performance?"

"No one gets a bonus for failing to abide by the fiduciary principles of the firm. We are making Mrs. Jacobson whole. Your bonus doesn't cover the amount we paid her—that's why you'll lose the deferred comp too if you don't sign."

Anger and discipline began penetrating the fog of stress. He knew he could immediately get another job on the Street. He knew that MD&S was just covering their asses. He was being sacrificed to the regulators on the altar of it's-not-our-fault. He never thought he would be the fresh meat thrown to the regulatory lions to save senior management. It wasn't fair, but it happened every day. He'd have another position before the day was over.

"I'll sign," David said, recovering some composure as he mentally ticked off the five firms he would contact tomorrow. Tomorrow—Christ, he remembered the group was coming to his apartment tonight for their regular biweekly get-together.

Exeter put the papers in front of David with a pen. David started to read the first one, but the rancid smell of his vomit in the room prodded him to sign and get the hell out of there. The fine print didn't matter—he had to sign or lose everything, not just the bonus. He thought of Meg. She would be devastated. He scrawled his signature on each page. A door slamming shut was all he could think about. Fil always said that when one door slams shut, just open another one. He kept repeating the mantra in his head. He decided he wouldn't tell Meg until he had signed on with another firm. Then he'd tell her it had been his idea to switch—better payout and all those logical reasons. Hell, he'd probably be able to talk his new employer into a signing bonus. After all, his reputation as a rising star was well known at other firms. Some of his present clients would follow him wherever he went. Yeah, when one door closes, open another door. He'd always seen the light at the end of the tunnel. He'd make MD&S regret what they had done. He was a survivor.

He rose unsteadily from the chair. Exeter handed him an envelope. David looked down at his name, and the return address sent a chill through his body: Securities and Exchange Commission. "What's this?" David looked from Exeter to Stoddard.

Stoddard, with a twisted, cruel smile, said, "That is a letter from the SEC, which, by the way, will be filed attached to your U5, barring you from the financial services industry for ten years."

David J. Hopkins-Wilson fainted.

*    *    *

David sat in his reeking clothes on his apartment's sofa. His personal effects were in a box by the door. He slowly came out of the daze of the last hour. After fainting, he had been revived and escorted out of the building into a company car, where the box of his personal items was already on the back seat, and driven home. The fleeting thought of opening a new door tomorrow had evaporated like a mirage when he'd been told he was barred from the industry for ten years. Hell, why ten years? That was the same as being barred for life. He had no idea what he was going to do. How to reverse this debacle was the immediate question. How? He didn't have the money for an attorney. His wife was the type he needed, but he couldn't ask her to take on MD&S—they were clients of her firm.

The putrid smell overwhelmed his senses. He struggled to his feet, stripped naked, and decided to just throw away the two-thousand-dollar suit, tie, and shirt.

Thirty minutes later, David lay naked on his bed, staring at the ceiling, trying to pull together a plan. The most immediate task was creating a menu for tonight and going to Whole Foods three blocks away to get the ingredients. His mood lifted. Being a foodie was his love in life. He did all the grocery buying, menu curating, and cooking for himself and Meg. It was the time he locked out all the problems of the world and just focused on enjoyment. That's what he'd do the rest of the day and evening. Tomorrow would be the time to tell Meg and figure out what he would do with his life. He'd get his deferred comp and 401(k) account transferred so he could use them as a bridge to the future. He closed his eyes and saw his hand on a new doorknob, opening a door to a new future.

# CHAPTER 2

"David, come on and join us. You planning on staying in the kitchen all night?" Sherm called from the living room, where he sat between his wife Carrie and David's wife Meg, with both arms on the back of the sofa and each hand playing with one woman's hair. Meg's head tilted slightly toward Sherm. Joe and Cindy Albertson looked at each other. They were surprised at Sherm's blatant signaling of future complications for the group. The apartment David and Meg rented was typical Manhattan, but it had one unique feature. The bedroom was tiny, overwhelmed by their queen-sized bed, and the living/dining area was small, but Meg had arranged the sofa, two chairs, and the side tables so that, when they had more than five, they could bring over some of the six dining chairs to make seating for more. The unusual feature was the kitchen. It had a Wolf six-burner gas stove, a Subzero refrigerator, a Wolf microwave, and long counters of prep space. There was no dishwasher. That didn't bother David or Meg; they wouldn't have used one, since none of their porcelain, silverware, or crystal was dishwasher safe. Best of all, the apartment was only two blocks from the Union Square green market and three blocks from Whole Foods.

"Be right there," David called back. He walked out of the kitchen holding his bourbon glass. "We have fifteen minutes, so drink up, conquerors of New York City. Sherm, don't you think the Wild Turkey Rare Breed is more enjoyable than playing with my wife's hair?" Sherm moved his arm from the back of the sofa behind Meg. David sat down on the couch arm, giving his wife a peck on the cheek. She half-smiled and reached for one of the three sesame-seed crackers smothered with Abbaye de Belloc French goat cheese and red pepper jelly.

"Carrie, try some of this goat cheese David discovered at the green market last weekend. It goes heavenly with pepper jelly," Meg said, handing a cracker to Sherm's wife.

"So, Joe, how goes online retailing?" Sherm asked.

"It's going. We just closed on our first round of venture capital, giving us enough to go live for at least eighteen months. Thank you, Meg," Joe said, raising his glass in salute. "If it wasn't for Meg's legal guidance, I'm not sure we would still be in control of the business."

"Who's handling your social media marketing?" Carrie asked.

"Cin is doing it herself," Joe said, patting his wife's knee.

Cindy added, "Strictly social media at this point. We intend to introduce various approaches to marketing in a way that lets us determine the effectiveness of each approach so we don't lose control of what works and what doesn't. By the way, David, I read rumors on Facebook and LinkedIn today saying your firm is in hot water with the financial cops for some bad things done to clients. What's up?"

David felt his face begin to burn. He took a sip of his bourbon and looked over the glass at these three friends who had gone to Harvard Business School with him; Carrie, who had earned her MFA from Harvard at the same time, and Joe's wife Cindy, whom Joe had met in NYC two years ago. The five Harvard grads had stayed in contact through these formative years since graduating. When Joe married Cindy, he'd had two best men, and she'd had two matrons of honor.

Sherman Church, called Sherm, and his wife Carrie worked in tech for different start-ups. Sherm's firm was growing faster, and he was reaping the rewards. Joe and Cindy were building a start-up online hardware store focused on supplying tools and such to millennials living in big cities. Together, the Albertsons' income was barely adequate to maintain their lifestyle, so when it was their turn to host the biweekly gathering, it was usually a picnic in Central Park.

David said, "You know, the same old BS. It'll blow over as it always does. What you need to know is that tonight we're having Wagyu beef with diced potatoes and a small side salad of arugula, toasted pecans, cherry tomatoes, and my secret salad dressing. All the ingredients are from Whole Foods this time—the Union Square green market was closed today. For dessert, there's hot spice cake from Breads Bakery with a dollop of vanilla bean gelato from Whole Foods."

"A dollop, eh? Is that a word in the dictionary or secret foodie jargon?" Sherm asked. He drained his glass and shook his head as the bourbon burned his throat. "Whew, Meg, now I see why you chose David over me."

"Among other skills," she retorted with a grin.

"Touché," Sherman said, lifting his empty glass in salute.

David got up from the couch arm using his wife's knee to assist him, which he squeezed gently, and started to the kitchen. "I've got to go check on the Wagyu and begin plating this culinary extraordinaire. Dinner is served in seven minutes."

When they were getting married, David and Meg asked their families to give them fine porcelain and sterling silver tableware, even if the giver had to just present them a gift certificate from a jewelry store. From the beginning, they wanted to have only the best in their life. They had selected Herend Rothschild Bird porcelain and dinner-sized Tiffany sterling silver tableware. Meg had scoured antique stores in Boston and New York and assembled a collection of Steuben air twist glasses. This expensive tableware was not just for company; they used it whenever they ate at home. It was their little reminder that they were special and going upward in their careers. They were the only ones among their friends who had this constant reminder of their destiny. It made no difference that it took extra time and effort to handwash and dry these pieces. That effort, in and of itself, was a reminder of who they were and where they were going.

"That was fun. You really outdid yourself with that meal—maybe you should have been a chef instead of a financial consultant. By the way, what was that about MD&S and the regulators?" Meg said, as she dried a dish from the dish rack.

"Nothing much. There was a complaint by an eighty-year-old client when one of her investments tanked." David didn't look up as he took another dish from the soapy water in the sink.

"That shouldn't have made the internet. It happens all the time." Meg continued drying.

"Well, she'd been with the firm for fifty years, and the investment was a firm-created 'product,' as the new MBAs call 'em, which seemed safe but blew up in a way no one thought possible."

"But she approved it, right?"

"Yeah, but not necessarily. The investment is in her IRA, and that brings it under the Department of Labor Fiduciary Rule. The DOL and the public investor legal bar, no offense, have been impatiently waiting for an opportunity to cream a firm and its people for supposedly putting the firm's and the professionals' interests before the client's. The DOL and SEC came in with both barrels blasting." David let the water out of the sink and dried his hands.

"That doesn't seem fair."

"Fairness no longer enters into it. Whether any of the lambs working in the business know it or not, the regulators have served up the financial relationship business to the wolves on a silver platter. Just in case the ambulance chasers don't have the brains, the regulators give them perfect twenty-twenty hindsight to help them out. You'll make millions in corporate law, but you'll seem like a pauper compared to these guys—excuse me, and gals."

"Who was the unprofessional shyster in the fiasco?"

David hesitated, devastated by Meg's description. What could he say? Was this the right time to tell her? "Just a new guy. You wouldn't know him."

"At least it wasn't you. I thought bonuses were being given out today. Did you get yours? Wasn't it a six-figure amount?"

"Tomorrow. Tomorrow is the day. Yeah, it's supposed to be six figures."

Meg dried the last dish and reached to put it on the shelf, stretching to show the leanness and flexibility of her body.

"Thanks for helping me with the dishes," David said.

"You're welcome. Now," Meg said, turning to David and kissing his neck, "I'm going to take a shower, get in bed naked but wet between my legs, and wait for you to do me long and rough."

"Sounds like a plan. I'm going to have another drink and will be in when I hear the shower stop." David forced a smile as he watched her walk to the bedroom. He knew the Sherm effect was at work. Meg and Sherm were soulmates during graduate school before she caught him in bed with Carrie. No matter what, she was obviously still attracted to him. David was assured of sex after every biweekly get-together. His benefit, at least. When was he going to tell her? Tomorrow, maybe? His stomach churned as he realized he had no idea what he was going to do for a job.

# CHAPTER 3

David called out to the closed bathroom door, "I'm going. See you this evening. Have a good day. Love you." He looked one last time in the closet door mirror, straightened his tie, put on his suit coat, and picked up his briefcase. He fought back the feeling of the absurdity of this charade. It was necessary.

He took the stairs down two at a time and pushed through the glass door onto the street. Looking to his right, he could see the tents the vendors were setting up for today's green market in Union Square. The green market was the major plus of living in this part of Manhattan. With the market, it was easy to overlook the grittiness of the area. Mix a lot of commerce with young up-and-comers, and you had the Union Square–Gramercy Park–Washington Square–Flat Iron area of the city. The neighborhood's vibe was different from other neighborhoods. The fast, get-out-of-my-way swagger of young professionals had always been its hallmark. The fresh-out-of-college or grad school transplants demanded the opportunity to rake in their share of the pot of gold at this end of the rainbow since the late 1800s. The creed "fake it till you make it" had become reality. What they didn't and couldn't show, if they wanted to keep their place in the crowd, was the insecurity that built day by day as naive self-confidence was ground down by the reality of survival of the fittest. Daily life in the city, where everything costs more—what locals call the mafia tax—was doable if a person had thirty hours in a day. Figuring out how to stretch junior-level income to pay rent, grocery bills, laundry, and the happy hour tab for networking on top of student loan payments was what burned out most wannabes.

David wanted to go right and walk through Union Square, but knew he had to disappear before Meg came down the stairs, so he turned left and briskly walked to Fifth Avenue, turned right, checked his watch, and was confident that Mass would be over before he reached the church. A few blocks later, he slipped into the side door of St. William's. Candles burning and the aroma of incense in the air reminded him of another less stressful time, a time when childhood activities and the discipline of the nuns and priests were the guiding light. He was an only child, but no doting parents had spoiled him. He was raised in Savannah, Georgia, a southern historic port city, by a single father who never mentioned David's mother. His father was kind but indifferent to his son. As a skilled carpenter, he worked when he wanted to and didn't seem to want to, most of the time, so the two of them barely got by. Catholic school education was just another way for his father to avoid exerting himself. The entire twelve years required uniforms, so he bought David two sets each year, one to wear and one for the laundry basket. David learned to iron, cook, and do laundry out of necessity. He didn't mind. He had no idea he was from a lower socioeconomic level than most of the other kids. What he did know was that he liked school and the interaction with the teachers, who he believed knew more than anyone else in the world. He liked being an altar boy. He always volunteered for funerals and weddings, where a gratuity was standard. Unlike other guys, he stayed an altar boy until he was old enough to get a part-time job at the grill around the corner from St. Jerome's School for Boys.

David sat in the last pew of St. William's, staring at the altar, remembering the happiest years of his young life. Filip Kowalski, Fil for short, had influenced his life more than his father and all the nuns and priests at school. Fil was alone, had come to this country when he was eight after World War II, and left school in ninth grade. He went back to Poland as a young man, going from job to job for four years, but realized that living under communism was brutal. Returning to the US, he found his calling in his thirties when he bought a used flat iron grill and other utensils that were being thrown out by a restaurant supply store. He rented a rundown store front and went into business. He set up Fil's Grill in that small space on a busy street around the corner from a park. Hamburgers, hot dogs, chips, and ice-cold drinks were what he sold. Nothing else. Customers could get chili, relish, ketchup, and mustard on the dogs and cheese, lettuce, tomato, raw onions, mayo, ketchup, and mustard on the burgers. As he'd said over and over, "KISS, David, KISS. Keep it simple, stupid." The business was steady and profitable, earning Fil a comfortable living by being open from eight thirty in the morning to four thirty in the afternoon.

When David first appeared at his door looking for afterschool work, Fil had turned him away, saying the grill didn't need anyone. David went back every day for a week offering to sweep the place for a dollar or wipe the tables for a dollar.

Finally, after a week of showing up, Fil asked him, "Why do you want to work here?" David told him the truth: he needed a job, this place was close to school, and he thought it was a neat business, serving people what they wanted. Fil hired him at fifty cents an hour for two and a half hours after school and nine hours on Saturday. "The first time you miss a day, you're fired," Fil said.

David learned everything. The bathrooms needed to be spotless, even though the clientele tried their best to mess them up. The pine wood floors needed to shine, even though mayo, ketchup, mustard, and sticky soft drinks had splattered and spilled on them during the day. The wooden tables and chairs were spotless when David left in the evenings. After a year, when David was a sophomore, Fil added cleaning the grill to David's duties. That same year, Fil showed him how to have enough chips and food on hand but not so much that it would go bad. By the time he was a senior in high school, David was running the place while Fil sat at the counter, reading the *Wall Street Journal* and kibitzing with the regulars.

David applied to Princeton on a lark and had been accepted. An academic scholarship, some grants, and part-time jobs let him squeak by at college. Holidays and summers, he worked with Fil. At the Christmas holiday his college sophomore year, David arrived back in Savannah, Georgia, to find his father had moved and left no forwarding address. David was eighteen and homeless. Fil let him sleep on a sofa bed in his one-bedroom place. Three years later, David graduated from Princeton, returned to Savannah, and found out Fil had been diagnosed with terminal pancreatic cancer. David turned down the three job offers he had, lived with Fil, ran the grill, and took care of Fil until he died. It was only then that David found out Fil had a daughter in Poland he had never seen. They had written to each other off and on over the years. It was clear from reading the letters that the daughter was not well and had spent most of her life taking care of her mother. David operated the grill until he could sell it. Taking the sale proceeds and what Fil had in the bank, he wrote the daughter a letter and sent her the money. David applied to Harvard Business School, determined to be a success.

The thought of success jolted him back to reality. What would Fil say to him now? David knew. He could hear Fil's accented voice loud and clear, just as if the man were sitting in the pew next to him. "When a door slams in your face, turn and open another door."

Okay, Fil, how do I find another door? he thought. He sat there, willing his mind to put aside the panic of being jobless and barred from a brokerage job for life, having to tell Meg, and worrying about their future, which took two high-paying careers to sustain. He needed to think as an analyst. That was it! He could go to LinkedIn and search for analyst jobs on the buy side. That was the answer. The buy side. An analyst's position could lead to a portfolio manager's position. Investing rather than selling. He had a Harvard MBA. He could start right away on a CFA designation. A chartered financial analyst designation would be a door opener. Since the CFA test was offered twice a year, he could have the CFA designation in less than two years—assuming he passed each level the first time, which was challenging since as many as 50 percent of the test takers failed each year. Open a door. He had a plan. With a plan, he could easily explain to Meg and, at the same time, show her how they were going to get through this. His 401(k) money and deferred comp would cover his share of living expenses. She'd understand. They were a couple, a team, lovers. This was just a bump in the road. All couples go through tough times. For better or worse, the vows went. Rough times melded a couple into one loving being. When a door slams shut, open another door. He had a plan.

David looked at the altar and told Fil he loved him, missed him, and thanked him for showing him the way through this mess. Yeah, Meg would understand, wouldn't she?

# CHAPTER 4

The menu had to be perfect. Long Island duck, orange glaze, haricots verts, and a few, very few fingerling potatoes basted in olive oil and Provence herbs were her favorites. Good food and wine would put Meg in the right mood. Leaving St. William's, he returned home and changed into a wool shirt, jeans, brogans, and his Barbour jacket. He picked up his green market canvas shopping bag and went to Union Square with a bounce in his step. A door was opening. A plan to start another career was exciting. A plan and a purpose always cleared a path forward. Starting on the Park Avenue South side of the market, he took his time inspecting and selecting the best-quality produce for the right price. He knew his meal had to be perfect to show Meg everything was going to be okay. By the time he got to the Broadway side, he had the fresh ingredients for an over-the-top dinner. Something elegant and simple. Something that wouldn't dirty too many dishes, so they could go to bed early and hold each other after making love, both understanding they were in this together.

David set the table with candles and decanted a Bordeaux merlot while keeping it below room temperature. He had texted Meg earlier and told her he had a surprise, asking what time she would be home. It was now seven thirty, so she was late, but that was fine. He took another sip of wine to steady his nerves. Over and over, he practiced his presentation out loud, just as he would for the job interviews he knew were coming. He had sent out twenty-five resumés through LinkedIn today. His strategy was underway. He was opening a new door. He could do it. At that moment, the apartment door opened.

"Sorry I'm late. This case I'm on is complicated and time consuming." Meg threw her coat and briefcase on the sofa and turned, seeing the table for the first time. "Well, what's going on here? You got promoted? I hope so because I found an incredible 1880 antique sewing desk for the apartment. It's expensive, but its provenance is impressive. Got a glass of that for me?"

"Sure do. No, I didn't get promoted. Meg, I'm changing careers—well, sort of." David handed Meg her glass of merlot and couldn't control the shaking in his hand. "I'm leaving MD&S and going to be an analyst."

"What? What do you mean, you're leaving MD&S? You're the fair-haired boy. The up-and-coming client relationships superstar."

"Not anymore, Meg." David's well-planned script went out the window. "I've been fired."

"Fired? How? Why? This can't be happening. Oh my God, wait! Jesus, you were the one. Are you the dumb schmuck responsible for that investment crap, the one that screwed over that old lady?"

"Yes, she was my client. I was told that the investment was appropriate. I was told that, but I knew it wasn't appropriate, and I sold it to her anyway. I really messed up. Now I'm the scapegoat. Nevertheless, I put a plan in place today. I sent out twenty-five resumés to buy-side firms today for an analyst position. I'll probably hear back tomorrow and have something by the end of the month."

Meg slumped into a chair at the table. She looked at David, her face contorted, her brow wrinkled, and her eyes as wide as saucers. "How?

How could you do this to me? How could you? Son of a bitch. This isn't real. How could you?" Now she wasn't looking at David, just at her wineglass, and shaking her head from side to side. "What am I to tell them at the law firm? I'm under review for senior associate status, one step away from partner. They're not going to give me a promotion knowing my husband is a cheat and got fired from his job. I'll be tainted goods, even though it was no fault of mine. Goddamn it, how could you do this to me?"

She looked up at David. The hurt in her face was gone, replaced with pure rage. Her beet-red skin signaled the inferno within her. Her eyes were watery but huge, with sparks almost visible. One hand was on the table and one trembling, trying to hold the wineglass.

"Meg, please, calm down for a minute. I can explain. I have a plan for how to explain it to people. It will look like a normal progression from client relationship to analyst on the way to portfolio management. It can be positioned right. I don't know how much I'll make, but my 401(k) and deferred comp can be tapped to carry us through. Please calm down and see the plan."

"Calm down? You've been fired. For all we know, you might not be able to get another job in the industry. You don't think everyone is going to know what you did? Are you a moron? Jesus, I thought you were brighter than that." She shook her head in disgust.

"Let's eat dinner, have some wine. I've fixed your favorite duck, green beans, and fingerlings, with a special dessert from Breads Bakery. Everything will work out, I promise." David moved to the kitchen to take the duck out of the warming oven.

Meg jumped to her feet, knocking over the wineglass, which shattered on the table and splattered wine everywhere, while her chair tipped over backward. "How can you even think of eating at a time like this?" she snarled, storming off to the bedroom. David heard the bedroom door slam, and to his surprise, the lock turned. Cold adrenaline moved through his body. Fear paralyzed him. He looked around the kitchen and dining area. Was this another slammed door? David told himself he needed her, and it couldn't be. He poured himself another glass of wine. She'll calm down, he told himself, and then we'll talk it through. Give her some space and time. They were lovers and partners for life. Their vows and marriage certificate proved it.

When he had finished cleaning up and putting away the food, he heard the bedroom door lock click. David smiled. She was calming down. Using her head. Probably figured a way for the two of them to make it work. Now, together, they would plan.

Meg stalked out of the bedroom into the living room, grabbed her briefcase, and went back to the bedroom. She slammed the door, and the lock clicked again.

David sat there. He couldn't believe how loud the bedroom lock sounded when it turned. What did it sound like? He couldn't figure it out. Suddenly, it came to him: a revolver cocking. He poured another glass of wine and sat on the sofa. His plan would work. Calls to some of his buddies from school would start networking. Hell, he was a member of NYSSA, the security analyst society. They had a whole group helping to place out-of-work professionals. David turned on the TV and channel surfed. He turned it off, unable to concentrate or take an interest in anything. Deep inside, he knew Meg's reaction was not that of a loving wife who stood by her man. Every time he allowed this thought into his mind, he got a cold, weak feeling in his stomach. He drank his wine, waiting for her to unlock the door. Meg had made the same vows he had—in sickness and in health, for better or worse. He wasn't going to beg. Going to the kitchen, he poured another glass of wine and returned to the sofa. A few minutes later, he got up again, went to the kitchen, brought the wine bottle back to the living room, and put it on the coffee table in front of him. May as well get anesthetized, he thought. Two more glasses, and he laid his head against the back of the sofa for a minute.

David jerked awake when he heard a revolver cock as he dreamed of standing on a balcony looking into a dark hole. Light was streaming through the living room windows. He looked down at the empty wine bottle. God, he thought. I drank the whole bottle. At that moment, he heard the bedroom door open. He immediately closed his eyes and pretended to be asleep. He wondered if Meg had come out during the night to apologize for overreacting, saw him asleep, and left him there. When she spoke to him, he'd pretend he just woke up and be positive with her.

Meg walked into the living room and crossed over to the apartment door, opened it, and walked out. No hesitation, no words, nothing.

David kept his eyes closed until the door shut. Open a new door, open a new door—he kept repeating what Fil had taught him. He just lay there, the back of his head and neck aching from the wine and his position on the sofa. Getting up was step one. There were probably several responses to his resumés. He'd wait just a few more minutes. Just relax. Then, he realized it was Saturday.

His whole body jerked up straight as his eyes flew open. Meg shouldn't be going to work this morning. Her firm had new rules: associates had to take Saturday off, Sunday too. They could work twenty-hour days from Monday to Friday, but they had the weekend off to spend with their families. Some crap about work–life balance to make up for the semi-slave conditions Monday through Friday. Where was she going? Obviously, she was going to her office, but why no good-bye, I'll be back later, kiss my ass, or anything? David sat there. He looked around the room. The few oil paintings on the walls, the two antique tables, and the early eighteenth-century cabinet holding the Herend porcelain were items that were proof of their togetherness and shared future. Were they a lie? Were they just a facade for two people who really didn't like each other? David knew he was sincere. He loved Meg. Loved her from the first time he had met her.

*   *   *

Meg was Sherm's fiancée. Both of them were at Harvard Business School, affectionately known as HBS, and intended to get married the day after graduation. They were the golden couple. Meg wore her auburn hair shoulder length, parted on one side, with the length shorter on the right and longer on the left. The hair framed her hazel eyes, button nose, and small mouth, accentuating all three features. Her golden facial complexion added mystery to her face and caused anyone looking at her to wonder if her coloring extended all over her sensuous body.

Sherm was not an athlete, nor did he obsess like his contemporaries in the gym about trying to build a model's body—he had a model's body without effort. The people he met saw nothing but an aura of success. His sandy hair went with his brown eyes. He was always dressed correctly, not in the jeans-and-T-shirt uniform students wore. He wore collared shirts, chinos, and loafers—nothing fancy to take away from his natural magnetism. When he graduated, he connected with a Hong Kong tailor, sent his measurements, and wore only tailored suits with a white breast pocket handkerchief and gleaming polished lace-up shoes. Associates, superiors, and clients knew Sherm was brilliant, elegant, and sophisticated, but they couldn't put their finger on why.

Meg and Sherm were top of their classes academically. She was dual enrolled in HBS and Harvard Law. Sherm was the one their classmates knew would one day make billions and Harvard would name a building for him. The summer after their first year, Sherm was Sherm. He went to McConnell's Pub with David and some friends while Meg worked on the *Law Review*. Carrie Brevard, the waitress, was cute and friendly. Sherm turned on the charm, acting the big shot he thought he was, always a little condescending to someone he thought was beneath him. It took only thirty seconds for her to cut him off at the knees. The entire table broke out in loud and rambunctious laughter, all at Sherm's expense. Before the evening was over, Sherm had her email and was focused on restoring his pride. It turned out that Carrie was a graduate student working on her MFA in art history, with an emphasis on fifteenth- and sixteenth-century European art. When school began, Meg dumped Sherm after she caught him in bed with Carrie. He moved into Carrie's apartment in graduate housing, and they were married that Christmas.

Meg was devastated and humiliated. She put up a good front, but David knew the truth, since he was Sherm's best friend. It was easy to "be there" for Meg, boosting her ego, taking her to the places she wanted to go, helping her save face, and, at the same time, taking pressure off Sherm. David and Meg threw themselves into their studies. David learned almost as much about business law as Meg did. She climbed the masthead at the *Harvard Law Review*. She proved to everyone except David that she didn't need Sherm. He knew the truth. She was shattered. David doted on Meg, helping her with her studies, taking her to school functions, and going to concerts and parties. All the while, he convinced himself he was playing a role to help Meg and his friend Sherm. He only fleetingly admitted to himself that he reveled in being seen with someone as attractive as Meg. Before long, he and Meg were a couple, and David didn't care that he was second choice and caught her on the rebound. She was his, and he loved that fact and her. Was it all a lie for Meg? Well, he'd find out now. She had to unlock their marriage door. Would she? He stirred and forced himself to get up. If he was going to open a new career door, it wasn't going to be done sitting on the sofa.

# CHAPTER 5

David took two Aleve and a cold shower, then shaved. Looking at the hoodie and jeans in the closet, he hesitated and shook his head. *I need something better, something that will say who I really am,* he thought. He reached for an Orvis plaid shirt and a pair of khakis with his brogans. He checked his email and LinkedIn. Nothing.

He grabbed his Barbour, a knit cap, and canvas market bag and headed to the green market. It was a chilly, clear-blue-sky day, and walking to the green market lifted his spirits. He loved Union Square and its farmers' market. He even loved the square when there wasn't a market.

Over the last 150 years, people have believed the square was named for the pro-Union rallies there during the Civil War. Others thought it was named for the many labor union rallies at the turn of the twentieth century. Neither story is correct. The name Union Square began because of the acute angle where Bloomingdale Road, now called Broadway, intersects with Bowery Road, two of New York's main streets in 1811. The Commissioners' Plan of 1811 ordered a survey, and in 1815, the commissioners decided to form a square at the "union" of these two streets. Even fewer people know that the square is over a potter's field, as are Madison Square Park, Washington Square Park, and Bryant Park.

Union Square, whatever its origin, is a vibrant place on Monday, Wednesday, Friday, and Saturday, as vendors and farmers entice New Yorkers with fresh produce. It is a foodie's heaven. The rest of the week, it's a place to go play chess with guys sitting on wooden crates, listen to someone protesting something—it doesn't matter what—or just sit on a bench and watch people as they wear their lives on their faces. What David knew was that Union Square always lifted his spirits. He wasn't sure why and didn't try to analyze the joy he felt as he stepped into the square. What he knew was that he felt a kinship with the entrepreneurs hawking their fruits, vegetables, baked goods, meats, homemade liquors, and plants displayed on wooden boxes and tables under their own tents. He read all the handmade signs at each tent. The urge to rewrite the signs to make them more sales oriented was strong. The whole shopping experience gave him excitement and joy. On other days, he enjoyed rooting for New Yorkers jousting with the realities of city life. To David, being in the square was being in a society of real people trying to do the best they could every day.

David started on the east side of the market and worked his way slowly toward the north and around to the west. He didn't get too far. At the third tent was an old man and his young grandson. On three sides of their space, the vendor had arranged tiered boxes containing apples, pears, dried beans, beets, cabbages, carrots, onions, parsnips, several types of potatoes, winter squash, and turnips. The old man was sitting in a folding aluminum chair reading the Wall Street Journal while the grandson stood ready to help any customers. Each produce box had a hand-lettered sign sticking out haphazardly.

David was studying the white potatoes when the grandson said, "Hey, can I help you?"

Without thinking, David said, "Hay is for horses." The young boy's smile disappeared.

"I was just kidding. That's something a friend of mine used to say whenever I said 'hey.' These potatoes look really good. As a matter of fact, all your produce looks good. I may be back."

David moved on.

"Don't mind him, Charlie. He's just one of the big-city smartasses. He won't be back," the old man said, not even looking up from his newspaper.

Two hours later, David was back at the tent. "Hi," he said, laying his still-empty canvas bag on a box of beets. He turned his attention to the old man. "I'd like to make you an offer. I'll exchange a day's work for enough fixings for dinner," he said with a smile.

The old man looked David over. "Nope, that's not fair. I tell you what"—he looked at his watch—"you work the rest of the day and help us pack up, and I'll pay you fifty dollars if we sell out. If we don't, I'll pay you twenty-five, and you pay for whatever produce you want."

David smiled. "Agreed."

"All right. I'm Dex, and this here is Charlie." Dex held out his hand.

David felt Dex's iron grip and said, "I'm David."

He took his place at the tables with Charlie. Dex sat back down and resumed reading the paper, keeping an eye on David. Charlie kept up an endless chatter, and David ignored most of it, but nodded his head appropriately as they bagged produce for customers and made change. Just after lunch, David and Charlie were discussing their favorite potato variety when a man appeared in a white chef's coat. He selected vegetables and brought them over to David and Charlie. David started putting the items in a bag, while Charlie added up the cost.

"Hurry up, will you?" the man said. "It's eighteen dollars, for Christ's sake."

Charlie blushed and looked at Dex.

"Having a frustrating day?" David asked with a smile. "I am too. Say, are you looking to put together a vegetable plate, or are you going to serve pork with these? I really like pork loin basted in olive oil, with just a touch of dill and basil, along with the veggies you've got there. Put everything in a roasting pan, have two glasses of wine, and it comes out perfect."

"Really? What oven temp do you use?"

"It depends on the oven. Mine at home is set at three seventy-five. In a commercial oven like you probably use, you might consider three thirty."

"Thanks. I appreciate the idea." The customer turned to Charlie and said, "Look, I'm sorry for my shortness. Hope you have a good rest of the day." Charlie smiled and nodded.

When the customer was gone, David stood next to Charlie and said, "Charlie, when you get a little older, you'll be able to tell the customer who is having a bad day from those who are just negative, nasty people. In selling, which is what you and your grandfather do, you must ignore those who are nasty and sell them whatever they want to buy. You're good at what you do—always keep that in mind." He smiled at Charlie. Dex just continued sitting with his paper in his lap, listening but saying nothing.

They didn't sell out, but they came close. Before breaking down the tent and boxes, David selected what he needed to make a creative dinner for himself and Meg. He was confident she would be home on time, and they would have the conversation he blew last night.

Dex came over and handed David fifty dollars. "Look, David, if you have nothing to do Monday, we'll be here early Monday morning. If you work all day, and we have a good day, I'll pay you a hundred for the day. No charge for what you have in your bag."

"Thank you. Yes, I'm likely to be free on Monday. If I am, I'll be here early," David said, helping Charlie load the van. He turned to Charlie and said, "Have a good weekend, Charlie." David smiled, waved at Dex, and started toward his apartment.

*　　*　　*

"Granddaddy, I need to talk to Granny."

"It's too late, Charlie. We had a long day at the market and still have to restock the truck. Maybe in the morning before church. I'll get you up early."

"It can't wait. Please, Granddaddy, I've got to talk to Granny now. Please, Granddaddy," she pleaded, tears streaming down her face.

Dex glanced over at his granddaughter. She looked so vulnerable, huddled in the corner of the truck seat as they headed back home to Calumet Farms. Her legs were squeezed between the gear shift and a cooler on the cab floor. Empty and partially empty produce boxes filled the back of the truck. It had been a decent day at the green market. Dex couldn't figure out what had gotten into Charlie to make her so emotional. When she wanted to talk to her granny this bad, it had to be something important. Glancing at her again, he saw she was rocking gently back and forth, as she had done all her life when she was confronted with something she couldn't comprehend. It was like life was too much for her. Her grandmother Mary had known that when these moments of overwhelming stress gripped Charlie, the best thing to do was to hold her and whisper in her ear that everything was going to be all right and Granny would take care of her.

Dex stifled a sob by coughing. Since Mary passed three years ago, Dex didn't know exactly what to do. He knew Charlie missed not talking to her grandmother and being held by her, but he also knew he couldn't replace his deceased wife. He'd done the best he could. Charlie compensated in times like these by asking to go to Granny's grave and talk to her. He knew how large the hole in his own heart was and couldn't imagine the hollowness Charlie felt inside. He blinked rapidly to keep from crying.

"Okay, Charlie, you can go have a conversation with Granny. It's getting dark. You'll need a flashlight. Look in the glovebox, and get it. Turn it on to make sure it works."

She opened the compartment and started pulling out maps, a box of tissues, loose papers, and finally a small black flashlight. She kept turning it over in her hands, over and over.

"I can't find the button, Granddaddy. I can't!"

"Okay, Charlie, remember what I taught you. Take a deep breath and calm down. You don't see a button to push on the side, because that's not where it is. Look at the end. Try twisting the end of the flashlight."

Charlie twisted the end of the light. "I twisted it, Granddaddy, but it still doesn't come on. It's broken!"

"Did you twist it as far as it would go?"

"Yeah."

"Remember to say 'Yes, sir.'"

"Yeah. Yes, sir."

"See how the back end of the flashlight is round?"

Charlie turned the small tube around in her hand. "Yeah. I mean, yes, sir."

"Push on the round end of the flashlight."

She pushed and the light came on.

"Okay, it works," he said. "Now turn it off."

She did as she was told.

"Good. Now, until you get out of the truck—" At that moment, Dex gripped the steering wheel hard as a wave of pain moved through his hip and groin area.

"What's the matter, Granddaddy?"

"Nothing, Charlie. I just had another thought. Put the flashlight in your shirt pocket until we get home. Then you'll have it when coming back from seeing your granny."

She did as she was told. "Granddaddy, are you going to give that guy a job with us at the market?"

"I don't know. What do you think I should do?"

"I don't know either. He was a big help with the people. I'm not sure, but it seemed like we sold more for a Saturday market. Don't you think?"

He didn't answer, but instead asked, "How about you? Do you think you could work with him? You know, this is a partnership, you and me and Calumet Farms. You must be good with bringing him on."

"Do you think he knows I'm a girl?"

"Don't know. I figure we'll have to tell him up front. How do you feel about that?"

"I don't know. I guess all right. I guess it would be like having a big brother, don't you think?"

Dex was more worried about a different sort of relationship. "I guess so. I tell you what. If he shows up Monday morning, we'll see how he does. We'll see how things go. That okay with you?"

"Yeah."

"Yes, sir."

"Yeah. Yes, sir."

After restocking the truck at four farms, Dex turned off the paved highway onto the gravel road that went from the back of the farm over the hill and down to the farmhouse on the front side. When he got to the top of the hill, he stopped the truck and killed the engine. "Charlie, look at me."

She continued to look at the tombstone just off the road. She had already opened the truck door.

"Charlie, look at me."

Charlie, with one foot on the running board and still half in the truck, looked at her grandfather.

"Promise me, Charlie, you'll not take the shortcut through the woods or across the fields. Promise me you'll stick to the road. Promise now."

"But it's shorter going home through the woods."

"Promise me, Charlie."

"I promise."

Dex stepped on the gas after Charlie got out. He didn't know why she had to see her granny or how long she'd be there. He just knew he had to get the truck parked and get back to the top of the hill.

He parked by the barn and got out of the truck. Another spasm of pain shot through his hip and groin as he put weight on his legs. He reached up under the seat and pulled out his Glock 26 nine-mm pistol. He shoved the gun into the waistband of his pants. Feeling behind the seat for his messenger bag, Dex rooted around in it till he found his pillbox, shook out two, and swallowed them without water. He closed his eyes, waiting for the pain to subside. He said a silent prayer to his deceased wife: Mary, please help me find an answer to what will happen to Charlie when the pain gets too much. As the pain subsided, he breathed deeply. He then headed back up the hill through the woods, using just the ambient light from the half-moon and stars.

Charlie stayed about an hour. Dex watched from the tree line, his heart aching for her and for himself. She moved from sitting against the tombstone to finally lying on the grave in a fetal position, talking constantly to her dead grandmother, the only mother she had ever known.

Dex and Mary had only one child, a daughter, Edith. They wanted more, but Mary couldn't have more, so she spoiled Edith. Dex always thought she was compensating for her own tough childhood full of sadness, betrayal, and cruelty. She wanted more for her daughter and didn't understand the temptations open to young people who felt they were above reproach. By the time Edith was in high school, with the natural rebellion of any teenager experiencing raging hormones, it was obvious that Mary had given in to Edith too many times. In her senior year of high school, Edith left her mother a hateful note and disappeared into the night. Dex could forgive Edith for running away, but he could never forgive her for the note. Mary had read that vile epistle over and over. Each time she did, the light in her eyes and the smile on her face seemed to fade away more and more. Dex had tried to take the cruel words away, but Mary never let him. It was as if she saw it as her punishment for the mistakes she had made with Edith. She went through the motions of being a wife and partner on the farm but without the joy and happiness she had in the past. Every night, she left the porch light on and the front door unlocked in case Edith came home.

One November night, two years after Edith had left, they were sitting in the front room reading and sewing. They heard a car coming up the gravel road. Dex reached into the box next to his chair and took out his pistol. Mary put her sewing down and just sat there. They heard a car door slam and gravel being thrown as the car sped away. Dex jumped up and threw open the door with his gun ready. He saw a frail, emaciated, and pregnant Edith leaning on the porch post. Mary let out a cry and pushed past Dex to envelop her daughter in her arms.

They carefully put Edith in the truck and raced to the hospital. The doctor said she was between eight and nine months pregnant, addicted to drugs, and close to death. Edith went into cardiac arrest, and the doctors performed an emergency C-section and delivered a drug-addicted baby girl. The doctors had little hope for the baby, but Mary knew that God was giving her another chance to be a mother. She named the baby Charlotte after her own mother.

Dex and Mary buried Edith on the hill, in the middle of and overlooking the farm. It had the prettiest view of any spot on the farm. Looking in any direction other than at the grove of hardwood trees, the rolling hills and fields could be seen for miles. The family had always had their picnics and outings up there. It was the right place. Mary placed Edith's note in her casket before saying her final goodbye to her daughter. When Dex tried to console her, Mary would say, "Edith came back to me to give me the greatest gift she could, her daughter. She really did love me. Now, for all the rest of my life, I'll not have to wonder if she's okay. I'll know where she is."

Charlotte was different from birth. By the time she got over the drug addiction, it seemed evident that she was slow in developing. She didn't talk until she was four. Her eyes darted around like bees in a field of flowers. She was restless and unable to concentrate on anything for long. She became easily frustrated and threw fits more often than other children.

Mary handled it all with grace and patient love. Slowly, she began to mold Charlotte's responses to her surroundings. The two were inseparable. Starting in fourth grade, Mary chose to homeschool Charlotte. Dex always felt that this decision was only partly because of Charlotte's "slowness." It had more to do with Mary's fear of Charlotte getting in with the wrong crowd the way Edith had.

Charlotte rose to her knees, leaned forward, and kissed the ground of Granny's grave. She went over and touched her mother's headstone. She then started home, heading for the wood's trail rather than the gravel road.

Dex smiled, moved behind a big oak so he wouldn't be seen, and followed her home.

# CHAPTER 6

Not one of David's resumés elicited a response. After a few days, he sent out another twenty-five to smaller buyside firms and family offices. It was like all fifty had just vanished into thin air. On the days he was not earning pocket money at the green market, he put on his best suit, shirt, tie, and HBS lapel pin, and polished his shoes to a blinding shine. He made the rounds of the offices where he had submitted his resumé. Most wouldn't see him. The few who did were friendly but apologetic that they didn't have an open position (even though they were advertising an open position on LinkedIn), or they didn't want to consider him until his situation with MD&S was resolved, since many of their analysts were in a dual role that interacted with the sell side. Some institutions were seeking outside investments in the firm's proprietary funds, thus requiring their analysts to have an active and clean SEC broker registration. Every time David was turned away by a receptionist or heard excuses from a managing director, it stirred turmoil within him. He was angry that this one mistake was obliterating years of diligent study in the best schools, as well as the hard work he'd put in at MD&S. At the same time, Fil's training and counseling molded the rejections into a steely determination to prove all of the jerks wrong. All he needed was a chance. Why didn't they see that?

This morning, David had to pee badly, so badly it hurt, but the only bathroom was through the bedroom, and that door was locked. He wasn't going to go over and pound on the door, demanding that his wife—supposedly for better or worse—unlock the door to allow him to pee in his own bathroom, where he was paying half the rent. He would go to the public restroom in Union Square. At least he would be gone before Meg got up. Just then he heard the ear splitting click of the bedroom lock and the turn of the handle. He feigned sleep, as he did on non-market days, to avoid facing his wife's hostility. Squinting, he watched her go over to the dining table. She did something at the table, turned, looked at him, and stalked out of the apartment. David jumped up and went over to the table. On it was a note that read:

Don't bother with dinner tonight. I'll be working late. I think we should talk tomorrow. Be coherent in the morning.

"Damn," David said under his breath. Well, it's something, he thought. She finally wants to talk about their situation. A first step. At least her anger was dissipating. A good step. Maybe someone in her office knows someone at one of the firms where he'd applied who can put in a good word for him. David had a list of the firms he had contacted. She didn't say anything about his sleeping on the sofa, so maybe the chill-out was over. He looked at his watch. Christ, he needed to get moving. That old guy and his grandson should arrive soon. Part of the deal was helping them unload the truck, and this was Saturday, so the day should be busy. In the shower, David felt a weakness come over him as he realized Meg had not said in the note that she loved him, kiss her ass, or anything personal. It was all business.

He didn't have to cook a big dinner, and he better lay off the wine. He wanted to be on top of his game. He thought about what she might say, and how he would have an intelligent and uncontestable response for her. She can set the rules for this meeting, but he'll come out the winner.

*　*　*

David was waiting at the market, where he had been working for the last four market days. He watched the Ford Econoline van with the name Calumet Farms on the side pull into its regular space. The old man got out and walked to where David was standing.

"Good morning, Dex," David said, shaking the man's hand.

"Howdy," Dex said, walking to the van's back doors.

"Where's your grandson?"

"I'm alone today. You interested in working?"

"Yes, sir."

"Good. Give me a hand with this tent, and let's get set up."

The two of them worked quickly and steadily, setting up the tent, boards for displaying the produce, the boxes of fruits and vegetables, and Dex's chair next to the money bag. The tent flaps fluttered in the stiff, cold breeze coming from the north.

Dex began putting the produce boxes on the boards in the order in which he removed them from the truck. David followed suit for a minute and then spoke up. "Mr. Dex, do you mind if I rearrange the produce a little differently?"

"How come? I've been doing it this way since I've been coming to the market. It works."

"Yes, sir. I understand that. Some of our customers are professional chefs, and others are what are called 'foodies.' They have a sense of what goes with what when cooking. I just thought it might be worthwhile if we arranged the produce the way these food lovers think about pairing items on their menus, that's all."

Looking at David, Dex was silent for a minute. He went over to the chair, sat down, and said, "Suit yourself." David quickly started rearranging the offerings and signage. Using Dex's marker and cardboard, he began adding small signs for the rearranged produce, highlighting menu ideas and benefits for the cooks.

The day was busy from the start until they ran out of produce an hour earlier than usual. Without being asked, David started breaking down the displays and tent and loading them and the empty boxes into the van. As he was working, Dex sat in his chair and watched. When he'd finished, David said, "Hope your grandson is feeling better next week."

"Why do you say that?"

"Well, I just thought he must be feeling bad, since he wasn't with you."

"My grandchild is fine. She just has a cold. She's not here, because I wanted to talk with you if you showed up."

"She?"

"Yeah, she. Charlie, I call her, but her real name is Charlotte. Charlie is what some people call "slow," if you know what I mean. Been that way all her life. We lost her mother at Charlie's birth and her grandmother three years ago, when she was eighteen. She dresses like a boy so other people won't mess with her, if you know what I mean. Charlie stayed home today so I could see how you work and have this conversation with you. Before I go off on a tangent, here's your money for today. Count it." Dex reached into his shirt pocket and pulled out some folded bills and handed them to David. David stuck them in his pocket without counting them. "Ain't you going to count it?"

"No, sir. You wouldn't cheat me."

"How come you doing this day work for peanuts?" Dex asked, staring at David.

"I lost my job because I made a mistake. A big mistake, and I haven't found anything else." David looked directly at Dex. He felt the same sense of openness that he had the first time he told Fil why he needed a job.

"You steal something or break the law?"

"No, sir. I didn't steal anything. As for breaking the law, no, sir, I didn't break the law, but they, the regulators and my former employer, said I broke some rules." David went on and told Dex the entire story, including recognizing, even before doing it, that he shouldn't. "So," he added, "if you don't think you can trust me to help you, I'll understand." David looked at Dex just as intently as Dex stared back.

"Me and Charlie will be here at seven thirty on Monday. If you want to work, be here then. One last point, David. Let me make it clear: you need to think of Charlie as your kid sister. Understand? Don't betray that trust. Don't let anyone get the idea that she is a girl. It's for her own good."

"Yes, sir, Dex." As Dex drove off, David thought of Fil. He knew Fil would say a door was opening. He said over and over not to look at the door being opened as bad or good. Any door that opens for a person can lead to a successful life. Grabbing the opportunity and doing a good job were what counted. Fil was smart. David also thought about his HBS education, and the fact that this week should have been dinner with the group. It was Sherm and Carrie's time to host. He knew he was the topic of conversation, but he didn't know if he was roasted or supported. He wondered if his wife took up for him. Heading home, David patted the money in his pocket and felt upbeat until he realized that none of his friends had reached out to support him. Friendship was hard to define and seemed to evaporate during the storms of life. In his mind, he heard a door slam and a lock click.

# CHAPTER 7

Coherent she'd said. How about cooperative? Why not? Weren't they married? They were supposed to be together, side by side, forever. She felt hurt, but he felt abandoned. Well, he'd show her he had a plan—a real plan for them to make it through this bump in the road, the most challenging time, the kind the vows speak about—to come out the other end better and stronger, together. He'd show her he had a part-time job, making $100 a day, cash, four days a week. He wouldn't tell her how much he loved the job. He could actively search for a full-time job two days a week and schedule interviews for those days. it wouldn't take long to get a good-paying job again. She'd see. He had a plan. By ten thirty, he decided he could have one Wild Turkey Rare Breed. By eleven thirty, he realized she was not coming home. Must be doing one of those all-nighters the lawyers in NYC were famous for, even if it was the weekend. Did anything really get done with all-nighters? Perhaps not. He did not have another bourbon. Then he realized he could go sleep in their bed. If she came home, she'd be too tired and crawl into bed with him. Maybe, just maybe, they'd touch and break out into the best makeup sex ever known to man—the best scenario for their marriage. David put the whiskey bottle away and went into the bedroom. He decided to sleep naked. That always worked with Meg. She loved to see him naked. She said he had the best body of any guy she'd ever seen naked, quickly adding that there weren't too many. Opening a door—that's what he was doing, the last thought he had before drifting off.

David was only half awake when he heard footsteps on the landing outside the apartment door. He looked over and saw that it was seven Sunday morning. He guessed the all-nighter at the firm was over. He threw back the covers and stretched as far as he could. His erection was fading but still half present. He got out of bed as he heard the apartment door lock turn and the consistent creak of the hinges blare like a bugle. He opened the bedroom door, still naked, and stepped into the living room. He stopped abruptly, and so did Meg. They looked at each other, he in all his nakedness and she in a loose-fitting hoodie, jeans, and hiking shoes.

"What are you doing here?" Meg blurted out. "You're not supposed to be here."

"Why not? I live here. I pay the rent. These are my furnishings. You told me to be coherent this morning. I have every right—." David stopped mid-sentence as Sherm came through the apartment door, carrying two obviously empty duffle bags. He stopped just behind Meg. David's eyes grew wide as he looked from Meg to Sherman and back to Meg. "What is he doing here?"

"Stop it, David. He's here as a friend to help me pack up my clothes. I didn't expect you to be here, and I needed someone with a car to help me get my things."

"Well, why didn't Carrie come help you? Does she even know Sir Galahad is saving the damsel in distress? Anyway, you told me to be coherent, don't you remember? We're married. Made vows to stick together, for better or worse, remember? Let's talk this through. I have a plan that will work."

"Cut the crap, David. Why don't you go and put some clothes on," Sherm said, moving around Meg, putting the duffle bags on the table, and taking a seat on the sofa. "It won't take long for Meg to get her things, and we'll be gone. Why don't you go down to Breads Bakery, have some coffee and a bagel, and when you get back, we'll be gone."

"Thank you for your concern, Sherman. I want to discuss the situation with my, repeat, my wife. We don't need any interference from you. I suggest you get out of my apartment. Obviously, you're interested in driving a wedge between my, repeat, my wife and me. Go on. Get out of here before I call the cops or throw you out myself." The emotions of the entire situation welled up inside David, his fists clenching and unclenching. He leaned forward, his face red, and his breathing hyper-ventilating. Meg knew David's temper, even if she had only seen it twice, and he'd never directed it toward her. She motioned for Sherman to leave.

"Sherm, please go and wait in the car. I can handle this. When I'm ready, I'll call you to help with the bags."

"No, I'm—"

"Sherm, please," Meg said. David's anger drained, and his insides turned to ice. He recognized the tone of voice Meg used in pleading with Sherman. It was the same loving tones she used when they were hot and heavy before Sherm hooked up with Carrie. He knew right then his marriage was over. His nakedness and the foolishness of it focused his mind on the reality of the situation. He looked at Meg as Sherman walked out the door. Everything he was and everything he had expected for the future vaporized because of his stupid mistake. How can that be? How could his life have been so fragile? He felt his resolve draining away, his willingness to fight for what he obviously didn't have. He turned and went into the bedroom.

A few minutes later, he came out barefoot, dressed in his jeans and a T-shirt. Meg was in the kitchen making tea. She poured the hot water into two cups and dunked a tea bag in one and then the other.

She pushed one cup across the counter toward David. "Let's be civilized about this, David. I came to get my personal things. You know, clothes, makeup, that sort of stuff. I've arranged for a mover to come and move my share of the furnishings out of here. I thought we could talk about how we're going to split the good stuff. Do you think we can do that in person? You know, as two adults, who want to be friends when this is over? Do you think so?"

"Meg, what happened to those vows we said? Don't they count for something? What about the good things we did together? Doesn't all that count for something? How could you react like this? I lost my job. Okay, I did something incredibly stupid, I admit it. But I'm not a crook. I'm not a murderer. I'm not a molester of little children. We have something special. I'll find another job. Hell, if necessary, I'll find another career. Just allow me the strength that comes from having my wife standing by my side during this challenging time." David looked at Meg as he spoke. When he finished, he was spent. There wasn't any more he could say. Meg loathed weakness, and he realized that his pleading was a sign of weakness in her eyes. He was surprised when she spoke.

"Look, David, I need time and space. I've taken a small apartment closer to the office. I'm working six or seven days a week right now on a big case, and I'm leaving tomorrow evening for Dallas. I'll be gone for at least two weeks. A moving company, Three Italian Muscle Men, is coming tomorrow to get my share of the furnishings. You and I have to divide up the furnishings now, so I can give them a list." Meg reached into her bag and pulled out a handwritten list. "Let's go through each room and divide things up, okay?"

David, resignation on his face, said, "No. You take everything. Leave me the mattress and one chair. I'm going to get dressed and go out. Lock the door behind you. Tomorrow, I've got to be at work by seven so the movers can come after seven. I'll be back by six, so they need to be gone by then. Is that doable?"

"Yes, I'll be here most of the time and make sure they're gone before six. My plane doesn't leave until eight, anyway."

"Let me shower and get dressed, and I'll be gone." David turned and walked into the bedroom, and shut the door.

# CHAPTER 8

"The market's waiting, Charlie. A whole new week is waiting," Dex said, sticking his head into her bedroom and reaching in to flip on the light. "Your blueberry pancakes and bacon will be ready in fifteen minutes."

Charlie sat propped up against the door window of the truck cab with her head resting on a pillow kept in the truck for her. "Do you think David will be at the market today?"

"Most likely, honey. He was a big help last week, don't you agree? I get the feeling he's lost."

"Lost? You mean he can't find his way home? Doesn't he know where he lives? Shouldn't we help him?"

"Not that kind of lost, Charlie. Sort of like when a person doesn't know what to do. Sometimes something happens that causes a person to be confused, and they don't have anyone to talk to."

"You mean like when I need to talk to Granny?"

"That's right."

"But I have you and Granny to talk to. You think he doesn't have a granny or granddaddy to talk to?"

"I don't know. It's not our place to pry. He's a good worker, and intelligent about business."

"Is he going to take my place?" Charlie asked with hesitation in her voice. Dex looked over at his granddaughter, put his hand on her shoulder, and tugged her ear lobe.

"There isn't a soul alive who could take your place."

"Really?" Charlie looked at Dex with a grin. She rested her head on the pillow and closed her eyes. Dex put both hands on the wheel and thought, Mary, help me solve this problem before it's too late. Did you send David to us? Give me a sign of some sort, please.

They entered the city on the Henry Hudson Parkway. Charlie still had her eyes closed when they got to Ninety-sixth Street. Dex nudged her gently, and she opened her eyes. "We're at the river, honey," Dex said. "I thought you'd like to see the boats and ships."

"Yeah, I like the river." Traffic was sparse, and daylight began to break over Manhattan. At Twenty-third Street, they turned left, away from the river, and headed across town. "This is my favorite street." Charlotte gave Dex a running account of the stores and people hurrying about. At Park Avenue South, they made a right, and shortly after, they pulled into their spot. David was there, sitting on the curb, reading the Wall Street Journal. His jeans and hoodie were old and comfortable. He folded the WSJ and walked over to the truck, where Charlie was rolling down the window.

"Good morning," David said. "Charlie, you sure look ready for a big selling day." David looked at Charlie and smiled.

"She's ready to go. Monday isn't the best of days, so if you want to work, we'll sure like to have another hand selling."

"Yes, I'm in, and we'll do the best we can, right Charlie?"

"Yeah."

"If you're finished with that paper, I'll take it to read." The three of them started unloading the truck and setting up the stand for business using David's new arrangement.

David said to Charlie, "While you weren't here on Saturday, I kind of rearranged the produce and signs. Is that okay with you?"

"Yeah, I guess so. How come?"

"That guy who was frustrated the first day I was here. He's a chef somewhere and what I call a 'foodie.' They're totally focused on what they're going to serve. If we arrange the food so that when they see something they want to buy, the other items they're likely to serve at the same meal are next to the one they intend to buy. Just a reminder for them to buy the other items, as well. Does that make sense?"

"Yeah."

"Yes, sir," Dex interjected from his seat.

"Yeah, yes, sir." Charlie corrected.

"Great. Let me show you how these displays might help us sell more."

When they were finished setting up, David reached into his jeans pocket and pulled out a twenty-dollar bill.

"Saturday, when you paid me, I just put the money in my pocket without counting. You accidently gave me one hundred and twenty dollars instead of the hundred we'd agreed on, so here's your twenty dollars back."

Dex took the twenty-dollar bill and said, "Much obliged. You could have kept it, you know."

"I guess so, but I wouldn't have earned it. We agreed on a hundred dollars. You shouldn't be out twenty dollars just because you miscounted."

"You're right, son. Charlie, take this twenty and go get us three coffees and something sweet to munch on. You know where I'm talking about, right?"

"Yeah, Granddaddy. David, do you want sugar and milk in your coffee?" Charlie asked.

"No thank you, Charlie. Black is fine."

The market's open area was buzzing with excitement and chatter, with vendors still setting up and early bird customers rooting through the chaos looking for the special finds before the crowds came. Charlie started across, stopping every so often to look back and wave to Dex and David.

Dex watched Charlie go and, turning to David, said in a low voice, "Son, I need to emphasize something to you. As I said Saturday, Charlie is slow. Your taking time to explain things to her is good; just don't expect too much. She doesn't understand adult ways too well, because she has been sheltered by her granny and me from the harsh realities of life. Try not to get frustrated with her because she will ask a million questions."

"Yes, sir."

"She doesn't know anything about hormones, boys being different from girls, or how and where babies come from. She does know you stirred something inside her. That's how she got the cold, lying on Granny's grave talking to her. Do you understand?"

"Yes, sir."

"Good. I know you're married. Remember, Charlie is your little sister, understand?"

"Yes, sir."

"Good, because if you were to hurt her or try to do anything with her, I'd be really disappointed." David had no doubt that Dex was not exaggerating.

"I'm asking you to protect her as if she was your kid sister. It's not her fault that she's the way she is. Guys would try to take advantage of her if they knew she was a girl, and a pretty one at that. You have any questions?"

"Yes, sir. No, sir, no questions."

"Good. If you want, you can help us every market day. Depending on how we do, you'll make no less than fifty dollars and maybe a hundred. I'll pay you at the end of every day. You okay with that?"

"Yes, sir. That's fine with me." David felt his heart skip a beat. The money was helpful and would give him steady spending money to survive. He was sleeping on the couch, which was probably leaving that day. That was okay; he had money in his pocket. Tomorrow, he could go on Craig's List and post his apartment for sublease for a few months while finding a cheap place to crash until he and Meg could reconcile.

*  *  *

Monday was a slow day at the green market. Every minute seemed to drag by. There were fewer buying customers than usual due to the cold and overcast day, and they just seemed to pick up the produce, roll it around in their hands, sometimes smell it, and then put it back. Finally, Dex said to Charlie and David, "OK, we've sold what we can. Let's pack up, go home, and load up for Wednesday." After the truck was loaded, Dex gave David folded-over money. "Not a good day, son, but that's the way having your own business is. You seemed to be off center all day. Anything I can do to help?"

"No, sir. I'm fine. Just a little domestic problem," David said as he put the money in his shirt pocket. He walked the two blocks to the apartment. Wondering what she took and left dominated his thoughts. He thought about the intricately carved marble top oval table where they had displayed their growing collection of sterling silver photo frames with pictures documenting the important times in their life together. He was confident she would take it. The small military campaign desk used by a Union army staff officer he expected she'd leave for him, since he used it daily as his place to sort bills and mail. Did he regret telling her to take everything? Not really. If their life was over, he didn't want any part of her to remind him what a fool he'd been. At least she probably won't take the old table and six chairs they used as the dining set. It wasn't an antique. Just something they picked up for fifty dollars when they first came to New York. No value whatsoever to anyone. As he climbed the steps, he remembered the unique artsy table, handcrafted by a woodworker from upstate New York. They found it on one of their many excursions on the train when they were just starting their jobs. They had gone back to the guy's shop several weekends in a row. They hopped off the Metro-North train as it went through Hudson, and offered him what little they had, promising him they would treasure the table all their lives. He had even turned it over and signed it. "To David and Meg, may this table bring you everlasting happiness, as it has to me. Horace Longfellow." It always sat by David's leather wing chair. Whatever book he was reading was there to pick up. At least he'd have his throne to remember this life he'd had. He turned the key and walked into a completely empty one-bedroom apartment with an envelope taped to the refrigerator door, telling him he would hear from her lawyer.

The days were getting longer, and David liked that. Besides not being as cold, more produce was sold, and he earned more on the good days. David felt less stress than he had since his life fell off a cliff. He unconsciously swung the paper bag of vegetables Dex had given him. He was a half-block away from his third-floor walkup when he noticed the guy leaning against a black sedan in front of the building. Even though there was nothing unusual about the guy or his car, David felt the hair on the back of his neck stand up. As he got closer, the guy pushed off the car and reached inside his coat pocket. As David turned to go up the stairs, he heard the guy say, "David J. Hopkins-Wilson?"

David stopped, a queasiness in his stomach, and turned. "That's me. Can I help you?"

"Yes, sir. This is for you." He approached David, holding out an envelope.

David hesitated, thinking about refusing, but he realized it was futile. Intuitively, he knew the papers in the envelope were from Meg, and all his plans to win her back were a pipe dream. He folded the envelope, put it in his jean's pocket, and looked at the bag in his hand. He no longer felt like going up and cooking a veggie plate for himself all alone. A friendly face, some company that respected him, that's what he needed. He kept walking to Tenth Avenue, turned right, and walked two more blocks to McGinty's.

Sitting at the bar alone with a beer and a plate of free hors d'oeuvres, he stared into the mirror behind the bar, realizing that staring back was a guy whose life was in turmoil, even as he tried to ignore the fact. He felt he had one foot in his old life and one foot in his new life, and the two were steadily drifting apart, stretching him to the point where he was going to fall into a black hole from which there was no return. Pushing a piece of pita bread lumped with humus into his mouth, he took a gulp of beer. He reached into his jean's pocket and pulled out the envelope. Inside were divorce papers with a cover letter from Meg herself. It was formal and matter-of-fact, sterile of any emotions. She wanted half of his IRA/401k to cover her student loans, all the furnishing she had already taken, and she wanted him to absolve her of any liability for the apartment rent. Finally, she gave him an ultimatum. He had two days to accept this no-fault divorce, or he would have to get a lawyer, and they would fight it out in court. David knew the second choice would be a disaster, taking at least the other half of his IRA/401k and years. "Eddie, another Bud and a pen, please."

# CHAPTER 9

"Granddaddy, what's wrong?" Charlotte and Dex were sitting on the front porch.

"Nothing, honey. Just need dinner and bedtime." He struggled out of his rocker.

"But you're all red and sweating," she persisted.

"I'm fine, Charlie. Come on. Let's put together some dinner." Dex put his arm around her shoulders and ushered her into the kitchen.

Charlie washed the dishes, while Dex went back to the front porch with his glass of tea. When he heard the water running, he reached into his shirt pocket and pulled out a small silver box, opened it, and took out three pain pills, swallowing them fast with a chaser of iced tea. He put his head back on the rocker and closed his eyes. He felt the tension from the pain beginning to ease and being replaced by his real problem. It felt like his days and nights were consumed by trying to resolve the unsolvable: What will happen to Charlie when his painkillers don't work anymore? Who can he trust to take care of her and the business? There was no one. Disaster was looming. All he could see in his mind was a speeding train headed toward a trestle that wasn't there anymore. He felt his heart skip a beat just thinking about it and coughed involuntarily.

Dex sat and rocked, thinking about the years he and Mary had done this, sitting in the dark, rocking and looking at the stars. They didn't even talk much, both knowing what the other was thinking. When Edith was little, there was always chatter as her half-size rocker sat between theirs. Even Edith, as she grew older, sensed that this peacefulness didn't need conversation. In the eighth grade, the year before the druggies started pulling her away, she'd gotten an A on a science project about the stars seen each season from their porch. His mood changed abruptly as he thought about the downward spiral his beautiful little girl had experienced a year later. No one at her school or the law cared. He went to both seeking help, but they all said the same thing: there was nothing they could do unless the group got caught breaking the law. That was a lie, and he knew it. They didn't want to do anything because that would have taken courage and upset their easy life. When the sheriff came calling after Edith's death and the disappearance of the three guys responsible for her death, Dex had fed the sheriff's own words back to him: "When you can prove I had anything to do about those dirtbags, come see me. Otherwise, have a good day, Sheriff."

The screen door slammed behind Charlie as she came onto the porch and sat in Mary's old rocker. "Charlie, I've got an idea I'd like to run by you. If you don't like it, I want you to be honest with me. Okay?"

"Yeah."

"Yes, sir," he corrected her.

"Yeah, yes, sir."

"You know your granny will know if you're not honest?"

"Yeah. Yes, sir."

"I've been thinking. We have a good little business growing vegetables, buying veggies from our growers, and selling them at the Union Square green market. Don't you agree?"

"Yeah, yes, sir. I really like seeing and meeting all the people."

"I do too. I'm getting to the age when I'll need some help."

Charlie turned and looked at Dex with a wounded look. "That's twice you've sounded like you're unhappy with me. Don't I do good, Granddaddy?"

"Charlie, darling, I'm not talking about you. I couldn't do it without you. I'm just getting older. There will be a time when I need another guy to do the heavy lifting that only a guy can do."

Charlie's eyes began tearing up. "Granddaddy, don't talk like that. You're all I have. Please don't talk like that." She reached over and grabbed his arm. He put his hand over hers. Dex decided to drop the subject. He'd have to find another time and another way to broach the subject.

# CHAPTER 10

David sat on the curb, sipping his Starbucks black arabica, and reading the paper when the familiar white van came around the corner. He smiled as Charlie stuck out her arm and waved vigorously. The three of them had become a team during the last several weeks, with each settling into a routine on market days. It always amazed David how neatly the truck was packed. He wondered if that was Dex's doing, or perhaps Charlie's feminine nature was a factor. He didn't raise the issue; he just admired the work. Within twenty minutes, the van was unloaded, and the tent was ready for what the three hoped would be a big day. The week had started slowly on Monday but picked up markedly on Wednesday, and Friday was close to the best David had seen, so today should be even better. Dex had been more than fair with what he paid, and David felt flush. He thought about enjoying Sunday by splurging and going to a decent restaurant. Reading cookbooks, the only thing Meg had left, was spurring him on to find a unique restaurant for a Sunday lunch where the menu would be different.

As expected, the crowd began building early, taking advantage of the cloudless blue sky, the slight breeze, and the mid-50's temperatures of April. Sales were steady, with David and Charlie helping the buyers and Dex handling the money and the cash box. Just before lunch, there was a lull in the flow. Charlie turned to David and said, "How come the people you help always buy two of what they want, and the people I help only buy one?" Dex looked up from reading David's WSJ, surprised by Charlie's question, and interested in David's answer.

"Charlie," David started, in a loving voice, "you do a good job helping customers. You should be proud of what you help them buy."

"Yeah, but your customers buy twice as much as my customers. How come?" Charlie folded her arms in front of her. It was apparent that she wanted an answer.

"Okay, I don't suppose you've heard of FAB?"

"Yeah, it's a laundry detergent Granny used to use. I don't know if it still is, 'cause me and Granddaddy use Tide."

"Not that FAB, Charlie. The FAB I'm talking about is a method of selling. Let me explain." David reached over and picked up a pear. "Charlie, what is this?"

"You know, a pear."

"That's right. Now, what are the features of this pear?"

"What do you mean by features? It's a green pear."

"Yes, it is. It has a smooth skin, it has juices inside if you bite into it, and it has a core, which can't be eaten, but has seeds if you want to grow more. Right?"

"Yeah, anyone can see that."

"Yes, they can. Those things I described are the features of this pear. Right?"

"Yeah, I guess so."

"Okay, now think of those features and what advantage they give a pear?"

"Huh? I don't get it."

"You now know the features of this pear. Thinking of those features, turn them into advantages for the buyer."

"Huh? They taste good, don't they?"

"Sure, but that's a benefit for the buyer. Why do they taste good?

"Because the juice is sweet, and it runs down your chin, silly."

"Bingo, that's the advantage of this pear. It is juicy and sweet."

"Yeah, and good."

"Now, since the pear is juicy and sweet, what benefit does that give the person who buys the pear?"

"Their pies will be better. They will have a sweet chin. Their children will love them more. They will ..."

"Bingo, you now know how to sell using FAB – think of what the features are, think of the advantages those features give a buyer, and think about how those advantages translate into benefits for the person buying."

"Yeah, that makes sense."

"You want to look at the FABs for all this produce."

"Yeah."

All afternoon, Charlie tried to use FAB selling principles, fumbling through in the beginning and getting better as she would lean into David and whisper a question. As he whispered back to her, her confidence in herself slowly replaced her hesitation and fear. Dex knew, as he watched the two of them pack up, that any resistance Charlie had to bringing on David full time was over. Mary may have sent the solution to his future dilemma.

# CHAPTER 11

David was energized by Saturday's sales at the green market when he awoke Sunday morning. Lying on the mattress on the studio apartment floor, he marveled at how he had so far opened a not-so-pretty door and found contentment, if not happiness. He silently thanked Fil and told him he loved him. The rent in his studio was cheap because the heating system was broken and there was no air conditioning. That didn't matter to him. This was the ultimate crash pad. He left early and stayed out late. The days he wasn't working at the green market were spent at the main library on Forty-second Street, one of the museums, a Starbucks with his laptop since he didn't have internet, or in the park reading a book. He had quit looking for a job in the securities business. He loved what he was doing, but he knew he couldn't continue to do it much longer. This job was not resumé material. He didn't care. He respected and felt close to Dex and Charlie. He knew a secret and had the trust and respect of Dex to keep that secret. That meant something to David. Everyone else thought he was a cheat. Dex had understood, without being told, that David had made a mistake—that was all. It wasn't a character flaw—just a mistake he could and would learn from. There was something different about Dex, strangely different. He had that same quiet toughness Fil had. David knew Fil had seen hard times; maybe Dex had too.

Dex seemed to always know what he wanted and how to get it. He never got riled, David thought, remembering a time when a customer was aggressively hostile to Charlie for making a mistake with his change. Dex never raised his voice, but the tone turned cold, dangerously cold. The customer realized it, and so did everyone milling around the tent. The customer muttered something, snatched up his potatoes, and hurried off. In awe of that kind of commanding presence, David began studying Dex and his attitude and mannerisms, searching for the key without success. Dex was a mystery. Charlie was another matter.

Without conscious thought, David's hand slid under the sheet and rubbed his penis to an aroused level. He had realized Charlie's face was beautiful. He wondered what the rest of her looked like under that baggy shirt and those khakis that were big enough for both of them. What a delightful idea, he thought, feeling his erection as hard as steel. Almost immediately, David remembered Dex's warning and the look in his eyes when he delivered it. Like someone had stuck a pin in a balloon, his erection deflated in an instant. Sister, little sister, that's the focus. David threw back the sheet and lay there naked, looking forward to a fun Sunday, the first in a while. There was life after the financial markets, he thought, rolling off the mattress onto the floor. He did twenty push-ups before standing. He went over to the only chair, holding his clothes from the night before, and took the clothes and hung them up in the only closet. His underwear was in a cabinet on the wall above the hot plate, small fridge, and sink.

David, book in hand, entered the Highline at the Thirtieth Street entrance. At the top of the stairs, he made the decision to go south, away from the Hudson Yards development, looking for a spot to read and people watch. Marveling at the new art, graffiti, and redevelopment underway, David saw an unusual sight: A young woman, bright red hair, in black and white striped pants, with white polka dots on a black top. She was sitting with her feet on the curved bench, with earbuds, and reading a book at the same time. She was stunning. What enhanced her uniqueness was the stark white building behind her with rows of big black dots and a three-story black and white portrait of an Asian man looking like he was about to deliver a karate blow to an enemy.

"Hi, mind if I sit here," David asked, smiling.

"What?" She looked up, pulling one earbud out, a frown on her face.

"Mind if I sit here?"

"Do whatever you want," Musee said, putting the earbud back in.

David sat down a couple of feet away. He opened his book and started reading. He realized she was prettier than he'd first thought. His eyes darted from her breasts to her green eyes. Wow, he thought. This is why I came to the Highline. While he was furtively looking at her, she cut her eyes from her book, looking at him. Both jerked their heads back to the front. Seconds later, they both snickered and burst out laughing. Musee pulled the earbuds out of her ears, closed her book, and turned to face David. He closed his book and turned to face her. "I'm David," he said. "Come here often?"

"Whenever I can. I'm Musee, spelled like French for museum. I work six days a week, so that doesn't leave much time to get here," she responded.

They played the twenty-question game like two young people who have been hurt but still yearn for one-on-one contact with the opposite sex, cautiously filling in some of the personal traits to avoid rejection. David, letting his biological hunger dictate his timing, finally decided that the opportunity was greater than the risk of rejection.

"Say, I'm going to Untitled at the Whitney for lunch. Care to join me?" he asked. "Oh, my treat, by the way," he said, trying to tip the scales in his favor.

"Untitled?"

"You know, the Danny Meyer restaurant at the Whitney."

"Sure, but I can pay my own way."

"Whatever suits you, but there's no ulterior motive or obligation implied."

"Sorry to hear that," she said, smiling.

They started walking south on the Highline, pointing out graffiti, art, interesting foliage, the views of the Hudson, and the skyline.

David continued making direct eye contact with Musee whenever they looked at each other. They were carrying on the conversation with the third set of questions and more personal subjects that rounded out knowledge of each other. The longer they talked, the more they were immersed in a bubble created by the deepening chemistry between them. Their first course of fish tacos had been served and cleared, while the two of them discussed in detail how they could make a similar first course with certain ingredients found at the deli or the bodega on the corner near their place. "In my opinion," David started saying, "the best—" He stopped mid-sentence looking out the exterior glass wall. A young man and woman got out of a black car. He had on a dark suit and preppy striped tie, and she was wearing a dress obviously from a designer store. Sherm took Meg's hand, and they walked into the Whitney as a couple. David's chemistry bubble with Musee popped. Musee turned to see what he was looking at.

"Know them?" she asked, turning back to David. "They make a power couple, for sure."

"Hmm, I thought I did, but I was wrong. Sorry." He reflexively touched her hand and smiled. "Where was I?"

"You were here, and then you were gone. Glad to have you back." She smiled and crinkled her nose.

They finished the second course, made a joint decision to pass on dessert, and lingered over their glasses of rosé.

"Do you live around here?" Musee asked.

"Not officially," David fudged. "How about you?"

"Yes, on Thirty-ninth Street between Ninth and Eighth Avenue. Not exactly a palace, but I can afford it, and I don't have to share with a roommate," Musee signaled.

"Good for you. Sounds like a nice place."

Musee took a deep breath. "Wanna see it?"

"You bet," David said grinning and gesturing for the bill.

"I'm going to the girl's room. I'll meet you outside," Musee said, smiling with her eyes.

Carrying on an easy conversation, they walked down the Highline and the rest of the way down Ninth Avenue to Musee's.

*　*　*

David jumped out of bed when he heard the doorbell buzz. Musee lay on her back without any covers. David looked down at her as he slipped on his jeans. He'd never been with a true redhead or blonde and was mesmerized by the translucent nature of her skin and the paleness of her pubic hair. The buzzer sounded more insistent, and he grabbed his wallet and went to pay for the pizza they'd ordered.

He didn't know the time, but the afternoon and evening had been more than he had ever dreamed possible. He'd had unexpected hookups before, and they were nice. This was more than a hookup to him. He didn't know what it meant to Musee, but it had done wonders toward helping him remember that he still had a social life ahead of him. His ambitions for success were rekindled, as well. He wanted to conquer the world and knew he could. He was standing at the counter that separated the galley kitchen from the dining table pushed up against the sofa back with chairs at each end, pouring two glasses of merlot, when Musee entered the living room wearing his shirt, and apparently nothing else. He moved around the counter as she sat. He placed the wine and the pizza on the table and sat opposite her. They both devoured a slice of pie without speaking. Then David said, "Wilson."

"What?"

"Wilson, that's my last name. He looked into her eyes. I'd like to see you again, and again. I'm David Wilson. I'm in between regular jobs, but I work four days a week with a family from upstate. It's temporary until I find something permanent in the food business. May I have your phone number and email?"

"O'Hara is my name, Maureen O'Hara, like the movie star. She was my mother's idol. Before you ask, yes, I get kidded a lot, but that's okay—she was beautiful and so am I." Musee crinkled her nose and smiled. "My contact numbers are 111-768-4269 and redh@hemail.com," she said. "You're quite a guy, David Wilson. I hope you do call."

David reached in his pocket, pulled out his phone, and started typing. "Great, eh ..., look I'm not good at playing games, and I'm out of touch with the proper protocol, so if you don't have a problem with it, I'll not wait the proper three or four days to contact you. I'm going to call you tomorrow night just to make sure I'm not dreaming all this."

"I'm good with that."

They finished the pizza, chewing between grinning at each other. David put the pizza box in the trash bag and set it by the door. He turned to Musee, who was standing a few feet behind him. "I guess I'll need that shirt," he said, closing the space between them.

"Take it off of me," she said softly. As he stepped closer and started unbuttoning the shirt, she leaned closer and whispered in his ear, "Why don't you do me one more time for good luck?" David moaned and took her in his arms. They backed up so Musee could sit on the edge of the table with her legs wrapped around his waist. Their eyes were wide open, searching the other's eyes as aggressively as their tongues explored their mouths. Then it happened. A release. A release from the bondage of self-doubt, insecurity brought on by others, and the loneliness of their existence up to now. It wasn't just an orgasm; it was a realization at the core of each of them that they were worth loving, and they were loved.

# CHAPTER 12

Musee felt the tension of expectation when she entered Raksin's Fine Fashions. Her interview was at nine thirty, which was her regular time for moving through her department giving last-minute sales ideas to the floor staff. Prepping the sales force was crucial, so she just compressed the time interacting with each one. She kept busy while running over and over in her mind why she should get the merchandise manager's job. It was clear she deserved the job. Mr. Raksin had always been fair and acted in the best interest of the store. Her section had built up a significant following of career women ages twenty-five to fifty. More importantly, Musee had trained a sales force that was the talk of the business. It wasn't her fault that they didn't stay longer than two years. Everyone who left went to work for a competitor at a higher salary. Mr. Raksin could have paid them what they were worth. Musee had proposed an incentive plan in which the sales staff's total compensation would actually reduce the department's employee costs as a percentage of sales to the lowest in the store. He said it wouldn't work because the other departments didn't have the same trained sales associates. The logic of his statement was lacking, since the incentive plan could be adopted by other departments. Still, when she became the merchandise manager, she could implement her ideas in a greater part of the store. Then, when those sales improved and profits rose, her next stop would be either general merchandise manager or store manager. She was ready. This was what she had worked for.

*   *   *

"Ms. O'Hara, thank you for your interest in improving our store. Your section has had a good year, and it's clearly because of you. As you know, Eddie Green has left, and his position needs to be filled. I know you are interested in the position. Frankly, you would be my first choice, but my brother Jules's daughter, Hannah, is working as a buyer in our other store. Jules sits on the board of directors and owns 35% of Raksin's. He wants his daughter in the merchandise manager position."

Musee stopped listening at this point. Her mind was disbelieving. Mr. Raksin said that she was the best person for the job, but she wasn't going to get it. It didn't matter that she had proven herself through an attractive floor appearance, the best-trained sales staff, increased sales, and a healthy profit margin. She had been told all her life that if you worked hard at something and were successful, success would be recognized. That may be so, except when working in a family business, where blood is thicker than experience and hard work put together. No, no, no, this can't be happening, she thought. She turned her attention back to Mr. Raksin, who was saying, "...so what I want to offer you is a raise and the opportunity to work as the assistant to the new merchandise manager, and a promise that when my niece moves up, you will follow in her footsteps."

"Excuse me, Mr. Raksin. You want me to train your niece to do the things I do best to improve sales? You want me to do the heavy lifting for your niece?"

"Well, I wouldn't put it that way, Ms. O'Hara. I prefer to think of it as asking you to be a team player on the first rung of the management team here at Raksin's. You have a future here, and I assume you enjoy your work and the reputation you're building here." Musee sat stone still looking at Raksin spin her situation, stroke her ego, and hold out the carrot of more pay. She got by on her current salary but just barely, with her student loan payments. There were five more years of those payments. She thought about what a waste it had been borrowing money to go to college. It looked like she was still hampered by not having the right name, being in the wrong place, and being in a career where the hired help was just that—the hired help, not really seen as equals. Her heart pounded loudly in her ears. She wanted to tell this little weasel where to go and to shove this store somewhere, but she didn't. She automatically put on her smile mask and slightly nodded her head when she thought he said something nice about her.

"Well, Ms. O'Hara, are you ready to be a member of the management team?"

"Yes, sir, but you haven't said what my raise will be."

"I still have to run it by the board, but you can expect it to be in the two hundred dollars a month range."

She was dumbfounded. She couldn't believe Raksin expected her to impart everything she knew to his niece for less than fifty dollars a week more. Musee kept her demeanor neutral. She wanted to buy time to figure out what was best for her.

"Mr. Raksin, yes, I do want to be a member of the management team. What do you say to making that raise three hundred fifty dollars a month? I'll be putting in a lot of overtime training your niece, so that's only fair, and you have always been fair in your dealings." She smiled her mask smile.

"Well, Ms. O'Hara, I'm sure I can convince the board to go along. It's a deal."

"Thank you for this opportunity, Mr. Raksin. I'm sure you won't regret it."

"Thank you, Ms. O'Hara. Next Monday, Hannah will be moving into Eddie's old office, and the two of you will begin this new opportunity for both of you." He stood, and so did Musee. They shook hands.

*   *   *

She poured more wine and emptied the glass in one long swallow. She sat there, tears streaming down her cheeks, mixed with mascara, giving her a movie monster look. She realized that she had never in her life felt so totally alone as she did at that moment. She ripped off another chunk of bread, yanked it apart, put in some ham and cheese, and took a bite. She choked as the mouthful of thought food— what she called this binging—collided with a sob coming from deep inside her. She poured more wine and took a swallow. The thoughts outlining her dilemma tumbled through her mind. What could she do? She was trapped. Her student loans were over thirty-five grand, she had less than five hundred in her checking account, no savings, her income barely covered her expenses, and she'd just been told that what she thought was her future was no future at all, unless she quit and went somewhere else. If she quit, she couldn't survive more than a month. If she tried to use her experience in retailing, she would be starting over at the bottom without any likelihood of a better outcome at the next store. In retail, if you want to go big-time, you've got to own your own business. She wanted her own store more than anything else in this world. She knew how she would run it, how to treat employees so they wouldn't want to leave and go elsewhere, and how to treat customers. She broke some more bread, wiped her face with the back of her hand, and poured more wine. She took the hunk of bread and dipped it in the wine without even looking at the glass. She was *museeing*—that's what she called it—taking both sides of a dilemma and discussing it out loud. Something deep inside her, she didn't know what to call it, refused to allow her to wallow in self-pity for long. She felt the energy seeping through her body. Not anger—anger was wasteful. Determination was a better word. No, steely determination she decided to call it. She couldn't command it to surface, but she knew, when it arose on its own, that everything would work out. There would be pain, but pain she could handle. A solution was what she wanted, and this spirit rising in her would give her the solution. That much she knew for sure.

As she thought about the problem, there were three alternatives. First, quit and find another job. The five hundred dollars in her checking account, which wouldn't last a month, ruled that out. Quitting was not an option, so she turned to the next option. Passive aggressive attitude at work. Sabotage Hannah's efforts while smiling all the time. That would work; she was confident of it. She could continue to use this approach while looking for another job in the city. The only problem was that her own reputation would suffer, and she would be splattered with Hannah's failure. Besides, she could be sure that Mr. Raksin would see to it that all his contemporaries, who went to the same Shul, would hear bad things about her work habits. That's the problem with being Irish in a Jewish profession. Passive aggressive wouldn't work. That left only one alternative. Musee would teach Hannah everything she needed to learn. Musee, however, would make Hannah's life easy. Musee would do all the work Hannah would let her do. That way, Musee's knowledge and experience would continue to grow. She would develop her contacts in the industry. She'd learn from the manufacturers and buying offices. As the departments started growing in sales and profits, and Musee had no doubt they would, Hannah would get the credit, but Musee would get the experience and knowledge. For how long? Out loud, Musee said, "The next five years will be the goal for getting myself ready to go on my own. The raise I receive will all go into a brokerage account for my transition from employee to owner." She liked hearing it out loud, so she continued.

"I'm the owner of my future, and I'm going to make it the best it can be. No one is going to stop me because successful people make a habit of doing things failures don't want to do." She stood up, and fell back on the sofa, dizziness overtaking her. She giggled, pleased with herself. You go girl, she thought.

# CHAPTER 13

"So, we're in agreement," Dex asked, looking over at Charlie as they drove into the city Monday morning.

"Yeah," said Charlie, grinning, and looking at the river and its barge traffic.

"Yes, sir."

"Yeah, yes, sir."

"Okay, we'll invite David to dinner in the city tonight and ask him then. He'll have to give us an answer, then and there, and return with us to Calumet Farms tonight."

"Is he going to live in the spare bedroom?"

"No, he's going to live in the farmhand's bunkroom in the barn."

"Won't he be cold out there in the winter?"

"Don't worry, Charlie. We'll make it real nice for him."

"Yeah."

"Yes, sir."

"Yeah, yes, sir."

"Now, Charlie, don't you go and say something to David before I do tonight."

"Okay. I can't wait to see his face. It's exciting."

"Now, honey, keep in mind. This will be a big change for him. He might have other plans or not want to move out of the city or might have a girlfriend, or something. He just might say no."

"But he likes us. I know he does," Charlie said, nervously wringing her hands and looking at her grandfather.

"That's why we want to break this news to him carefully. Not spring it on him when he has work to do. Okay? Promise?"

"Yeah."

"Yes, sir," Dex corrected her.

"Yeah, yes, sir. But I don't know why we can't ask him right away."

"Say that you promise."

"I promise," Charlie said, looking out the truck window as they turned onto Twenty-third Street. She took in the sights as they went from Manhattan's west side to Park Avenue South. It was her favorite part of the trip. The bustling crowds, the many different types of businesses, and the neon lights that were always on, even in the daytime. Dex turned right on Park Avenue South. Charlie was grinning excitedly. As they passed Seventeenth Street, Charlie saw David sitting on the curb, drinking his Starbucks and reading the paper. She rolled down the window and waved.

"Don't forget, Charlie. Don't say anything."

"I won't." As they pulled to the curb, Charlie jumped out and said, "Hey, David," while still grinning from ear to ear.

"Hay is for horses. Don't you know that?" David grinned back at her. "Morning, Dex. It looks like there's going to be a busier time than usual, the way the crowd is building. That's good. Charlie, let's get this show on the road. It's going to be a FAB day. I can feel it."

"Yeah," she said, opening the rear doors of the truck.

David wasn't sure what was going on, but he knew something was up. Several times during the day, Charlie started to say something to him, then look over at Dex, who would slightly shake his head, and she would straighten the vegetables. By closing, they had sold everything but a couple of potatoes, three red peppers, and some carrots. "Dex, you mind if I have these for dinner?"

"You can have them, but Charlie and I are going to take you to dinner tonight. Nothing fancy; just a neighborhood Italian restaurant over on Second Avenue and Eighty-fourth Street, call Elio's. They have excellent pasta, meatballs, seafood, decent beer and wine, and the management and wait staff are as outstanding as the food. My treat. You in?"

"Say yes, please," Charlie interjected. David felt he now knew what Charlie was so excited about all day.

"You bet. Wouldn't miss it," he said, holding the thumbs-up sign.

Charlie ordered a nonalcoholic frozen daiquiri with two cherries and a slice of orange. Dex and David ordered cold draft beers, neither one caring what brand it was. After ordering dinner, David said, "Charlie, you are a natural salesperson. You picked up the FAB sales language in a remarkably short time."

"Yeah." Charlie beamed with pride from the compliment. "Ask him, Granddaddy. Ask him now."

"Let's wait until we eat, Charlie," Dex said.

"Please, Granddaddy, now."

David had a sense that something serious was happening, and that he was deeply involved. "Ask me what?" He looked at Dex instead of Charlie.

"Well, I guess this is as good a time as any," Dex said, taking a swallow of his beer. "Look, David, it's obvious Charlie likes working with you. I think you have real smarts about you, particularly when it comes to business. I also kind of know that you have some problems right now, so that may be weighing on you. If it is, say so. But Charlie and I want to make you an offer. We want you to join us in our little business as a full-time person. If you say yes, there's a catch. You'd have to move to Calumet Farms and learn the whole business, not just the fun part at the market." Dex stopped to see David's reaction to what had been said.

"I'm not sure I understand everything, but go on," David said, staring intently at Dex, whose stare was just as steely at David.

"Calumet Farms is more complex than it looks. We source our produce from twenty-three small seven- to fifteen-acre farms in and around Columbia County. These growers only sell to us; that's why we have a steady supply of high-quality produce."

"Do you have them under contract?"

"Something like that. I'll explain the arrangements later, assuming you say yes. The business is six days a week, two days at the farm collecting and assembling what we sell the other four days. Sunday is a day of rest. It's long hours and hard work. No need for a coat and tie. If you join us, you'd be expected to do everything, learn everything, and, I might add, come to me, and only me, with any improvements you feel could make the business more profitable. I figure that Harvard MBA will get you a list of improvements right away."

"How'd you know I have a Harvard MBA?"

"Son, you wouldn't be sitting here if I didn't know all I needed to know about you. You told me about the mistake you made. I know I can trust you with my money and my granddaughter. I know you're smart. What I don't know is how you make decisions, but I'm about to find that out."

"What do you mean?"

"Charlie and me are offering you a partnership, of sorts. You'll move to Calumet Farms and live in the farmhand's room in the barn. It has a small bathroom with a shower, but it's nothing special. We'll fix it up better if you say yes."

"Internet connection?"

"Not yet, but I'll call in the morning, and it'll be in by the end of the week."

"When do you want my decision?"

The waiter brought their food. "I'll have another beer," Dex said to him. "How about you, David?"

"Sure."

"Charlie, you want another drink?"

"Yeah, please." She turned to David, "Say yes, please."

David looked back at Dex. "When do you want my answer?"

"When we finish dinner," Dex said, taking his fork and a spoon and using them to twirl some spaghetti on his fork while never taking his eyes off David. "When Charlie and I get in the truck, you'll either be coming with us, or the offer is over."

"I see. What about my things. When do I get them?"

"We'll stop by your place, and you can get what you need for the next few days. You can take one of our trucks Thursday and come down and get the rest."

David looked at Dex and then at Charlie. His first thought was how hilarious his classmates at HBS would think this was. His second thought was how he was being handed a future on a silver, or in this case, a wooden platter. He grinned and winked at Charlie and looked back at Dex and said, "Don't need to wait to finish eating. I'm in if you'll have me. Everything I need to get from my apartment can be gotten in ten minutes. Thursday needs to be getting ready for Friday and Saturday." Dex looked down and said a silent thank you to his deceased wife Mary. He knew she had sent David to him and Charlie.

*  *  *

I'll be down in a couple of minutes," David said as they pulled up in front of his apartment building.

"I'll help you," Charlie said.

"No thanks, it won't take long. You'd better stay with your grand-daddy, so he doesn't get scared."

"But I want to help," Charlie insisted.

Dex put his hand on her arm and said, "Charlie, let David get what he needs. You stay with me."

"Okay," she said frowning.

David entered the building and started up the three flights of stairs, taking them two at a time. When he got to the second-floor landing, he called Musee's number. It rang as he entered the apartment and started putting what clothes he had in plastic garbage bags. He put the phone on speaker and let it ring, assuming her voice mail would kick in. He ended up with three garbage bags of clothes, cookbooks, computer, and bathroom items. Musee's phone continued to ring. He shut the phone off, thinking he would call later, when he was sure she would be home. He grabbed the two lightest bags in his right hand and the heaviest in his left. His thought was the irony of being a Harvard grad and everything he had in the world fit in three thirty-gallon bags. He bounded down the stairs to an open door he couldn't have dreamed of four months ago. He thanked Fil for teaching him to believe in himself.

Later that evening when he was sure Musee would be home he dialed her number again. It rang. He let it ring over and over, the sound finally penetrating his excitement about his new future. She's on a date, he thought. Like a balloon with a leak, his mood slowly changed.

# CHAPTER 14

David woke early, just as the first light filtered into his bunkhouse. At first, he was confused, but it took only seconds to remember the door he'd opened to a new life—one totally different from how he'd been living for over eight years. He pushed back the covers and stumbled into the bathroom to take a shower. Dex had said the day began with breakfast at seven. He had just under an hour to see what he had chosen as his new home.

Leaving the farmhand's two-room apartment in the corner of the barn, he looked around at the rest of the barn. It was big. Although it didn't show signs of livestock, there was a loft with a ladder. The ceiling of the apartment was part of the floor of the loft. Moving toward the back of the barn, he saw a set of double doors and a Ford tractor, an old one at that, sitting inside. A stool and some clean and folded rags were around the well-kept machinery. On a table and pegboard against the back wall was an array of tools, old but clean and free of rust. A cabinet held drawers with screws, nails, and parts, all neatly arranged. David slid open the door leading out the barn's side and stepped out under a pole shed with two vans with *Calumet Farms* stenciled on the side and a pickup truck. All three vehicles appeared in good condition but showing wear from their age. David looked over and saw the van they had come home in last night, parked by the gravel road cutting through the farm. Three vans, he thought, so they must rotate them, or maybe one of these is used for spare parts. All three were Ford Econoline vehicles from the same general time period.

The barn sat on the slope of a hill. David walked up the hill, and at the crest, on a plateau, he saw two graves. He walked over and read the head stone, which said Holmes. There were two footstones, one reading Mary and the other Edith. No dates, just the names. David understood that the dates really weren't necessary. Those who loved these individuals didn't need a reminder of the time spans of pleasure and then pain at their loss. Just as he did the few times he'd visited Fil's grave, he looked around for a pebble or small stone to leave on the headstone, evidencing his respect and visit. Turning around, he understood why these two were buried here. He could see for miles. Even the fencing separating the various farms and roads seemed to vanish, as the broad sweep of the valley and hills stretched out, the patchwork of fields, some tilled, some with orchards, and some with row crops, looked like a quilt. Facing the graves again, he thought about the heartache Dex and Charlie must feel. He looked at the grove of trees that stretched down from the hill. The trees were mature, with saplings reaching for the sun where an older tree was either dying or had fallen during some weather event. The grove was dense; however, David could see a slight path leading into the trees. He decided to follow the path. The temperature was noticeably cooler the farther he went into the woods. Although the trail was nearly nonexistent, he only had to stop twice to make sure he was going the right way. The natural slope of the hill led him to believe that the trail would end up close to the farmhouse. He was correct. Coming out of the tree line, he saw the side of the farmhouse with its tall pitched roof, weathered white clapboard, and a set of steps leading up onto the wide porch that ran along the front of the house. He walked up the steps, trying to be quiet. On the porch, he looked across to the barn and his new life. Was this what he wanted? What about all the years of achieving in the success arena of Ivy League grad school and Wall Street? Was all of that sweat and toil for nothing? Would he ever go to a class reunion? Could he tell his classmates he was a partner in a truck farming operation? He caught himself as Fil's voice in his mind shattered his doubts about where he was: You make your own future when you open a door. Having a door to open and recognizing that fact is all you are due. The rest is up to you. David whispered, "Yes, sir. I understand. I love you. I'll make you proud."

"What did you say?" Dex was standing at the kitchen door a few feet away.

David jumped and turned crimson and muttered, "Nothing really, just talking to myself. Good morning, Dex. I thought I would look around before you and Charlie were up. If you're ready for breakfast, I'd like to fix it for the two of you."

"Sure, Charlie would like that. I've already eaten. I saw you leave the barn and thought I'd let you explore on your own. I assume you saw Mary's and Edith's graves at the top of the hill. One day, I'll be there with them. Come on in. Charlie likes to have pancakes, bacon, butter, and a gallon of syrup on the days we don't go to market."

"Sounds good to me. Sure you don't want any?"

"Well, maybe a short stack of two would be nice."

"Got it."

David walked into a kitchen almost square in dimensions, with counters and appliances running around three sides. On the porch side, there was a double-hung single window. On the side facing the grove of trees and the top of the hill was a double-casement window with glass panes that cranked out. Underneath the window was the sink. There was no dishwasher. A white electric stove with oven was to the left of the sink. On the farmhouse's back wall was a decades-old white refrigerator. Between the stove and the refrigerator was a small, aged microwave oven. The Formica countertops were black and worn in spots, with other places reflecting burns where something too hot had been put down. The upper cabinets were on the refrigerator wall while the lower cabinets were on three sides of the room. On the counter were kitchen gadgets: an old wide-mouth jar holding wooden spoons, green canisters with white lettering announcing Sugar, Tea, Coffee, and Cookies, a green breadbox, and an old bottle, one David imagined someone had found buried in the dirt, held a single paper flower.

Dex saw David look at the flower and said, "Mary used to keep fresh flowers in that old bottle when she ruled this kitchen. She said, 'No kitchen should spend a day without flowers rewarding the woman who kept the family well fed.'" He hesitated for a minute, looking off through the sink window. "Since she died, me and Charlie haven't had the want-to to plant flowers, so Charlie bought that paper flower on one of our market days shortly after Mary passed. She put it in the bottle. Didn't ask me for money or anything, just went and did it. She misses her granny a lot. Me too. Enough of that. Look around and you'll find everything you need. I'll go start waking Charlie up. We have a lot to load up for tomorrow's market."

The kitchen's fourth side had a beat-up old kitchen table with two leaves hanging down. A place mat was at each side of the table's center. David went over and lifted the table's front leaf, felt underneath for the wooden brace to secure it, and turned to find what he needed to make pancakes, bacon, butter, and gallons of syrup.

David committed himself to the business of Calumet Farms. This first day, he went with Dex and Charlie to pick up produce from growers. "Our system is fairly simple," Dex explained, as they drove along. "We have twenty-three small farmers spread around a radius of sixty miles from Calumet. Each farmer has seven to ten acres, except for two who have shown they can manage fifteen acres. We sit down with each one at the beginning of the year and come to an agreement about what they will plant that year. I keep a master annual notebook and specific farm notebooks that record what the yearly crops should be, who is growing what this year, and what they grew in past seasons. These notebooks show the yields they received for every type of produce they have grown on their land each year. When possible, everything is grown organically. When necessary, we use the minimum amount of nonorganic fertilizer."

"They let you have all this information willingly?"

"We won't go into it all now, but yes, they give me the info and are open to suggestions about what we need them to grow each year. This relationship between the farmer/producer and Calumet is critical to our success. Sort of like your relationship with your clients in the past. If both sides are respectful of each other, a partnership works well."

"Why a notebook and not a computer?"

"We started before those things became popular. My notebooks are part of me. Yeah, I could put everything on a computer, but then someone else would know what I did and how I did it. That's even if the computer wasn't hacked. Besides, one morning I might go to turn the darn thing on and find out everything is gone. When they tell you to back up your stuff, they're really telling you it's almost guaranteed your computer will crash. No, sir, my notebooks work just the way I want them to, and no one except me, and eventually you, knows what's in the book."

"Amen to that."

"This next farm we're going to belongs to Walter Evans. He goes by the name of Walt. His wife is Jo, and they have three daughters: Millie, who is fourteen and plays basketball for the local junior high; Karen, who is eleven, and in the fifth grade; and Cindy, who is eight and in the third grade. The younger two take dance lessons. All of them get good grades and are active in the Pineville Baptist Church Youth Choir." David scribbled notes on everything Dex said.

"Walt is my favorite," Charlie chimed in. "His girls are re-e-e-ealy nice. I like seeing them when they're home. Ms. Jo always has some cookies when we come. They are so-o-o-o good."

"Back to the system," Dex said. "Each year, I rotate what farms will be picked up on what day and let them know. That way, they can plan when to harvest their target produce, depending on my schedule. As you can see, Tuesday is a long day. We pick up according to the specific produce in such a way that we can position the goods in the boxes, handling them only once. So is Thursday, when we pick up for Friday and Saturday. Friday night and Saturday night, after market, we fill in for Saturday and Monday's green market."

"Have you ever thought about going another step and having some canned or pickled or stewed produce to make the extra margin?"

"Yes and no. When Mary was here, we had discussed it and sort of started taking steps in that direction. Then she became sick. It just dropped."

"Okay. Just a thought."

"Keep it in mind for when you've absorbed all of the rest of the operation."

"Hmm, I'll probably be older than you when I've figured all this out. Charlie will be pushing me around in a wheelchair," David said, smiling at Charlie, sitting between the two men.

"No, you won't," she said, punching him on the shoulder.

It was after nine that night when they arrived back at the farm. They'd had lunch but no supper. David said, "How about I grab a few of these vegetables and throw together a mix of steamed veggies. Any meat in the fridge?"

"Sure," said Dex. 'There's ham in there and fresh bread in the breadbox. Let me clean up, and I'll help you."

"Naw, I'll help, Granddaddy. You get a glass of tea and sit on the porch."

"Sure, Charlie, good idea," David said.

David rooted around the kitchen, trying to remember where certain pots and pans were from his morning search and found the items he needed. Charlie pointed out the obvious places and items and set the kitchen table for three. After dinner, Dex said, "Charlie, how about you clean up and get ready for bed while I talk to David some more on the porch."

"Yeah."

"Yes, sir," Dex responded with a smile on his face.

"Yeah, yes, sir," Charlie said while clearing the table.

"Lord, I'll never win," Dex said, shaking his head. "Just like her granny. Come on David, bring your tea, and I'll fill you in more about the operation."

Sitting in the rockers, with a breeze being channeled between the hills around the farm, David thought about how interestingly simple and at the same time complex and beautiful this whole endeavor was. He waited for Dex to get settled and begin.

"David, you asked if the farmer/producers were willing to give me information about their operations. Well, they do so because they are my partners. In the beginning, it was just Mary and me planting, harvesting, and selling from a roadside stand over there." Dex pointed to where the driveway met the highway. "It didn't take long before we had a reputation for quality produce and friendly service. When we got some money put away, I figured we would buy the land right around here and expand, but I realized there was just so much work the two of us could do without risking the quality of the produce and our quality of life." Dex took a sip from his glass. "Boy, this is the time I'd really like a cigarette. Mary made me quit back in my thirties. Said she wasn't goin' to be a widow with all this work to do. Little did we know." He looked off into the distance. The rhythmic squeak of his rocker screamed the agony he felt.

"Anyway," he resumed after a few minutes, "she was active in the Pineville Baptist Church Ladies Circle and became aware of a young couple that had fallen on hard times as tenant farmers trying to eke out a living on the wrong kind of land. I knew of a good ten acres not too far from here, so I bought it and made the farmer and his wife a proposition: If the farmer agreed in writing to stay on the land for twenty years, and work with me, following my directions as to what to grow, and have the produce ready when I want it, after those twenty years, the land would belong to them. We'd split the revenue sixty-forty, Calumet and them, with me paying for all the seeds and supplies."

"Wow, what a deal."

"It might seem so to you, but it was a hard sell to this couple and others in the beginning. Dirt people, and I don't mean that in a bad way, because that's what I am, too. Dirt people are fiercely independent, close-to-the-earth people. They're good people in almost every way. They could only see it as being slaves controlled by someone else. They were afraid I would put too many restrictions on them. At that time, they didn't have any children. They wanted to be able to drive off at a whim and move somewhere else. There's probably a hippie song to that effect."

"How'd you get them to take the deal?"

"I didn't. Mary did. She got the wife at one of the Ladies' meetings, where the ladies of the church helped young people less fortunate than themselves without making them feel like it was charity."

"How'd they do that?"

"In this case, they asked this young wife and a couple of others like her to help sort out donated clothes for those in need. You know, a person might know they don't have anything, but they really don't know they're poor, or, really, they don't admit they're poor. Well, this young wife was helping, and Mary noticed that she was drawn to helping fold the baby clothes. Well, you didn't have to hit Mary in the head with a frying pan. She was smart as a whip. She moved over to that table and started talking to the young lady. Sandra is her name, and quietly, without anyone else hearing, Mary began to tell her about me, us, I guess, and what we wanted. She used that FAB thing you talk about, but she didn't know it. She started describing the benefits the two of them and their future children would have, not having to worry about anything, as long as they worked hard, and one day they would have their own land and be able to pass it on to their children, or afford for their children to go to college, or whatever path God put them on."

"It must have worked."

"Patrick called me that same evening to see if the offer still stood. They got their land twenty years later. We found another five acres close to theirs and started all over again, with them farming the fifteen acres. Sandra was pregnant at the time we started and had a girl. The daughter now has a good job in the medical field as a radiology assistant. She has a family of her own, over in Albany. Patrick and Sandra had a second child, John, who is a major in the Army. When his twenty years are up, he intends to move back here and farm like his dad. That'll be in three years if all goes well. You'll have to find a plot of land for him at that time."

"We will."

"That we, David, will be you and Charlie. I'll be joining Mary before then."

"You look fit as a fiddle to me, as they used to say, Dex."

"Looks and reality are two different things. I've got health issues we won't go into now. Just understand that you have to pay attention and get up to speed quickly. There's one more lesson for tonight, and then I'm going to turn in. My attorney and CPA are one and the same—a guy by the name of Win Oakley. He and I grew up in the same neighborhood a long time ago. When I moved here, I found out he had come here after law school. I felt and still do that I could trust him, to a certain extent. The key words are 'I' and 'to a certain extent.' He may think he can get the upper hand if I'm not around. Just be wary. I used him to draw up the original contract with my first partner, but he doesn't know about the rest or who those partners are. He does my taxes so that the IRS knows an enrolled CPA does the work. That makes a difference. He thinks he knows everything, but he doesn't. I'll introduce the two of you when the time is right. Now I'm going to follow Charlie up to bed."

Dex slowly got up, picked up his empty tea glass and David's, and went inside. David sat for a couple of minutes, realizing that the situation he had stumbled on was going to be as challenging as his prior profession. Suddenly, he looked at his phone and saw that it was after ten. He dialed Musee's number and started walking to the barn. She never picked up. He was beginning to fear that he'd just been an afternoon stand, a hookup, to her. He felt foolish; he'd thought there was a deeper connection. Anyway, he'd have internet by the end of the week, and he could reach out that way. Maybe she would at least send a forget-it-stupid email and give him closure.

*   *   *

Doing the work of a merchandise manager without the authority or pay convinced Musee that nothing else in her life could go bad. Maybe even dropping dead would be an improvement. She willed herself to be positive at work, making sure her departments had the right signage, the correct stock on the floor, the dressing rooms were clean and neat, just the way she knew her best customers considered their own lives and businesses.

Being second fiddle to someone who didn't know enough about career fashion to fill a thimble but had the right DNA was excruciating in the short term, even if the long-term goal was the grand prize of her own store. Could she keep it up? she wondered. Hell, yeah, but it would have been easier if that glorious Sunday afternoon had panned out. She looked across the sales floor without seeing anything but David taking his shirt off her and looking deep into her eyes as he made love to her.

I'll never sell that table, she thought. Why did he disappear? Was she just another piece to him? Without realizing it, she shook her head and muttered out loud, "No!"

She took a deep breath. Maybe he had to go out of town on a job interview. Maybe he lost his phone—I saw him put my numbers and email in it. Yeah, that's it. He lost his phone. Where did he say he worked? He's between jobs; that's right. God, please make that Sunday as important to David as it was to me.

"Musee, Jack Flynn from Ballentine Suits is here to see you."

"Who? From where?"

"He says his name is Jack Flynn, and he represents Ballentine Suits."

"Okay, I'll see him in the lounge area."

Musee went to her office to get her order book and went to the lounge. She looked up and saw a statue of a Greek god, or at least a replica of a Greek god. She immediately imagined what he looked like naked, his broad shoulders rippling with muscles whenever he moved his arms. His waist was at least ten inches smaller than his chest, and his glutes were trying to rip out the seat of his pants. When she glanced at his face, she saw the most mysterious brown eyes below bushy eyebrows she had ever seen outside of a romance novel cover. She felt her face flush.

"Hi, I'm Maureen O'Hara, assistant merchandise manager for business wear." She held out her hand.

"Good morning, Ms. O'Hara. I'm Jack Flynn." He shook her hand with a firm grip, but not quite like guys trying to establish their dominance when they meet a woman for the first time. His handshake was confident. "I represent Ballentine Suits. You've never chosen to do business with us. May I ask why?"

"Your quality is not what our customers want, Mr. Flynn."

"I've heard you're direct, Ms. O'Hara, and I appreciate that, so I'll be direct as well. Ballentine Suits has been bought by a private equity company that specializes in retail acquisitions. We're committed to improving quality and taking market share in the women's business space."

"And how do you propose to do that, Mr. Flynn?"

"Please, call me Jack."

"Okay, Jack, how do you intend to do that?"

An hour and a half later, Musee had placed an order for four styles in three sizes as a trial order, with the stipulation that she could return them immediately if the quality did not meet her standards. She had also agreed to attend a dinner party Ballentine was throwing for merchandise managers and their assistants at the Fifth Avenue home of the firm's CEO. She knew the dinner was a prelude to something more intimate. Jack was the closest thing she had ever seen to a woman's fantasy—at least her fantasy. She sat at her desk, twirling her pencil. She thought about what a hookup with Jack would be like. She thought about that incredible Sunday a few weeks ago when she knew she had found out what love was all about. Her eyes watered up, and she took deep breaths to avoid crying. Why hadn't he called, as he promised he would? Why hadn't he at least emailed to say it was over? She thought about Jack, here and now. She thought about his firm, which had taken over a lousy business and could, no, would, make it better. She pictured him naked and in bed with her. She felt her body heat rise. He was here and now. David was fading away the longer he went without contacting her. She closed her eyes. David is out there. He gave me not only the physical love I needed at that time, but he gave me unconditional love, not dependent on my "behaving" or doing some act that was degrading, she thought. She realized that in one afternoon he'd boosted her self-esteem constantly, and with a sincerity that could not be faked. David might not ever materialize again, but he'd ruined her for casual hookups. She wanted a real relationship with a person—like David.

She picked up her phone, looked at Jack Flynn's business card, and texted, "Order still stands, but cancel me for this evening. Never mix business and pleasure. Thanks, Maureen O'Hara."

# CHAPTER 15

The weeks went by faster than David had thought possible. Four days a week they were selling from the tent at Union Square and two days filling the truck with produce to sell. Friday and Saturday they did both, not finishing till well after ten both nights, while beginning before five every morning of the week. Sundays were unusual for David. Dex let it be known from the beginning that he was expected to go to church with Dex and Charlie. He explained that most of the farmers they associated with went to the same Pineville Baptist Church. Dex went on to explain that religion was both social and spiritual. He emphasized, looking directly at David, that a person needs both. The social was for the present, and the spiritual was for those times when an extra hand on the plow of life was needed to keep the rows straight. David heard the message loud and clear. Every Sunday, some wives and children of their farmer-partners always wrapped Charlie in love and attention. David was surprised that he enjoyed the fellowship, and the sermon each week made sense from a here-and-now perspective. The parishioners could relate the message to their daily lives. In the Catholic Church, the emphasis was on the hereafter. He joined Dex and Charlie in "their" pew three from the front. David went in first, then Charlie, and Dex sat at the end. All of their world now knew that Charlie had an adopted big brother, and Dex had an adopted son capable of running his business. What no one knew was just how extensive that business was.

David had settled into the farmhand room and was content—with one exception. Daily, he called and emailed Musee without so much as a return voice message or email. He was lonesome for someone of the opposite sex to talk to, flirt with, and at least pretend he had a chance to get into an intimate relationship. There were times at the green market when the verbal sparring with young good-looking customers raised his testosterone level to a painful plateau.

The morning routine developed naturally. David was up at four, took a quick shower, put on jeans and a T-shirt, and went over to the house to put on coffee and breakfast. He varied the breakfast, sometimes cereal, more often fruit, eggs, bacon, toast with butter, and an assortment of jellies. Some Sundays, he made pancakes. Both Dex and Charlie commented on how long it had been since they woke up to the rich smell of coffee and good food. David was pleased to be cooking both breakfast and dinner for the three of them. The few times he thought about his prior life, it was not with longing. He recognized the tension and falseness of those stress-filled years.

It was a Wednesday morning, the first week of May, when David walked into the kitchen, flipped on the light, and was startled to see Dex sitting at the kitchen table. He hardly moved, but David could see perspiration and a grimace on his face. "Morning, Dex. I'll have the coffee on in a minute. Everything okay?"

"Yeah. I've decided to let you and Charlie go to the market without me today."

David didn't turn around or ask why. He said, "Yes, sir. She and I can handle it, no problem. Have you told her yet?"

"Not yet. She'll be down in a few minutes. I want it to be your idea.

I'll stay here and get some book work done." David poured a cup of coffee and took it to Dex. He looked hard at him and could see that he was in a lot of pain.

"I've got some Aleve in the cabinet. Want some?"

"Yeah, give me three before Charlie comes down."

David went over, shook three pills from the bottle, and took them back to Dex. "Hold on to these until I can whip up some breakfast. You don't want to take them on an empty stomach. I'm fixing pancakes so take 'em after you've eaten and had some milk. That'll help protect your stomach." He went back to the counter and started to mix the batter after turning on the griddle to preheat it. "Anything I need to know about today?"

"Naw, I should be all right in a little while. After y'all leave, I'll go lay down for a while. I'll be all right. Listen, Charlie is real sensitive to something happening to me, so it'd be best if nothing is said as to why I'm not going in today."

"I thought you were doing bookkeeping and planning for the fall crop planting."

"You're right."

Ten minutes later, after Dex had eaten his pancakes and taken the Aleve, David walked out into the hall and called, "Charlie, you coming to breakfast today or tomorrow?"

She appeared at the head of the steps and said, "Tomorrow? What about today?"

"I was just kidding. Come on. I've got a surprise for you. Grand-daddy has agreed, after much persuasion, to let you and me go to market alone while he works on the books and fall planting schedule. That okay with you? You think you can keep me in line?"

"Yeah, I'll teach you how to FAB sell."

"Oh, you will, eh? I tell you what, whoever sells the least has to clean out the truck this evening, and, to make it worse, do the dishes after dinner."

"You're on. I'll beat your you-know-what off."

"You wish. I'll dirty so many dishes that you'll be up till midnight. Here you go—pancakes, bacon, and sliced pears. Dig in. You'll need the energy to keep up with me."

As they were leaving, Charlie kissed Dex. "I love you, Granddaddy. Don't be mad when David comes home crying."

"Treat him gently, Charlie. You know his feelings get hurt easily." Dex looked at David and nodded slightly. They shook hands, and he said, "Have a good day selling, you two. I'll be waiting on the porch when you get home."

# CHAPTER 16

Charlie didn't seem to attach any significance to Dex staying home as she and David continued to knit the bonds of siblings. The green market was busy. David and Charlie sold most of what they'd brought. She asked a lot of questions about every subject under the sun. He would explain the answer to her question, but he quickly realized that she didn't always understand the answers or the meanings of some of the words he used. He took time to formulate the answers so that she could grasp much of their meaning. He thought of Albert Einstein's words: "If you can't explain it to a six-year-old, you don't know the subject yourself." David felt spurred to meet that challenge. He didn't know the extent of Charlie's special needs, but he knew that if or when something happened to Dex, she would be devastated and afraid. The trouble was that Charlie wanted to know about a lot of different things. Why do we use paper bags for the produce rather than plastic bags? Why are we in the same spot at the market every time, instead of going over to the other side? Why do the weather people always get the forecast wrong? Why can't people go down any street they want in the city? Why are the songs on the radio so short? Why are soldiers in faraway places? The questions went on and on. It was like Dex's absence turned on the spigot of her curiosity, and she didn't know how to turn it off. Overall, he enjoyed the day, and Charlie's questions took his mind off the building concern caused by a serious health issue with Dex. Perhaps after dinner, Dex would be willing to give David an explanation of his physical status.

True to his word, Dex was on the front porch in his rocker. He still had on the same clothes he did that morning, and, most unusual for Dex, had not shaved. He did, however, have a pitcher of tea, three glasses, a bowl of ice, and a plate of cookies on the table.

"How'd it go, you two?"

"He's got to wash the dishes, Granddaddy," Charlie said, stepping onto the porch and grabbing a cookie, kissing Dex, and plopping into the rocker next to his.

"She didn't beat me by much," David said, winking at Dex. He handed Dex the cash bag and took the last rocker after pouring Charlie and himself a glass of tea.

"Well, I certainly hope you kids didn't have so much fun you forgot to sell everything."

"Naw, Granddaddy, we sold just about everything."

"David, how 'bout Charlie and I make the rounds tomorrow restocking. I'd like you to take the five names on my desk and go speak with the farmers about what would be best to grow in the fall, and what their needs will be."

"Sure, but we haven't discussed that issue yet. I'm not sure—"

"You can handle it. On the shelves behind the desk are my yearly logs for each farm, starting when they became part of our operation. You'll see what each grew in the fall of each year, their yields, the type of weather, and other incidental info I thought was important. Go over that information this evening, and you'll be ready. They're expecting you. I called them today and said you'd be around some time tomorrow."

"Sure, I'll start dinner and then get on it."

"Nope, I've made us some stew. It's on the stove, ready to eat. Why don't you fix us each a bowl and slice some bread. We can eat out here, where it's cool and pleasant. Charlie, how 'bout getting the folding table from the hall closet and setting it up."

*   *   *

At eleven, he stopped working and tried to reach Musee. He dialed the phone and let it ring until the automated voice told him no one was going to answer and clicked off. He then sent an email, trying to be light about it, but even he saw the desperation in the words. He shut off the computer, understanding more than ever the saying that repeating the same tasks over and over and expecting a different result is a sign of stupidity. He finished going through the logs around two in the morning. The thoroughness of the logs was impressive. Dex clearly understood the details of running a business, particularly one with independent partners ... at least almost independent partners. David closed the books, had his notes for tomorrow, and put the logs aside. His mind turned back to Musee. He refused to believe that she was so callous that their afternoon those many weeks ago was just a passing lark for her. The connection they had was real, at least for him, and his gut told him it was for her as well. Stripping, he fell into bed. It had been a long day, but he relished every minute. Even though he tried to go to sleep thinking of Musee, his mind would not leave Dex and the turn in his health. What would it mean for the three of them?

*   *   *

The first three meetings with the farmer-partners went well. David's confidence grew. The farmers introduced David to their wives and children. Discussions took place either at the kitchen table or on the porch. Iced tea and cake or cookies were served. The scheduling went quickly and most of the time was spent satisfying their curiosity about

David and his relationship with Dex. At the fourth, and most important meeting, David sensed a problem the moment he drove up in Tim Roy's side yard. Tim was working on his tractor.

"Good morning, Tim. How's it going?"

"Going good. Just changing the oil and filters on this hunk of iron."

"Smart. Treat them right and they'll last a lifetime. You have time to discuss the fall schedule?"

Tim put down his wrench and wiped his hands on a rag. "Sure, I have time to talk, but not about fall planting. I've been thinking. I've had a relationship with Dex for eleven years. No complaints, but I'd like to plant what I want to plant, sell where I want to sell, see how I do."

David's stomach felt queasy. This is what he feared—a top-notch farmer-partner sensing that Dex wasn't doing well and wanting to take advantage of the situation. David knew this was a test of him and his ability to hold Dex's creation together. David smiled and said, "Sure, Tim. I can understand your perspective. Your agreement with Calumet Farms has a provision for doing what you want done. Do you want to get an appraisal of the farmland and equipment, or do you want me to?"

"I can get it done."

"Fine. Will you be going to the Pineville Bank? It should be easy to get the loan there since you will only have to borrow 50% of the farm and equipment value. They're familiar with Calumet Farms. If you need a reference, suggest they call Dex."

"Will you be buying what I produce?" Tim asked.

"Probably not, Tim. We have two new farmers coming on board. If you find you have produce you want to offer to Calumet, we'll certainly take a look at it. You've been a good partner, and we appreciate everything we've accomplished together. Why don't we talk again next Tuesday? Will that work for you?"

"That's good. Tuesday will give me time to arrange everything, Thanks, for understanding, David." The two shook hands and Tim watched David get back in his truck. From the porch, Tim's wife, Julie, stood leaning against the post with her arms crossed and a worried look on her face.

*　*　*

Dex was on the porch when David arrived back at the farm. He sat straight, with both feet planted firmly on the porch, gently rocking. Sweat glistened on his forehead. "How'd it go?"

"Four of the five are done and looking forward to a good harvest. They all like the fall since it means money in their pockets when Christmas rolls around. We have one problem, a big one at that."

"Who?"

"Tim Roy."

"Figured that may be the case. What's the issue?" Dex asked with a slight grimace on his face.

"Dex, in my former job, we had a condition that we called the seven-year itch. A good or even great producer begins to wonder how much they could make if they were on their own rather than sharing their production with the firm. The question grows until they feel like they have to do something. Those who succumb to the urge leave and invariably find they're worse off than before. Those who investigated first usually didn't leave, recommitted themselves to what they were doing, and went on to much higher production."

"What's your point?" Dex said.

"Tim wants to tear up the partnership agreement. He understands the mechanism of getting an appraisal and paying you half of the appraised value."

"Did you buck him?"

"No. Having an unhappy partner is untenable for you. I suggested he pick the appraiser, go to Pineville Bank, and discuss the loans he'll need to buy you out and finance the fall crop. By the way, I suggested he use you as a reference if they asked for one. I told him we would speak again on Tuesday. Tim is a good farmer, and I suspect a reasonable businessman. He's going to find that the risks associated with going alone and borrowing money from a bank or third-party credit source is not as safe as having Calumet finance everything. If he stays, it should be a stronger relationship. If he goes, all of the other partners will see that Tim was treated fairly. We're bringing on more farmer-partners so while his expertise will be missed, we'll still have production capacity. I didn't get to speak to his wife, but she didn't look so happy standing on the porch. My bet is Tim is smart and will decide on his own to stay."

"You're right about not wanting an unhappy partner. You're also right about letting him figure it out. Now that you're back, why don't you fix dinner later. Have Charlie come and wake me when its ready. I'm going to take a nap. She's up on the hill talking to her grandmother." Dex slowly got up, stood a minute, and left the porch. David sighed and sat thinking for a few minutes. Thoughts about what will happen to Charlie, the business, and him when Dex died raced through his mind over and over. He didn't know how to prepare for the inevitable, but he knew he'd better figure it out fast.

# CHAPTER 17

"Hey, David, won't Granddaddy be happy at what we've sold today." Charlie had just finished using her FAB skills to sell two bags of vegetables to build a meal. This was the second day her granddad had stayed home, but Charlotte did not seem to attach any significance to his absence. After lunch, business slowed, and David and Charlie talked about various menus using the produce they had on hand.

"Charlie, can you handle things while I swap these empty boxes for more veggies from the truck?"

"Sure. I'll FAB anyone who comes in."

"It'll take a few minutes rearranging the boxes, so knock on the side of the truck if you need me."

Charlie was doing what she liked most other than FAB selling, watching the people in the market as they moved from tent to tent. She wondered who they were, what they did, and where they lived in this huge city. She was proud of how she and David had displayed the produce to make people think about meals and not just one item. She was proud of her handmade signs, too. David said they were better than printed ones.

Charlie watched a couple as they moved from tent to tent. They looked different. She was pretty, but he seemed prettier. Both wore jeans, not the ripped kind, but the kind that looked like they were never worked in. Both wore white shirts. Both wore boots that looked like hiking boots she had seen in catalogs, but they didn't look like the kind of people who did much hiking in the woods. They wore sunglasses, even though the sun was behind the clouds. She noticed that they both carried canvas bags that were sold on the other side of the market. In big green letters, the bags read Save The Planet Reuse This Bag. Charlie decided they were serious buyers and she'd FAB them and make David and Granddaddy proud.

As they approached the tent, Charlie said, "Hi. If you need assistance, let me know."

"Sure," the guy said, not looking at Charlie but picking up a peach and smelling it. "Meg, why don't we do what this sign says, and serve beets with off-the-cob corn along with the beef wellington medallions?"

"I told you I'd rather serve them snap beans and small white potatoes with beef medallions along with a bottle of Ridge Monte Bello. Don't you remember? We're serving tuna on toast points for a first course with the Chateau Montelena chard."

"This is the first I've heard of that. For God's sake, these are associates of yours, not clients. We could do the meal for half the cost. These people aren't going to put money in our pocket."

"You just don't listen, do you. I told you last weekend what the menu was going to be. Let me remind you: I had to leave Jackson and Perkins because my crooked husband got in trouble, and my little affair with you went public. It was sheer luck that I landed a new position so fast, and now, miraculously, we get to host Casteel, Harris, and Weitz's senior associates, the ones who can grease my way into senior associate or junior partner status, so yes, they are indeed the ones who can 'put money in our pocket.' If you want to scrimp, why don't we forget having a chef and his kitchen staff? That costs a hell of a lot more than the food and wine."

"First, let's be clear. You didn't tell me anything last weekend. Second, I'm not about to cook and clean up for anybody, so the chef and his staff are coming. But speaking of clean-up, I think we should get dishes and glasses that go in the dishwasher instead of those fragile *objets d'arte* you have. It's just stupid not to have usable easy-care stuff. Third, you're the one with a short memory. My partners and I—not 'sheer luck'—got you the position at Casteel. The senior partners know very well who you are. They just need our business, so you'll get a shot at senior associate or junior partner when you earn it. The chef and his staff make a statement about us and the fact that we're top tier. They're essential," Sherm said as he reached for her hand. Meg pulled her hand away and picked up a white potato.

Charlie stood watching this exchange and wondered why the two were together; they were so nasty to each other. She hadn't ever seen that type of relationship. She'd ask David on the way home.

"Yes, but the cost of the chef and staff is far greater than the food or wine. That's money we could invest in good antiques and art, things that we'll have for a lifetime that increase in value. What antiques and art people surrounds themselves with goes much further than a chef in making a statement about who they are."

"That's your opinion. Look, what people notice today are the experiences a person has. You know, going to exotic places, doing unusual things, and having a chef and staff at parties. People don't still value antiques and art. When you get a raise or bonus, you can siphon off some of the money for antiques and art. That's not for me." Sherm looked over at Meg and continued. "Another thing. As I said a minute ago, count me out for washing dishes and glasses."

"I thought we enjoyed our time washing the good stuff and talking about our day."

"We do, but it would be more enjoyable half-undressed on the sofa or the bed, talking and exploring each other."

Charlie made a mental note to ask David what he thought the guy meant by that. She continued lingering behind the table and listening intently to the two strangers.

"I thought we liked the idea of getting in the mood for sex. I didn't think that doing the dishes hindered that at all. We've been letting outside issues get in the way of enjoying each other. With all we've been through, we can't let that happen," Meg countered.

"We both work long, stressful hours. In a couple of years, or maybe sooner, we'll hit the jackpot when my venture goes public and your firm handles the deal."

Meg's head snapped around to stare at Sherm. "What do you mean my firm handles the deal? You're committed to Jackson and Perkins in a multi-year contract. You know it would be unethical for me to handle the deal—I have a non-compete contract with them that's in effect for another two and a half years."

"Don't worry. I'm getting one of my venture investors to demand that the company's IPO investment bankers use your new law firm instead of your old one. That'll let you off the hook. It's all arranged with your new senior partners. That's why they hired you." Meg's face turned red, and she narrowed her eyes.

"They hired me because of my experience and knowledge, not just because of a deal you worked out behind my back."

"Take it easy. You were being pushed out. You needed a job, because we couldn't exist on the small amount I draw from my business each month. This was a win-win-win for all three of us: you, me, and your new firm. That's the way it works, Meg. You're a big girl. I thought you understood that. Gee, I'm sorry for helping you get ahead. Come on, let's pay for these veggies, go home, and have a glass of wine."

Meg handed the string beans and white potatoes to Charlie, who weighed them and put them in one of their canvas bags, mumbling "Twenty-seven dollars, with tax." Sherm handed her thirty dollars, and she made change. She focused on giving them change and trying to remember the parts of the conversation she wanted to ask David about.

Just as Meg and Sherm were turning to leave, David came around the truck saying, "Here's everything we have left. Let's fill in and hope for the best." Hearing his voice, Meg and Sherm turned and stared at him. David looked at the two of them.

"I'll be damned," Sherm said. "I wondered where you disappeared to."

"Well, the two of you look good," David responded. "Hello, Meg. How are things?"

"Thanks to you, they're not what they should have been."

"Really? Last April, the two of you looked very much in love, walking hand in hand at the Whitney. I assume by now Carrie knows you're back together. How is she? How are Joe and Cindy? The old group is shrinking, I guess."

"Carrie and I are getting a divorce, thanks to you," Sherm snarled.

"Thanks to me? That's an interesting perspective," David said with a smile.

"If you hadn't tried to stick a bad investment in that old lady's portfolio, we'd still be married," Meg blurted out.

"You don't say. Let me get this straight. My mistake at work was the only reason you walked out on our marriage and ended up in Sherm's bed? You hear that, Sherm?" Meg started trembling.

"I didn't mean it that way."

"Come on, Meg. We've wasted enough time with this loser." They turned to leave.

"Sherm, before you go, thank you." David smiled and folded his arms across his chest.

Charlie sat down in the rickety lawn chair they used in the tent. She wanted to scream at the guy that David wasn't a loser; he was smarter than both of them put together. How did David even know them, and what did she mean they were married, she thought. She was glad she had gotten their money before they left. David would be proud of that. She started stacking the new produce, and David came over to her and said, "Charlie, remember when I told you that at some point you would learn the difference between people having a bad day and the just plain nasty people?"

"Yeah."

"You just saw what nasty people are like."

"Yeah, you should have heard them talking to each other when they first came up. I almost knocked on the truck, but I remember you said to sell nasty people what they want because we are salespeople. I sold them their produce before they left," she said and grinned.

"The best saleswoman in the world," David said as he winked at her and smiled.

"Who were they? What do they do? Why do they dress like that? Why did she say you were married?" Her questions kept tumbling out like a waterfall cascading down a mountain.

"I'll explain on the way home. Let's sell out and make Granddaddy happy."

On the ride home, David gave Charlie a sanitized and heavily redacted explanation.

*   *   *

The peak hot weather was over. A hint of the coming fall chill, with leaves soon painting the countryside shades of red, orange, and yellow, was on the minds of all three. Since Labor Day, the crowds had been building each market day. David looked forward to smelling woodburning smoke lazily coming from chimneys and leaf piles smoldering in people's yards. Sunday was his day of leisure, and he enjoyed sleeping until six. He had showered and put on a pair of khakis and a plaid collared shirt for church when he heard his name and a loud knock at the door to his sitting room. "David, David!" It was Charlie's voice. At first, his thought turned to something happening to Dex.

"Coming," he hollered as he opened the bedroom door. "What's the matter?"

Charlie giggled, and said, "You need to come to the kitchen right away." The giggle let David know the urgency wasn't Dex's health.

"Okay, Miss Giggles. Lead the way." She took his hand, and they walked briskly across the yard, with Charlie pulling on David's arm. They reached the porch, and she let his hand go and opened the kitchen screen door, holding it open and showing David the way in. He entered the kitchen and stopped, looking at Dex sitting at the kitchen table, a cake with a single candle sitting on the table and three plates and forks.

"Happy anniversary!" Charlie and Dex said in unison.

"Huh?"

"Charlie remembered last night that today would make five months since you became a member of our family and business. She wanted to do something to mark the occasion. Earlier this morning, she made her Granny cake, as she calls it. Most people want ice cream with their cake, but Charlie's cake don't need nothing. No, sir, nothing." Charlie sliced two big pieces and handed one to David and Dex, then cut a smaller piece for herself.

David put a forkful in his mouth and said, "Charlie, this is remarkable. How do you make a cake like this?"

"You really like it? Really? Honest?" Charlie said, holding her plate and fork, her shoulders hunched up, and a grin across her red face. "Granny taught me. We used to make cakes for the church socials. She let me do what I wanted. One day, I just started adding things and came up with this one."

"What's in it?"

"I don't know. I just add things."

"Gee, that's great. What things do you add?"

"I don't know."

"Would you let me help you someday? Would you like it if the two of us made one?"

"Yeah, that'd be fun. Maybe tonight."

"Sounds good."

"Granddaddy, I'm going to go tell Granny about the cake and stuff before church. Toot the horn when you're ready to go." Charlie said, clearing the table and putting the dishes and forks in the sink. She kissed Dex and smiled at David.

David moved to the sink and watched Charlie going up the hill. When he felt she was out of earshot, he said, without turning around, "How are you doing?"

"This is a good day." It was obvious to everyone except Charlie that Dex was not well, losing weight and short on stamina. Since the first episode, Dex had missed at least one market day every two weeks. Lately, his absences had increased to once a week. Even when he went, David had taken over the stocking of the truck with Charlie, or alone, driving to market, putting up the tent, unloading with Charlie, setting up Dex's chair next to the cash bag, taking down the tent, putting the boxes back in the truck, and upon arriving back at the farm, cooking dinner, and then going to restock the truck on Friday and Saturday nights. The farmers began working with David seamlessly. Dex chose to work with the five oldest relationships because he wanted to. In the time David had been with Calumet, they had added two more farmer-partners, with David taking the lead in negotiating and selecting the families. These two were new to truck farming, but they had the desire and love of the land necessary for success. In the coming year, one long-term farmer would get his full independence. Dex left it to David to handle the transition and to help the farmer see the benefit of maintaining the relationship.

David returned to the table with a fresh cup of coffee for both. "Dex, Charlie's cake is better than any I've ever eaten. I can't quite figure out what she has in it, but whatever it is, it's unusually good. I'm certain we could sell slices, quarters, halves, or wholes at an average of one hundred dollars for a whole cake. Is there a recipe?"

"Not that I know of. Since Mary died, Charlie hasn't wanted to bake a cake. This is something special. She was up at 4:30, came in and woke me up asking if she could make a cake for your anniversary. She did it all by herself this morning."

"Do you think she'd let me sell a few slices at the market tomorrow, just to see how people react?"

"Don't know. You'll have to ask her."

Later, while doing dishes, David washing and Charlie drying, he said, "I bet Granny was happy you made a cake again."

"Yeah, she was."

"You know what? I bet our customers at the green market would think it's the best cake they ever had."

"Naw, you really think so?"

"Yeah. I tell you what. Let's find out. We'll take a few slices of cake tomorrow and see if anyone wants to buy them. What'd you say? I bet we could get ten dollars a slice. What do you think we could get for a slice?"

Charlie got a quizzical look on her face and frowned. "I made this cake for you, not to sell. You don't like it?"

"I love it. You're right. Let's save this special one for the three of us."

"Yeah." Charlie's smile returned.

"Tell me about Granny, Charlie."

"She was really special. Hey, when we finish, let's go to the living room and look at the two whole books full of pictures of Granny, Granddaddy, Mommy, and me. Granny used to show me pictures all the time and tell me about each one. I haven't looked at them since she died. I mean, went to heaven."

"Great idea."

Dex, still at the kitchen table, nursing his iced tea, said, "Great idea. While the two of you do that, I'll go to bed." He leaned on the table for support as he got up  and brought his tea glass to the sink, kissed Charlie on the head, patted David on the shoulder, and headed to the stairs.

"This is where we'll start. Here is a picture of Granny and Granddaddy on their wedding day. They lived just south of Chicago in a town called Lincolnton." David looked at a beautiful girl of around eighteen or nineteen and a well-built young man in his twenties. She was smiling, and he appeared more serious than happy, looking directly at the camera with a stare that immediately caught the viewer's attention. Something about the picture was interesting, but David didn't know what it was. Charlie turned the page. "Here is a picture of Granny, Mommy, and Granddaddy when she was two years old. They had moved here to the farm by then. David looked at the photo and suddenly realized what it was about the wedding picture.

"Charlie, go back and let me see the wedding picture again." Charlie turned the page back, and David studied the facial features of the bridegroom. "They were a nice-looking couple." Charlie turned back the page and continued with her narrative of the various pictures. The family history was interesting, particularly as Dex's daughter started becoming a teenager. It was increasingly apparent in the photos that she was unhappy and not as connected to her parents. By her high school years, the photos were few, and the daughter was in only half of them. The number of photos began increasing after Charlie's birth and were of Dex, Mary, and Charlotte. The first of this new series was of Dex, Mary, and a new baby sitting on the same couch where he and Charlie were sitting now. Mary was smiling, but Dex looked serious and dangerous. *I've seen that look in the last five months*, David thought. *I would not want to cross him,* that's for sure. "Charlie, we have an early day tomorrow. You need to turn in. Four-thirty comes early."

"Yeah," she said, closing the book and putting it back on the coffee table. David went into the kitchen until he heard her close the door to her room. He went back to the living room and looked at the photo of the bride and groom again. Flipping the page back and forth between the first photo and the one a few years later, it became clear that the man's face in the two photos was completely altered. David wondered why.

# CHAPTER 18

Again, Dex couldn't make it to the market. A cold northwest wind signaled that fall was near, and his tolerance for the cooler weather was shrinking along with his weight and stamina. Charlie continued to appear oblivious to Dex's health. David grappled with the eventual demise of his friend and mentor, and its consequences. He thought about the word mentor. Fil was the first and most important. He'd been assigned one at HBS and one at MD&S. Together, the two hadn't had the patience, confidence, and business knowledge that Fil or this simple farmer had. He thought back to the first day he bargained for food with Dex. A door opened, and it was like winning the lottery. He realized his maturity and business sense were light-years ahead of where they were before his crash-and-burn at MD&S. Even though he was earning a third what he was at the brokerage firm, his needs were infinitely less than they had been before the divorce. He was as happy as he'd been in his life, yet he knew the day Dex died, all of this would be coming to an end. He also knew he would do what he could to keep Charlie with him. She was of age, so she could make the decision, assuming the courts would let her, since her mental condition was considered impaired. What should he do about ensuring that he and Charlie would remain together? Ask Dex, stupid, he thought.

"Charlie, you've done it again. The produce and your new signs look FABulous. I'll probably be washing dishes till midnight again. Feel like a cup of coffee and donut?"

"Yeah, you bet. Can I go get them?"

"Sure. Here's twenty dollars. Get both of us a cup of coffee and a donut."

"What kind you want?"

"I'll take a chocolate one. You get what you want. See the bread tent across the square?" he said, pointing to the west. Charlie looked over where he was pointing.

"Yeah, that's the McDougal's stand. Granny used to like their breads and cookies."

"Here's another twenty dollars. Buy some cookies for us to have with our lunch."

"Okay, what kind?"

"Why don't you surprise me. Buy whatever you like, and I'll like 'em too."

She started across the open space, mixing with the crowd of shoppers, looking back every few steps to make sure she could see David. He watched her and waved whenever she looked back. When Charlotte arrived at McDougal's, and he was confident she could find her way back, he surveyed the crowd, sizing up what kind of sales day it would be.

"Remember me? We were each other's good luck charms."

David recognized the voice, turned to his right, and was staring at Musee. "How could I ever forget you?"

"Evidently, easy since you never called or emailed after that afternoon."

"I called 111-768-4296 and emailed redh@hemail.com every day since the Sunday we spent together, and you never responded."

"Oh God, 111-768-4269, and that Monday, I found out my email was hacked, so I changed it. You did try! I can't believe it," she said, frustration spilling out of her voice.

"Why didn't you contact me?"

"For two reasons. First, you didn't give me your email or phone number. Second, at that time, I couldn't handle the rejection I felt would be coming. You know, 'It's not you, it's me. I just don't care for your whatever.'"

"There isn't any way I could think that was just a hookup. You were a tipping point in my life. Things changed for me rather dramatically the next day. I moved from the city and—"

"Here's your coffee, David," Charlie interrupted, holding out the cup for David.

"Thanks, Charlie." David took the cup. He looked from Musee to Charlie and back to Musee. "Charlie, this is Maureen O'Hara, better known as Musee. Musee, this is Charlie Holmes, my associate, along with Dex Holmes, Charlie's grandfather, who isn't here today." Musee looked at Charlie, immediately seeing through the manly disguise to her beauty.

"Now I understand," Musee said, turning to walk away.

"Wait, please," David pleaded. "Don't walk away. I couldn't handle losing you again." Musee looked at him, heard the honesty in his voice … the same way she did the afternoon he told her his last name and said he wasn't going to play games, and that he wanted to see her again. "Here, you take my phone and give me your email and number. I'll contact you this evening after we finish working. It'll be after nine, if that's okay."

"Sure, that's okay." Musee entered her info on his phone and handed it back. She looked at Charlie, still wary about her and how she fit into David's life. She smiled and left.

"She's pretty. Is she your girlfriend?" Charlie asked, biting into her multicolored sprinkle and chocolate-covered yeast donut, getting chocolate and sprinkles on the tip of her nose.

"You've got chocolate on your nose. Sprinkles, too," David said, pointing to his nose. Charlie took her finger, wiped her nose off, and licked her finger. "No, she's not my girlfriend. I don't have a girlfriend. Come on, let's sell all this produce and surprise Dex with what a good job we can do." David's elation poured into every task the rest of the day. Not even the customers who squeezed all the produce could stop his happiness. He wasn't rejected after all. The void he had felt was bigger than he'd imagined. Even so, it was filled in a split second with the beauty and obvious caring of Musee. His thoughts were of her and that Sunday afternoon, and the promise of more to come. Sex, yes, but more than that. A deeper relationship with someone who accepted him at the lowest point in his life. That's it, he thought. Unconditional acceptance—something he had never had from a lover before her. He smiled at Charlie. "I'm going to outsell you so bad you'll be doing dishes for years."

"Naw, I'm going to outsell you so bad you'll be doing dishes, even ... even when you go to heaven."

Charlie kept up a running commentary about the stores she imagined would be fun to go into as they drove down Twenty-third Street, headed to the Henry Hudson and home. When they made the turn onto the highway, she stopped describing the sights but remained looking out the window. Triggered by her excitement about sharing the good day at the market with Dex, it finally clicked that he had missed so many. For a moment, she attributed his absence to David relieving him of the chore, but she knew that her granddaddy liked going to market. It wasn't a chore. Like hit by a lightning bolt she put the signs together. He was not going to market as often, he was tired more often, he couldn't handle the full boxes of produce. David had to do the chores Granddaddy used to do. She continued to look out the window, afraid of broaching the subject with David. Her fears gradually rose to the point where she was overwhelmed and started to cry silently.

Still facing the window, she took a deep breath and said in a low voice, hoping she was wrong, "Granddaddy is sick, isn't he?"

David didn't answer right away. "Yeah, Charlie, your granddaddy is sick."

"Will he get better?"

"I don't know."

"Really?"

"Yeah, really. I don't know much about sickness." David glanced over to Charlie and saw the tears silently running down her face. He reached over and took her hand.

"Will you leave if Granddaddy dies?"

"No, Charlie. I'm not going anywhere. I don't think your granddaddy is going to die, but I'm not going anywhere. We're family. You and Granddaddy took me in and made me part of your family. While I don't know anything about sickness, I do know that if Granddaddy dies, you and I will be sad, but we will still be family. As long as you want to be family with me, we'll stick together."

"If Granddaddy dies, will we have to move away from the farm? Will I be able to talk to Granny anymore? Will we be able to go to the market?" The questions came in her rapid-fire cascade, with her voice and anxiety elevating higher and higher. "If Granddaddy dies, he'll go to heaven and be with Granny. That'll make him happy. He hasn't been really, really happy since she went to heaven." She wiped her cheeks with her shirt sleeves, taking her hand from David's.

"Tomorrow I'll make Granddaddy a cake. That'll make him feel better." She turned back to look out the window.

"Yeah, that'll make him feel better. You want to make the rounds with me in the morning, and then we make the cake together in the afternoon?"

"Yeah, yes, sir."

# CHAPTER 19

It was close to eleven when David finished cooking and washing dishes with Charlie's help. After Charlie went to bed, David took Dex a glass of iced tea out to the porch. He related his conversation with Charlie coming home. Dex just nodded and didn't offer any comments, suggestions, or opinions. David then told him about Musee, how they'd lost touch, and her showing up at the green market today. Dex smiled and chuckled, but again offered no comments, suggestions, or opinions. They talked a few minutes about the business, and then Dex unsteadily got up and went to bed. So much for sage fatherly advice, David thought, as he went to the barn and fired up his computer. Excitement wrapped itself around his fatigue. He figured Musee was probably sleeping by now. He ignored all his emails since they were either from solicitors or former classmates who wanted to sell him something. That world was so far gone it was like another planet light years away. He hit compose and started:

*How could I forget U? U entered my life at a time when*
*I needed U more than I needed anything but another breath*
*itself. When you didn't respond to my emails, texts, and calls,*

*my faith in the good in life withered like a water-starved flower. The only lifesaver was, and is, Dex, and his granddaughter, Charlotte, whom you met as Charlie today. They took the spark you had rekindled, fanned it gently, added kindling and more fuel through their acceptance of me as I am. U, however, were the spark in my life to give me unconditional acceptance. Before I met U, I would have distrusted that type of kindness, looking for an ulterior motive. Your unconditional sharing of your emotions and your body and soul that glorious Sunday softened my defensive shell. I did not disappear. I could not. With one afternoon and evening, U became the keeper of my soul and spirit. I want to see you again, if you'll have me. I don't know when. Dex is ill, I think seriously. He doesn't seem to want me to know how serious. Charlie is a special needs person. As beautiful and innocent on the inside as she is on the outside. Dex has not said what will become of Charlie if he passes. He must have a plan for her. He loves her as deeply as I've ever seen one person love another. My feelings since I've been here have grown to mirror Dex's. I can't leave her until I know she is in a safe place and cared for. She is both the sister I never had, and the child I hope to have one day. Why am I telling U all of this? I don't know. I just know seeing U today reinforced my vision of goodness and a bright future.*

*David*

He felt drained but relaxed, having said what he'd kept bottled inside him since that beautiful Sunday. His soul was free. He felt vulnerable but strengthened. He knew he should read the email over, wait ten minutes, and reread it before sending. He had brain dumped everything he felt right now, and females don't want a relationship with a whiner. He got to the first word, *How* ... and his finger hit the send button. What the hell, he thought. I feel good for writing it, even if she thinks I'm a wuss. Who's she going to tell, anyway? Read it to her girlfriends over a bottle of wine one evening? Okay, they can all have a good laugh at the wussy's expense. Would this door open or slam shut? He stood up, pulled his shirt over his head, and went to the undercounter fridge and took out a bottle of beer. He twisted the cap off and took a long pull.

*　*　*

Musee sipped her wine as she watched TV. She looked at her watch, eight forty-five. David said he would email her after nine. How lucky was it that she'd gone to the Union Square green market today? She started museeing.

"Don't get your hopes up, Musee. He may have been lying about trying to contact you. Why didn't he just come to your apartment, huh?"

She responded, "Because he thought I'd given him fake information. He knew the phone number; he just transposed two numbers. He knew my old, hacked email. He was telling the truth; I just know it. He cares as much about me as I care about him." She looked at her watch again. After nine. She went over and made sure the computer was on.

"That sure was a beautiful young girl he was with. I can't believe they don't have the hots for each other."

"He said she's the granddaughter of his employer. They acted more like brother and sister."

"Yeah, sure."

"That's enough of this negativity. What we had, have, is special. I know it is. Let's watch this movie. Before it's over at eleven, he'll email me." At eleven, she clicked out of streaming. She fought back tears as she climbed into bed. A second rejection from the guy she realized she actually loved was too much right now. Fifteen minutes later, she heard the computer ding.

✳   ✳   ✳

Ding went David's computer.

He jumped out of bed and went back to the computer. He pushed the MSG button and saw a message from redgirl690@hemail.com. Opening it, he read: L U 2.

A door opening ... again, he muttered to himself and smiled. His analytical mind, however, wanted to know how the relationship could develop, since they both worked six days a week and miles apart.

# CHAPTER 20

"Hey guys, where's Dex?" Terry asked, leaning on a stack of five boxes of snap beans, corn, mustard greens, turnips, and zucchini. His lanky frame, jeans coveralls, unlaced brogans, and rough and calloused hands were evidence of his occupation as a man of the dirt. His old, worn canvas coat had seen, and would still see, many seasons of hard but pleasurable work.

"He's good. Home working on the books. Charlie and I thought we'd pick up and enjoy this incredible weather. I can't believe it's this cool but not yet cold in October. Looks like you're havin' a good harvest."

"Awesome harvest. Everything is cookin' now. Audrey is excited. She's figuring a new quilted jacket from the internet is in order."

"Well, Christmas is right around the corner."

David grabbed a box and slid it into the van. "Will you have more for Friday?"

"I can have at least six boxes Friday for the weekend, but this is the last of the zucchini. How about some parsnips?"

"That's good."

"David, I saw Tim Roy at McAllister's Feed and Seed the other day. He mentioned that he was thinking about pulling out of his partnership with Calumet Farms." David tensed and stopped loading the boxes. Terry was another of Calumet's better farmers. Tim Roy had decided to stay in the partnership, but David was worried that other producers might choose to pull out, particularly as the church community could plainly see that Dex was declining.

David raised his hand to stop Terry from speaking, turned to Charlie, and said, "Charlie, will you please go get me the logbook out of the cab?"

"Sure."

David motioned for Terry to move closer to the barn.

Terry went on, "He, like anyone else, can clearly see Dex is having a tough time health-wise. He also told me how you handled his thinking about leaving the partnership. He feels strongly about you being one of us. Sort of a young Dex. I won't lie to you; some of us were getting anxious as to what would happen if Dex decided to sell Calumet. You've put those worries to rest. I just wanted you to know that." Terry handed David another box, nodding his head in respect, and turned to Charlie, who was walking back, flipping the pages of the log book.

"Need anything else, Charlie?"

"Yeah, Mr. Terry, do you have any mint and ginger root?"

"Sure do. Come on, Charlie, and I'll get you some." The two of them walked toward the farmhouse. David got in the truck and made some entries in the log book.

Loading the van went quickly, stopping at the farms on schedule and loading the variety of vegetables and fruit. At each stop, Charlie got some ingredients for her cake, visited with the farmer's wife and children, and focused on the ingredients she still needed.

By midafternoon, the van was full, and they were ready for the next day's market. Charlie had all the ingredients necessary for her cake. Back at the farmhouse, Dex was waiting on the porch. Charlie jumped out of the truck, ran to the porch, leaned down, and gave him a hug.

"Granddaddy, me and David are going to make you a special Granny cake."

"That's great, Charlie. I'm looking forward to having some."

Two hours later, the cake came out of the oven, and David had a written recipe. He couldn't help but think that the business and his life were running smoothly on all cylinders.

# CHAPTER 21

Dex lay on the bed, the sheets and his pajamas drenched with sweat. He'd always told himself he'd know when the time came. Everything was ready. He'd left David a letter on his desk that explained his will, the trust created by the will, where the assets were, about the safe, its combination, and, more importantly, who he could trust and who needed watching. If he was right about David, Charlie and the business would be fine. He knew he was right about David. Everything would be fine. He slowly turned his head toward the clock. Three-thirty in the morning, time to begin. He knew David would get up in thirty minutes. David always had breakfast ready by four forty-five. Charlotte would be up in an hour, and they would be gone to the market in two hours. He struggled to sit up. The pain was always the sharpest trying to sit up from lying down. He took a minute for the pain to subside and then stood. He stripped off his pajamas and left them where they fell. He put on his jeans without underpants. No need for both pairs today. He put on a plaid collared shirt. Never felt good, he thought, about those T-shirts the youngsters wear. Need a collar to look dressed. He slipped on his boots without socks. No need for those, either. He felt the day-old growth on his face.

No need to shave. As quietly as he could, he went down the stairs to the kitchen and sat in his regular chair at the kitchen table. He didn't turn on any lights. He liked the dark of the early morning. Sitting and looking at the blackness inside and outside the kitchen windows was one of life's small but immense pleasures. He waited for the first glimmer of light coming from the other side of the hill. Watching the day begin would be missed. He sat there, drumming his fingers on the table. His mind wandered over the past.

Mary had found the farm and brought him to see it. The owner had died two years before, and it'd sat empty. "It's got good bones, Dex. This is the place for us," she'd said, hugging him. He couldn't understand that she hadn't seen the broken windows where kids had thrown rocks into the house, or she didn't notice the raccoon droppings in every room on the second floor, or she didn't notice the water stains on the ceilings of both floors from the leaky roof, or the leaky faucet in both bathrooms and the kitchen, or the rotten boards on the wide front porch, or the shutters, all either missing or hanging from one hinge. When he started pointing out these issues, she responded with, "All opportunities come disguised as disasters, Dex Holmes. I have faith in your being able to fix anything." She had come over to him, put her arms around his neck, and said, "This is our new home. We're going to make a house full of babies here. What do you say we start right now."

She was right about everything except the babies. After the first, she couldn't have any more. There were two miscarriages until the doctor told them that trying for more was risking her life. That was the only time he'd put his foot down. He told her life without her would be worthless, that God had given them one beautiful child, and she needed to focus on that child. He went and got fixed. He continued drumming his fingers on the table as the faintest glow appeared at the top of the hill.

Every step of the way, they worked together building the business. No complaints about the long hours, the scraping by in the beginning, slowly building a life, finally developing the farmer partnerships. Every time they set up another one, Mary took the wife under her wing, brought her into the Ladies Circle at the church, helped with the children, counseled her when her husband wasn't what she thought he should be, and held her hand as she experienced the ups and downs of raising children. His fingers drummed harder and faster. When her own child started spiraling downward in high school, Mary kept up a brave face, not letting him or the others know what was going on. He knew, though. He knew because, in the middle of the night, when she thought he was asleep, he heard her softly sobbing downstairs in her chair, asking God why, night after night during those last three years, until one day Edith went to school and didn't come home. She'd taken up with three older kids. They disappeared for a while, and then came back to the area two years later. Dex asked Mary if she wanted him to go get Edith, and she said no. If she was coming back, it was because she wanted to, not forced to. In one forty-eight-hour period, Edith came home to die and give birth. Dex's fingers drummed on the table faster and more force- fully. He watched part of his Mary die that night, the part that had made her feel that love and God would conquer all. She turned to him that night and asked him to get those animals who had done this to her child. In all their life together, he never disappointed her. He didn't that time, either. The doctors told Mary that they'd saved the baby, but it had serious alcohol and drug addictions. Mary begged them to do all they could. She wanted that grandchild to replace her child, no matter who the father was or the circumstances of its conception. She felt it was God's way of making up for what he let happen to Edith.

Dex's fingers resumed their natural drumming rhythm as he thought about Mary's decision to bury Edith up on the hill, visible from the kitchen sink window. "At least I'll know where she is every night," Mary had said, with sadness in her voice. They named the baby Charlotte after Mary's mother. Dex later surmised that it would give some sense to the nickname Charlie. Mary was that way—always aware of what she was doing. Mary and Charlie regularly made the climb up the hill to put flowers on Edith's grave, or smooth the dirt after a rain, or just sit and talk. Mary told her stories of Edith when she was the age Charlie was at the time.

Dex kept drumming. He looked over to the kitchen window and saw the dawning day. What a beautiful time to be alive and well. His thoughts turned back to his Mary, the rock of his life, and the day he received the blow he thought would kill him. He and Mary went to the doctor because of a lingering cold she had. After x-rays and an exam, they waited in the doctor's office, holding hands and making plans for the next day's market.

The doctor came in looking serious, and got right to the point. "Mary, you have small-cell lung cancer, and it has spread to your brain." Dex felt like he couldn't breathe. She was too young for such a condition. She didn't smoke, drank very little, kept fit, and prayed regularly. There had to be a mistake. The doctor assured them it was no mistake. He offered Mary surgery, followed by chemo and radiation of the brain. It would be hard on her, but the process would buy some time.

"How much time?" she asked.

"Several months, maybe a year."

"And if I do nothing?"

"You've got maybe six months, four good ones and two tough ones."

Dex's finger drumming sped up. She didn't even ask my opinion, he thought. She looked at the doctor and said, "Thank you, Jim. This is the last time we'll see each other as doctor–patient. Come on, Dex. We have work to do."

On the way home, she told him what was going to happen, and it happened just the way she told it. Her trips up the hill with Charlie became a daily routine, as she tried to impart as much love and knowledge to Charlie as a little girl could absorb. Five months later, Mary said it was time. He put the pills and a glass of water next to her bed. He arranged the pillows so she could sit up and read her Bible. He kissed her goodbye, and he and Charlie went to market as they had started doing the month before. It took weeks for Charlie to come to terms with Mary being in heaven and her being able to go up the hill and talk to her granny, who had homeschooled her, taken her to Sunday school, nurtured her, and kept her innocent of the relationship between man and woman.

His finger drumming returned to a normal rhythm. He saw more promise of the beautiful day over the trees on the hill. He heard footsteps in the yard. David was coming. He thanked Mary and God for David. He was convinced she had guided David to him to make sure this very day would be all right. He heard the screen door open and felt David's presence in the room, and then the light came on. Dex stopped drumming his fingers.

"Morning," Dex said, startling David.

"Morning."

"You going to put on some coffee?"

"Yeah, anything special you want this morning?"

"Bacon, scrambled eggs, and toast usually hits the spot."

"You got it." David turned to reach up for two coffee mugs. "Anything I need to know?" he asked, with his back turned to Dex.

"Yeah, the house will be empty when you and Charlie get back from the market. This here key is to my study. It'll be locked when you get back. Take the key with you. Don't lose it—it's the only one. Don't let anyone, not even Charlie, in there until you have thoroughly searched it." David froze for a few seconds. "There may be some ladies from the church here. I've asked Pastor Tom to request that they not come tonight but to come after regular Sunday services in the morning, but they may be here anyway. Can't know for sure. They'll have enough food for a week. You might spread it so that some of our partners can take the excess home. I've told Mort at the funeral home that I want the service on Monday, so you'll miss the market. You'd better call them and make sure they know to keep your space. It'll be good for Charlie if y'all load up as usual Tuesday and be at the market Wednesday. On my desk is a note to Charlie. It should help somewhat, but she'll be scared. I suspect one or more of the ladies will want to take her home with them for a while. Unless she wants to go, say no. They won't like it, but be firm. Pretty certain Charlie will want to be right here with Granny, me, and you. You will have the right to do that. She'll want to spend a lot of time up on the hill, particularly when you get back from the market. It'll be dark. Make sure she has a flashlight. She likes to cut through the woods, which is not good, so I always make her go up by the road. Then I go up by the woods to watch over her when she's there and coming back through the woods."

"Got it," David said, now sitting at the table facing Dex, a cup of coffee in front of each. He picked up the key and put it in the change pocket of his jeans.

"Oh yeah, Ezel over at Pineville Granite knows what to put on the footstone. Mary and me are sharing the head stone. I'll be on Mary's left, Edith's on her right. Charlie will be at Mary's foot. There's room for more, if you ever need and want it." Dex looked up from his coffee cup and stared at David. "Don't know how she'll react. Don't know if she even knows how sick I am. I'm putting her in your care, because I know you'll take care of her. That's a lot to ask, but you're the only one I can ask."

"I understand." David choked a little, turned to look out the kitchen window, took a deep breath, turned back to Dex, and said, "Don't worry. We'll be together through this and whatever it takes to keep her safe." Both heard Charlie start down the stairs. David jumped up, wiped his eyes, and put two skillets on the stove.

"Hey everybody," Charlie called out, her regular morning greeting.

"Hay is for horses," David retorted, as he did every morning. "Got your coffee ready. Breakfast coming up in a minute."

After breakfast, David did the dishes quickly. When Charlie returned from upstairs, he dried his hands and said, "I forgot my wallet. I'm going to go get it. I'll meet you in the truck, Charlie. He walked over to Dex, who held out his hand. David took it and squeezed. "Won't let you down."

"I know."

Charlie grabbed a cookie from its jar, and Dex said, "Have a good day at the market. Beat David with that FAB stuff so he'll always have to do dishes. Listen to him. He can teach you a lot."

"Yeah, he's my best friend."

"Give me a big hug, girl. I love you, you know." He stayed in his chair, and Chalie leaned over and hugged him.

"I love you too, Granddaddy."

"Now, get going and make me proud."

"Yeah."

"Yes, sir."

"Yeah, yes, sir." She turned and ran out, letting the screen door slam behind her, the way she always did.

# CHAPTER 22

On the drive into Manhattan and all day at the green market, David kept up a steady chatter and an eagle eye on Charlie. She had been less vibrant and inquisitive since that night, weeks ago, when she asked if Dex was sick. David kept hoping she had reconciled herself, even a little bit, to the inevitable. She didn't seem any different from the day before. He began to relax a little and enjoy the usual Saturday crowds moving from tent to tent. Most had their save-the-planet canvas shopping bags, stained with the juices from countless fruits and veggies discovered and coveted at the market. With the exception of the tourists, who could be recognized by their cameras and the amazed look on their faces, the typical New Yorker had on jeans, the men's too baggy and worn low on the hips, and the women's had rips in the knees or thighs. He did notice the appearance of bell bottom jeans, the latest trend, harking back to the seventies. Another separate fashion trend he noticed was the resurrection of faux army field jackets on the younger shoppers. They were festooned with fake patches, some with the old peace sign, some with *make love not war* slogans, and some with bright colors and no real message. The New Yorkers were also distinctive because the women didn't wear makeup, both men and women didn't seem to comb their hair, and both sexes wore wire rim glasses. Since it was getting cooler, the traditional stretched-out T-shirt with some cutesy saying on the front or back was now covered by puffy quilted jackets in either black or brown, mostly black. The non-conformist, David thought, has to conform to non-conformity. Whatever they wanted to be and look like was okay with him, if enough of them spent their money at the Calumet Farms tent.

Charlie's two cakes went in the first two hours. She giggled when she told David they would have to bring three next week. They had a third cake for samples. David quickly stopped giving away samples and started selling the remaining part of the third cake as slices. Those slices went in the third hour. By closing time, the produce boxes were essentially empty.

"Granddaddy will be excited we sold both cakes and have orders for three more," Charlie said, resting her head on the side window. David was quiet as the pending horrific scene came closer and closer as they drove. The ride home was an hour and fifteen minutes. Usually, it seemed like two hours. Tonight, it seemed like about thirty minutes before David turned onto the gravel drive.

Charlie immediately sensed something was wrong. "David, there isn't a light on in the kitchen or on the porch. Why is Granddaddy sitting in the dark? He wouldn't go to bed before we got home." Fear gripped her voice. David rolled to a stop in the regular place and quickly jumped out and went to Charlie's side of the truck. She was halfway out of the truck when he reached in the open door and drew her to him. He embraced her in a bear hug and whispered in her ear, holding her head with his hand against his chest.

David felt his stomach flip as he said softly, "Charlie, Granddaddy has gone to be with Granny in heaven." He felt her slump in his arms as she let out a piercing wail.

"No! No! No! I need Granddaddy here with me. I need him. I don't know what to do without him. No! No! No! Oh God, give him back. Please. Please. I don't know what to do. I don't know what to do. I don't know what to do." She rocked back and forth in his arms, sobbing. "Please, please, bring him back. Maybe you're wrong, David. Please go look. I need him. I need him."

"I know, Charlie, I know. He's in a good place with your granny. He's not in pain anymore, Charlie, and that's good. I'm not your granddaddy, but I won't leave you. You'll still have me, Charlie. I promise." David was silently crying at Charlie's uncontrollable fear and panic. It wasn't like she didn't know he was sick; she did. But she couldn't connect sickness and death. "Let's go inside, Charlie, and I'll fix dinner. How about a sandwich?"

"I'm not hungry."

"I understand, but you have to eat something."

"No, I don't. I want to go to bed." She wouldn't sit down, standing there with her head down, her arms straight by her side, her lower lip pushed out.

"Okay, Charlie, I'll help you get ready for bed."

"I don't need any help," she said, turning and leaving the kitchen. He heard her running up the stairs. Okay, David, be calm, he thought. What do you want right now? To be left alone. That's exactly what Charlie wants. Don't crowd her. Let her grieve. Stay in the house until she's asleep, then go to the barn. Thank God the ladies from the church weren't here tonight. David went to the fridge, pulled out the fixings for a ham and cheese sandwich, grabbed a bottle of beer, and made two sandwiches, one for himself and one to leave for Charlie, in case she came down hungry later.

He sat in the kitchen, wishing he had his computer to email Musee. She'd know what he should do with a devastated twenty-one-year-old. He took off his boots and left them in the kitchen. Walking softly, he went to Dex's study and tried the door. Locked, just as Dex said it would be. I don't want Charlie to come down and see me in Dex's study, he thought. I'll leave it for tomorrow. He went to the living room and the photo album again. He was still puzzled by the striking difference in Dex's appearance in his wedding photo and in photos only a few years later. After a while, when he had been through both photo albums, he thought again how easily Charlie had remembered the details of the various photos, having heard Granny speak of the times they were taken. He sensed the quiet upstairs. Rather than go up and wake her, he went to the kitchen, put on his boots, and slipped out the door.

In his apartment, he got another beer and turned on the computer. He scanned the emails looking for one from Musee, but there were none. He hit compose and typed:

*Musee, an important part of my life ended today, and a more challenging part began. Dex, the farmer/merchant I told U about, died today. I had to tell Charlie when we got back from the market. She is grieving like no one I have ever seen grieve before. She is so sad and scared. She feels all alone and helpless. While I miss Dex and his mentoring, I'm at a loss trying to help Charlie. Dex believed in me, and I need to make a future for Charlie and the business. Charlie can't grasp the fact that I won't leave her helpless. I won't because she needs me, and because I promised a wonderful man who believed in me that I'd take care of her. With her special needs, she is too vulnerable for others to take care of her. I'm telling you all of this because it affects U and me and what I want our relationship to be. I hope U understand. The ladies of the church will be here tomorrow. The funeral will be held on Monday. Dex urged me to keep Charlie focused on the business, so we'll be picking up produce Tuesday and be at the market Wednesday. Since Dex is not here, and we don't have to rush back, I'd like to have dinner with U when U get off work. I'm sure Charlie would like that. She doesn't really have any girlfriends her age to talk girly stuff with. Would U mind? U can pick the restaurant, and the treat will be on me. I want to see U, if only for a short time and with a chaperone. Once U get to know Charlie, U will understand why she must be my priority right now. Please understand.*

*L U David*

He hit send and sat back. Finishing his beer, he went to the cupboard and pulled out some crackers and a jar of peanut butter. He got another beer and went back to the computer, expecting a response from Musee in the next few minutes. He went to the Wall Street Journal site and started going through the stories, taking a cracker, dipping it in the peanut butter, and sticking it in his mouth. Then came a swig of beer. Finishing the WSJ site, he next pulled up the London Financial Times site. He went systematically through the sections. What struck him was the artificiality of the news focus. Not the news itself, but the thought of how many people spent their entire lives, many hours each day, trying to glean a kernel of foresight into how the various events would influence the financial markets. Dex had always told him the whole process was nonsensical.

"Buy when it's obvious you're getting a dollar's worth of value for fifty cents or less. Otherwise, go do something fun," he used to say. "What's wrong with that?" he used to say. 'There won't be any more 'used to say.' He missed Dex more than he'd first realized. First Fil and now Dex. How fortunate he was, David thought, to have known these two giants. Even knowing death was near, in both cases, hadn't prepared David for it. No wonder Charlie, who wasn't familiar with death, was taking it so hard. It had been an hour and a half eating from the peanut butter jar, and still no response from Musee. Wonder if she's pissed, he thought. No, that can't be. We both hung on to a dream for over six months. This little blip can't break our bond. Can it? No. He had offered the dinner Wednesday night more for his sake than Musee's. Even though Dex was sure David could handle the situation with Charlie, he wasn't so sure. He'd try his best, but what if his best wasn't good enough? It must be, a voice in his head said. He switched off the computer, took his beer into the bedroom, stripped off his jeans, and got into bed. He picked up the open copy of *The Old Man and the Sea* that he was reading for the seventh time. Courage against all odds. Persistence in the face of adversity. A master-piece in just forty-seven thousand words. It didn't take David long to turn out the light.

He didn't know what time it was when he heard the noise. It sounded like the barn door opening. He lay still, waiting to see if it was a dream or his imagination. The next sound was unmistakable—the opening of the door to his sitting room. Then he heard her voice.

"David, you asleep?" The door to his bedroom opened, and she was standing there. In the dark, he could make out that she had on her pajamas and was clutching her Raggedy Ann doll.

"No, Charlie. Everything all right?"

She rushed over to the bed and got in with him. Consciously, he kept the sheet between their bodies. She started to cry. "I want my grand-daddy. I'm scared. There're noises in the house. Can I stay here with you? Please." David put his arms around her and drew her in to him. He put her head on his chest.

"Charlie, remember when you first found out that your granddaddy was sick?"

"Yeah, yes, sir." She wiped her face and nose on the sheet and pressed tight into him.

"Remember when you told me he would be in heaven with your granny and how happy he would be?"

"Yeah, yes, sir."

"You and me, we're sad because we won't—"

"You're sad, too?"

"Yeah. Your grandfather was like a father to me. I miss him a lot. What helps me is thinking of the good times we had, and his being in heaven with your granny and not being sick anymore, while the two of them watch over you and me."

"Yeah, but I'm scared."

"Hey, I've got an idea."

"Hay is for horses," she giggled.

"Smart aleck. Why don't we go back to the house. You get in your bed with all your dolls, and I'll sleep in Granddaddy's room, right next to yours, so if you hear any noise, I'm right there. That good with you?"

"Okay, that's good. Will you leave both doors open?"

"Sure. You go in the sitting room while I put on my pants, and then we'll go."

David was up at four. He went to the barn, took a quick shower, opened the plastic zipped bag, and took out a white shirt and navy suit. No ties were needed in the country, but they needed to know who was in charge. He got his dress shoes from the bottom of the bag. These are good people, but they would gossip if they thought he and Charlie were cohabitating without marriage or a chaperone. They needed to understand that he was all business. He grabbed his computer and went back to the house. Turning on the computer, he put coffee on. He decided breakfast would be light—toast, butter, and jam. The ladies of the church would have them swamped with food by lunch, and they'd expect them to eat. He heard a ding as soon as the computer cycled up. He went over and opened his messages. There was one from redgirl690. He opened it and read:

*Meet the 840-train at Pineville three thirty tomorrow afternoon.*
*L U 2 M*

His heart leapt. It reminded him of watching old movies on TV as a kid, when the bad guys were about to slaughter the good guys, and the cavalry appeared on the hill to save the day. He wasn't alone, and that meant Charlie wasn't alone.

# CHAPTER 23

Musee's plan was working. She sat back in her chair, put her hands behind her head, and stretched. Her desk was just behind her boss's desk, the merchandise manager and niece of the store president. Their secretary also shared the space, actually not much bigger than two standard closets. That's retailing, she thought. The selling floor space was infinitely more valuable than desk space. Besides, they were all supposed to be on the sales floor most of the day. She didn't care; her plan was succeeding. Her boss took all the credit, and Musee got all the experience and contact with the vendors and people that made career fashion work. Her rolodex was expanding steadily. The floor sales force loved her and her tips for helping their prime customers—career women from twenty-five to fifty. They put together complete outfits that made their customers look feminine but not sexy, powerful but not overbearing, smart but approachable. Each time a salesperson introduced Musee to one of their regular customers, Musee made a point of finding out as much as she could about the client, her profession, where she worked, and her opinion about what makes a woman stand out in her profession. Musee used signage creatively on the sales floor and taught the sales ladies the power of "a special item in the back room."

Musee was determined that she could last a little more than four years. At that point, her student loans would be paid, her credentials and contacts solid, and she would have some seed money to go along with her sweat equity. Even now, she had her Moleskine notebook of ideas and concepts she would put in place in her own business. Turning out the lights in the office, she slowly walked the sales floor of her section checking the stock and signage and noting anything that needed to be fixed before the store opened Monday.

Arriving home, which was always a treat for her, she put her briefcase on the desk, switched on her home computer, and took the bag with the deli beef pot pie to the kitchen, where she turned on the oven and slid the pie in. She filled a glass from a half-empty bottle of Mondavi Chablis. At the computer, she opened the MSG center. No email from David. She began her nightly out-loud conversation with herself.

"Musee, I certainly hope he didn't get tired of just talking and not doing."

"Don't be silly, Musee. He just hasn't had time tonight."

Leaving the glass on the desk and walking into the bedroom, she stripped off her blouse, bra, skirt, and panty hose. She felt the tension leaving her body. The blouse and skirt went in the closet, and the bra and panty hose in the laundry hamper. She wrapped herself in her favorite cocoon: sweats and slippers.

Back at the computer, she saw that there was still no message from David. "David Wilson, are you real or a mirage? Here one afternoon, gone for half a year. Here for twenty minutes at the green market, and gone again, except for some of the most loving emails a girl could get. Are you for real or just playing with me?" She sipped her wine.

"Musee, you really don't know anything about this guy. Maybe he's a smooth-talking gigolo. Is he married? Has he been married? He's educated, that's for sure, but why is he working for a farmer at the green market? He can't be making any money. Oh my God, Musee, what if he's homeless? That's why y'all didn't go to his apartment. Maybe he's destitute. Girl, you'd better be careful."

"Cut it out, Musee. He's not a perv or something. I'm sure he has a plan for life."

"But what if you're not in his plan?"

"Guys don't show those deep feelings without some reality to them."

The oven clock buzzed. Musee got up and slid the pot pie from the oven. She went back to the computer. No email. "Musee, get your work done. I'm tired and want to go to bed soon."

"All right, I'm just as tired as you."

The computer dinged just as she put a fork full of hot pot pie in her mouth. She grabbed her wine glass, gulped down a mouthful, and hit MSG. She opened David's email and took a sharp breath. The old man had died. David's grief was palpable. So were his feelings of responsibility for Charlie. His thinking about me during this crisis proves that he loves me. Musee sat straight in her chair. She held the plate up to her chin and took another fork full of pie. He's lost, she thought. He needs help. Guys his age don't know what to do with special needs females. All they know what to do with females is chase them for sex. He said the farm was right outside of Pineville. She minimized the MSG and Googled the Sunday Metro North train schedule. The 840-train was leaving right after lunch and gets to Pineville at three thirty. I could go in early tomorrow, get done what I have to get done this week, leave HR a note that I had a family emergency and need a few days' vacation. Musee tried to remember Charlie's size. The only thing she was sure about was Charlie's height. They were about the same. The rest was hidden in the baggy clothes.

"What if he doesn't want you there?" Musee said.

"Get serious, Musee. He'll love the help, and if he doesn't, he can bring me back Wednesday, and we'll know it's over. I love bringing things to a head." She quickly bought a ticket on the 840-train to Pineville. David, we're about to see if you've been telling the truth, she thought. She printed the ticket, put it in her bag, went into the bedroom carrying her wine, and got the duffle off the closet shelf. I don't need much—he said we could have dinner in the city Wednesday night. There'll be a funeral, so one professional outfit is necessary. She went to her closet and selected her best professional outfit with all the right accessories, just like she did for customers. Then she took out a pair of jeans and two blouses, one for hanging out, and a killer white blouse in case she had to compete with someone. Shoes and underwear made the packing complete. Then she stopped and wondered about Charlie. They had kept her disguised as a boy, so she probably doesn't have a real dressy outfit. Musee went back to her closet and put together what she considered her second-best ensemble, including shoes. The shoes might not fit, but she would look so good that no one would notice the shoes. She carried the duffle and put it by the apartment door.

Turning back to the bedroom, she realized that she had not emailed David back. She sat down, typed a short email, hit send, and shut the computer down.

Setting the alarm for five thirty Sunday morning, she got in bed and realized she was wide awake. "Are you crazy? This is too aggressive. Be coy. Can you handle his rejection?" The voice started making a case for safety.

"No. No. Victory goes to the bold. I'll take him at his word," she told the voice firmly. She tried to close her eyes, but realized there was something missing in this plan. She lay very still, going over every aspect of what she was doing. Then it dawned on her. David was single, good looking, and in his late twenties. Charlie was beautiful and in her early twenties. Musee was attractive and in her late twenties. The three of them would be living under the same roof for a few days. People would talk about the stud with two young women, so she needed a plan. What if he was engaged to be married? Then the two betrothed people would be chaperoned by the younger girl, and since his fiancée was there, the young girl would not have to worry about the guy. She hopped out of bed and went to her jewelry box, where she found a costume silver ring with a single blue stone. She placed it on the fourth finger of her left hand. She held her hand out to examine her new engagement ring and said, "Thank you, David. Yes, I'll marry you. Please get off your knees." She went back to bed, satisfied that she had thought of everything.

# CHAPTER 24

After getting Musee's email, David felt he could make it through the next two days. He went to Dex's study and unlocked the door. He left it open so he could hear Charlie if she started down the stairs. The envelope for David was in the center of the desk. He opened it and found Dex's letter. It read:

*David, my attorney/CPA, Win Oakley, has the papers ready for you to sign to get access to all these accounts. These accounts and what's in the safe in this room are your working capital for taking care of the business and Charlie. Remember when you first came I had you sign a card? It was the signature card for Box 431 at the bank. You'll find a key in the safe here, along with other important documents. Ask for Marie Goodman, the branch manager. She's expecting you. One more thing: think about what I said in our conversation about Win Oakley. You are the son I always wanted and didn't have until Mary guided you to me and Charlie. Dex*

David sobbed and took a deep breath. He quickly scanned the other papers, which turned out to be brokerage statements at four major firms and the business bank account. He thumbed through them and was amazed. Each one had more than two million dollars in assets. Two were in Dex's name, transfer on death to an irrevocable trust, and the other two were in the name of the irrevocable trust with Dex as the trustee. The trust was dated over ten years ago. David put everything back in the envelope and looked at the desk. It was a reproduction partner's desk with the standard number of drawers. There was a key in the center drawer. David took it and tried to lock and unlock every drawer. The key worked. He placed the envelope in a drawer and locked it. He put the desk key in his pants' change pocket. He looked around the room, searching for the likely place for a safe. He heard Charlie coming down the stairs. He walked into the hall and shut the study's door.

"Good morning, Charlie. You look very nice in that dress." Charlie had on one of her Sunday dresses, her sneakers, and was clutching her Raggedy Ann doll. "I thought we'd have a light breakfast, 'cause I'm sure the ladies from the church will bring a lot of food later. That okay with you? Your granddaddy left this note for you," David said, handing her an envelope.

Charlotte clutched the note in the hand holding onto her doll. "Since we're going to go talk to God, I wanted to show him what a good job Granddaddy did here on Earth, so He'd give him a good job in heaven. Can we have eggs and bacon?" she said, her smile turning into a frown.

"You got it." Easy, easy, David thought. Charlie was in a world of her own. He found that being a parent was more complicated than being a big brother. Musee could not arrive too soon.

The preacher arrived at seven thirty, and the ladies started coming at eight. The first to arrive was Henrietta Stombaugh, the current president of the Pineville Baptist Church Ladies Circle. She blew into the house like a whirlwind. "Morning, Ms. Charlie. Howdy, Mr. Wilson. The ladies will be bringing a few things to carry y'all over till after the funeral. What I'm going to do is make a list of who brings what, so you can have it. Has Simpson brought the sign-in book yet? Probably not; he's worthless. That's all right, I figured he wouldn't, so I brought one. Where should I put it? I know. Let's put it on the kitchen table. Everything's under control. You young people just don't worry a bit." David heard all that and thought superwoman had arrived. He visibly relaxed. He and Charlie were sitting at the kitchen table. Pastor Tom motioned for David to come in the hall. There was a man standing with him.

"Hi, I'm Mort Simpson. Dex didn't want a visiting time. Is that correct?"

"Yes, sir," David answered, nodding his hand.

"My man will be here today to dig the grave, and we'll be putting up the tent early in the morning. About how many chairs will we need?"

"Gosh, I don't know. What do you normally have?"

"Usually twelve. But this is for Dex. He was well liked and respected. I suggest fifty."

"Fifty?"

"Yes, and two tents to cover them. Don't think I'm crazy, but I believe you need to have two port-a-lets too."

"Why? This is a funeral."

"This is Dex's funeral. Paster Tom usually asks people if they have anything they want to say. If he does that tomorrow, we'll likely be here all day."

"Whatever you say is fine with me."

"Any particular time for the grave digging? He'll be on a backhoe, so it'll make some noise. And, by the way, do you know where he should dig?"

"Yeah, I think I know where to dig. Can he do it after three this afternoon? How long will it take? I've got to meet the three thirty train, and I'll take Charlie with me. I don't want her seeing the process of digging, if you understand."

"Yes, sir, I understand. He'll arrive after three fifteen and be gone by four fifteen. Can you come now and show me where to dig?"

"Sure, give me a minute." David went back to the kitchen and knelt in front of Charlie.

"Charlie, I've got to go with a man for a couple of minutes. Do you mind keeping Mrs. Stombaugh company so she doesn't feel lonely?"

"When will you be back?" Charlie said, frowning.

"Five minutes, top. I'm just going behind the barn, not far."

"Okay, I'll make sure she's not lonely."

*　　*　　*

Charlie put her doll in her lap and opened the note from her grand-daddy. She read, *My dear Charlie, I've gone to be with your granny and mother in heaven. I know you may be sad and scared. I trust David to take care of you. Listen to him; he has much to teach you. Know that your granny and I will be looking out for the two of you. Everything will be all right, I promise. Just make sure you FAB David so he has to do the dishes every night. Much love, Granddaddy.*

Charlie spoke softly under her breath. "Yeah, yes, sir. I love you, Granddaddy." What am I to do? What will become of me? Who will take care of me? Will David leave? Granddaddy, help me, please. Charlie's thoughts kept going in a loop. She sat at the kitchen table, clutching her doll and gently rocking back and forth in the kitchen chair. Some instinct told her not to suck her thumb in front of this woman. David will help me. What if he doesn't like me anymore? What if he leaves? The anxiety kept bubbling up and causing her to hyperventilate.

"Charlie, you want to put that doll away?"

"No, ma'am." She clutched the doll closer to her chest.

"Aren't you a little too old to be carrying a doll?"

"I don't know. Is David back yet?"

"I'm back, Charlie," David said as he walked into the kitchen. He looked past Charlie at Mrs. Stambaugh, and slightly shook his head. The ladies of the church were steadily streaming into the kitchen, bringing their food offerings, and paying their respects to Charlie, while nodding to David. They put ham, chicken, turkey, and tuna casserole on the sideboards closest to the sink. On the long sideboard, they positioned the green bean casserole, potatoes au gratin, tomato salad, rice and peas, mac and cheese, and stuffing. On the kitchen table, they placed apple pie, rhubarb pie, lemon pie, red velvet cake, chocolate cake, carrot cake, and an assortment of homemade cookies. Charlotte wished she had baked a Granny cake, too.

"David, do I have to give up Raggedy Ann?" Charlie looked over her shoulder at him.

"I tell you what, Charlie, since the kitchen is getting crowded, and Mrs. Stambaugh and these fine ladies have to arrange everything for lunch, why don't we go into the living room out of the way. The service will start soon, anyway. Bring Raggedy Ann with you. You good with that?"

"Sure."

*   *   *

Pastor Tom gathered everyone at Dex's together out on the porch and the yard to hold a shortened Sunday service. The church ladies had set up the kitchen table and counters buffet-style, and after the service everyone filed in, fixed their plates, and returned to the porch, some sitting in chairs and some on the porch edge with their feet dangling off. Others brought chairs from the dining room and sat under the trees in the yard. Quietly, in a low voice, one of the choir members began singing *Amazing Grace*. Everyone joined in at the chorus.

David looked around and realized this was truly the experience of a lifetime. Young, old, and children gathered to help and pay their respects to one of their own. It was all he could do not to burst out crying. What kind of man was Dex that he commanded this kind of love and respect?

After lunch, Charlie sat on the sofa, curled up against the arm, and held Raggedy Ann close. David sat in the upholstered chair next to the sofa that was Dex's place for watching television. He leaned over and said, "Charlie, you remember that young lady I was talking to one day, and you asked me if she was my girlfriend?"

"You mean the pretty red-headed one?"

"Yes, that one."

"Yeah, I remember. She was pretty."

"Well, she's coming here to help us this afternoon. She likes you and is sad that your granddaddy is in heaven. She wants to be your friend. Is that okay with you?"

"Sure. What's her name?"

"Maureen O'Hara. Everybody calls her Musee."

"That's her play name? Like mine's Charlie?"

"Yup, that's her play name. We're going to pick her up at the train station at three thirty. The three of us will stay here at the house."

David and Charlie were standing on the platform when the 840-train pulled into the station fifteen minutes late. Musee disembarked and looked around. Charlie turned to David and whispered, "She's still pretty." David took Musee's bag and gave her a friendly one-arm hug. Musee focused on Charlie.

"You must be Charlotte. I'm Musee. Is it all right if I visit you and David for a few days?"

"Yeah, yes, si—er, ma'am."

"Whoa. Let's get something straight right now. We are close to the same age. I'm Musee. You are Charlotte. We're buddies, okay?" Musee hugged her.

"Okay." Charlotte hugged her back.

"What about me?" David asked.

"Oh, yeah, you," Musee said, winking at Charlotte. "You can drive while we girls talk."

Musee linked arms with Charlotte, and they turned toward the parking lot. With her free hand, Musee found David's and squeezed it. She turned her face to him and mouthed, "Later."

At the house, David went upstairs and put Musee's duffle in the spare bedroom. Returning to the kitchen, he said, "You're in the spare bedroom next to the bathroom in the hall."

"Well, we won't have to cook for a while. This is awesome," Musee said, opening the fridge and looking at the counters.

"The funeral is here tomorrow at ten in the morning, up on the hill."

"On the hill?"

"Yeah, look through the kitchen window. When Charli—"

"Charlotte," Musee corrected him.

"When Charlotte's mother died, Dex and Mary buried her up on the hill. When Mary died, she was buried there, too. Now, Dex will be there. It's a beautiful spot. Char... Charlotte goes there often to talk to her granny. Now, she'll go to talk to both her granny and granddaddy, probably tell them about her new friend."

"Stay in my room." Charlotte grinned at Musee. "Can Musee stay in my room? Please?"

David looked at Musee, who looked at Charlotte. "If you'd let me, I'd love to stay in your room. We've got a lot of girl talk to do." Musee giggled and crinkled her nose at Charlotte.

"I'll go move your bag," Charlotte said, rushing out. As soon as she heard Charlotte clomp up the stairs, Musee grabbed David and gave him a passionate kiss.

"I've got some good luck for you later, after Charlotte's asleep," she whispered in David's ear. "Oh, by the way," she said, pushing away and holding up her left hand to display the ring, "we're engaged. Thank you for proposing." She looked at him and crinkled her nose. "Seriously, I thought the ladies of the community would be less talkative if they thought you and your soon-to-be wife were staying here with Charlotte instead of two gorgeous young horny females staying with this hunk of a man."

David chuckled. "God, you're amazing." He dropped to one knee and said, "Maureen O'Hara, will you marry me?"

"Get up. You're too late. I said yes last night."

It was long after midnight before David felt Musee slip into his bed. She was naked, and he explored her body. "Quickly," she moaned. "I've waited too long for you to be inside me." It was quick and intense.

Afterward, he whispered, "How long can you stay?"

"At least till next Sunday. I took a week's vacation."

"You're awesome. What you're doing with Charlie—"

"Stop. She's Charlotte. Charlie is in heaven with Granny and Granddaddy. She might have special needs, but I've only been around her for a few hours, and I think part of that is from being smothered. I don't know why that happened, but I think it did."

"I'll tell you something I've noticed since Dex died. Charlie always said 'Yeah' in answer to a statement or question to her. Dex would correct her to say, 'Yes, sir.' And she would say, "Yeah, yes, sir." Now, I haven't heard her say either. As to her being smothered, I'll explain that to you tomorrow." He caressed her breasts.

"Oh, God," she said, rubbing his chest and stomach. "Do me again, hard." And he did.

# CHAPTER 25

Monday morning, mourners started coming early. The sky was cloudless, and the air crisp. They drove up into the yard between the barn and the house, turning around so they were facing outward. No one drove up the hill or parked alongside the gravel road leading up the hill. It was a steady stream of vehicles, mostly trucks, some decades old and others brand new. The cars were mostly old, since they were of less use than a truck in this part of the world. By nine fifteen, the yard and all the land between the house and the paved road were full. Trucks were lined up on both sides of the paved road. At some point, the sheriff's deputies arrived and were directing people where to park so the road could be kept open.

At nine thirty, Pastor Tom arrived and looked at the gathering. "Praise the Lord. We're going to have a beautiful day." He turned to David. "When you and Ms. Charlie are ready, we can walk up the hill."

"There will be three of us, Pastor. My fiancée arrived from New York yesterday afternoon."

"That's fine. The whole first row is reserved for us."

"I'll go see if Charlotte and Musee are ready." He went to the foot of the stairs and called to Musee.

"We're ready," she replied.

Musee and Charlotte started down the stairs. David looked at the two of them, unable to speak. Musee looked professional and business chic, the poster woman for the young up-and-coming business achievers, in her light grey suit, white blouse with a red and black tie, and black pumps with a small, raised heel. Charlotte was stunning. There were no other words to describe her appearance. Her short hair was parted differently, not like a boy. She was wearing a black skirt with a grey silk blouse. There was a single strand of black pearls around her neck, with matching black pearl earrings. She had no makeup except the faintest color on her lips. She wore black closed-toe shoes with flat heels. As she came down the stairs, she showed the awkwardness of an insecure girl searching for approval.

"Char... Charlotte, you look wonderful. Your granny and granddaddy will be so proud to see the beautiful young lady they raised," David said, sensing from Musee's look the need to reinforce Charlotte's confidence.

"You really think so?" Charlotte said, looking back and forth from David to Musee.

"See, what did I tell you?" Musee said. "This is the new Charlotte, the beautiful young lady raised by her grandparents to make her way in the world." David noticed that there were no dolls in Charlotte's hands.

"Mr. Wilson, we had better get started," Pastor Tom said.

"Yes, it's a quarter till. Musee, you and Charlotte lead the way. Pastor Tom and I'll follow you two ladies up the hill."

The four of them were almost at the top when David heard a car coming up behind them. He touched Musee's arm, and they moved off to the side to allow the BMW 735i to pass. The car went past the gravesite and parked just past Mary's and Edith's markers. An overweight man in a dark grey suit and striped tie, along with his overweight wife in a light blue suit wearing bracelets that jangled as she walked, emerged from the car and walked back to the gravesite. Win and his wife arrived at the same time Musee, Charlotte, David, and Pastor Tom crested the hill.

"You must be David," the man said, holding out his hand to David. "I'm Win Oakley, Dex's family attorney and accountant. This is my wife Ellie, Charlie's godmother and first cousin of Charlie's grandfather." Ellie went over to Charlotte and hugged her.

"Let me look at you," she said. "Cousin Dex would be so proud of the fine young lady you've become." She held Charlotte at arm's length.

"Everyone, please take your seats. We'll begin," Pastor Tom said. The five sat in the front row. Ellie Oakley had tried to sit next to Charlotte, but Musee pointed David to a seat three from the end of the row and seated Charlotte next to him. She took the end seat. Win Oakley sat next to David, and his wife was relegated to the opposite side of her husband on the end.

The actual service was short. Pastor Tom then asked for a show of hands of those who would like to say something about the deceased. Many hands went up. Pastor Tom improvised some rules. "First, we'll start from the back and move to the front. Second, say your piece, but keep it short. Any rambling would be cut off by me. Third, when finished, take the shovel, and throw some dirt onto the casket."

Mourner after mourner, some individuals, some husband, wife, and children together, came to the front and spoke about both Mary and Dex. For the most part, they looked directly at Charlotte. They talked less about the helping hand Dex and Mary had given them through the years, and more about the respect the Holmes family had given and sought from the people they were involved with. When it came the turn for the front row, Musee looked at David and cut her eyes to Charlotte and back to him while shaking her head no. David turned to Win and said, "Win, do you wish to speak?"

"Sure do." He jumped up and turned to the assembled crowd. "Dex and I grew up together in Lincolnton, south of Chicago. I still remember when he met Mary and they got married. Ellie and I echo everything that has been said today. Our main concern is for Ellie's goddaughter and third cousin, Charlie. She has suffered a terrible loss, and just like all of you, we want to make sure she is protected and taken care of. Dex was a fine man, and his shoes will be hard to fill, but we're going to try to make sure his activities and affairs continue to run smoothly. May he and Mary rest in peace."

When Win sat down, David sat still for a minute, absorbing what had just been said and composing his emotions.

"Mr. Wilson, do you wish to speak?" Pastor Tom asked.

"Yes, yes, I do." David stood and turned to address the crowd. "No matter how happy we are that Dex and Mary are united again in heaven, those of us who have worked with them have an empty place in our hearts. We feel this sadness, but we don't want to fill this void quickly. We want to understand that our sadness is in direct proportion to the love and joy Dex and Mary brought to all of us. I didn't have an opportunity to know Granny, but Charlotte has spent a great deal of time over the last six-plus months making sure her granny's instructions about life and living were known to me." A ripple of laughter went through the mourners. "Tomorrow is Tuesday, and Calumet Farms will be back on schedule, just as Dex wanted. Charlotte and I will be around on our regular schedule. Since Saturday was a good day at the market, if you have some surplus, we'll take it. On behalf of Dex and Charlotte, thank you for being here, sharing your thoughts about this most unusual couple, and for being a part of Calumet Farms. The fine Pineville Baptist Church Ladies Circle has brought the family a gracious amount of food. Please come to the house and share in this bounty with us." He turned, picked up the shovel, and threw in three loads of dirt. He then nodded to Pastor Tom.

"Go in the way of our Lord Jesus Christ," Pastor Tom said.

⭑  ⭑  ⭑

The mourners at the house were noisy. David circulated, thanking people for coming. Musee, with Charlotte by her side, circulated, making sure everyone had what they needed to eat and drink. Charlotte introduced Musee to the people she knew, which was almost everyone. At first, she would say, "This is Musee, David's fiancée and my friend." Pretty soon, she just put her arm around Musee's shoulders and said, "This is my friend Musee."

David was standing in the kitchen, thinking about the funeral and what was said, when Win Oakley came up and said, "Is there a place we can talk without all this commotion?"

"Sure, let's go into Dex's study."

"Good. Let me get some papers from my car. I'll meet you in there."

David sat in Dex's chair, remembering Dex's comment months ago and his references to him in his letter: "Trust him to a certain extent." Dex didn't explain what he meant, but he only said things that were important. David didn't know what to expect, but he had been warned, and more importantly, he had paid attention to everything said at the funeral.

"Mighty nice service this morning," Win said as he settled on the sofa.

"Yes, it was."

"I've got the papers here necessary for you to have signature authority over Dex's business and personal accounts and the trust accounts. If you'll sign them, I'll get them filed first thing in the morning." Win put the folder of papers on the coffee table along with a Mont Blanc pen. "Charlie really looked lost at the service. With her special needs, it'll be important for her to be protected, just the way Mary and Dex protected her. Family is always important to a person who can't do everything for themselves."

"Charlotte will be fine. It was important to Dex that she have a stable environment, doing the things she knew and felt comfortable doing.

That's why we're going back to the market on Wednesday." David felt the coldness of adrenaline coursing through his body.

"Sure, sure. Just sign where I have the forms marked, and I'll be on my way."

"Win, leave the papers here. I'll drop them by your office tomorrow afternoon, when we're finished picking up for Wednesday."

"No need to do that. Sign now and save the hassle of coming by tomorrow. Besides, tomorrow is my golf day, and I can file them early; otherwise, I won't be able to process them till Wednesday."

"Win, we'll likely be doing business together in the future. Let me help you understand. I don't sign anything without first reading it and taking the time to think about what I'm signing. I'll bring them by tomorrow. Filing Wednesday is fine.

"Tell me something, Win. You said today that you and Dex grew up in the same neighborhood. A while back, Charlotte was showing me Dex and Mary's wedding pictures. He looked totally different than he did in the later pictures when their daughter Edith was a newborn. Can you shed some light on how he changed appearance? Was he in an accident?"

"You can say that."

"Huh? What do you mean."

"Dex wasn't always the kindly wise man you knew. He was a cold-blooded killer when he was young. We grew up in a rough neighborhood where the girls got pregnant early, and the boys started their lives of crime while still in high school, joining one local crew or another, all of which were associated loosely with a Chicago outfit. Dex wasn't interested in stealing and petty stuff where he could make a few bucks. That was for the other boys. Dex wanted the serious money, and serious money came from enforcing the rules, so to speak. By the time he was a junior in high school, he knew how to efficiently break a guy's arm or leg, or, in more serious debt collections, kneecap a guy. You know, hold a 22-caliber pistol to the guy's knee and pull the trigger. Fella never walked right again. By the time he was a senior, he had graduated to enforcing orders by killing those who didn't go along. He was good, too. The best for getting a job done without a lot of fuss or publicity. Give the job to Dex, and the guy just wasn't there anymore. He was making big, big bucks. He never was flashy about it, though. Not many people knew what he did because he had a day job in the local welding shop.

"After a couple of years, he met Mary at a local Catholic church social. She was as innocent as the new-driven snow. Well, Dex fell hard—real hard. He would have married her the first day he saw her, but she didn't come easy. More important, she wanted a husband with the potential to get her out of the neighborhood. Move up in the world. Not go to the Gold Coast, but move into the solid middle class, where people knew something besides whiskey and poverty. Mind you, she wasn't a snob—just someone who wanted to better herself and her future family.

"Dex convinced her that he had a good future as a welder and would one day own his own welding shop. So they got married. Shortly after, two things happened: Mary got pregnant, and she found out where Dex's money was coming from. Mary being Mary, she didn't make a fuss. She sat Dex down and explained why she was leaving him. No threat. No screaming. Didn't even ask him for child support for his future child. She told him she was not going to have anything to do with a killer and mob associate. That's the way she was, a strong woman who loved him but had her principles. Dex promised he would get out of that life, but he needed time. She gave him two weeks. He planned his own death, and the two of them disappeared. The next thing I know, they're here in Pineville, and Dex didn't look like Dex. The rest is history."

"That doesn't sound like the Dex I knew." David was taken aback by the news, although he had known that something, some big reason had caused Dex to alter his appearance. He was more concerned about what Win had said in his eulogy and Win's insistence that he sign papers now. He willed himself to focus on Win and establish a relationship with the attorney/accountant now.

Win continued, "That life was forty-something years ago. Mary changed him. He would have done anything for her."

"Tell me one more thing. What happened to Charlotte's father? Did he ever come back looking for her?"

"Don't know. The three guys Edith had been hanging out with disappeared shortly after her death. The sheriff went looking for them. He wanted to charge them with drug possession and giving drugs to a minor—Edith was still a minor when she hooked up with them—but he couldn't find them. Put out the word all around here. Never heard from them again."

"So, you don't think her father might reappear all of a sudden one day?"

"After twenty-something years? Not likely."

"Thanks, Win. You've been helpful. I'll drop these papers off at your office tomorrow." David stood up, making it clear that the meeting was over. Win stood up.

"I'll just get Ellie, and we'll be on our way."

Following Oakley, David walked out of the room and was stopped by Walter Evans and his wife Jo. "David," Walter said, "you can count on our farm and our help in any way you need. We owe a great deal to Dex and Mary." He looked at his wife and took her hand. "And we know that Dex picked you to keep Calumet together. From what I've seen, you're the man for the job. We're with you."

David took a deep breath, stifling a surge of emotion. Jo spoke up. "David, understand that any time of the day or night I'm available to help with Charlotte. There are some issues a woman can understand about a young girl that a man can't, if you know what I mean. Me and my girls will do what we can to help you."

David took another deep breath, feeling he was about to lose his composure with the love and support he was being offered by people who had known him for less than a year. His mind flashed to his group of friends, whom he'd known for over seven years through HBS and work, and the fact that they abandoned him when he needed friends more than ever. These thoughts shone a harsh light on the different worlds surrounding the two crises. Finally, he swallowed hard and said, "Walt, Jo, thank you. I can't express my feelings correctly, but I want you to know how important your support is to me." Jo pulled him in for a hug. Walt shook his hand and embraced him.

Thinking there was nothing more that could bolster his good feelings about the future, he was stopped in the hall by Tim and Julie Roy. "David, we want you to know we're here for you. Anything, anything at all. Just let us know."

Julie spoke up. "Charlie ... Charlotte ... will need a mother's touch through this ordeal. I'm available to help. We, all of the Pineville Baptist Ladies Circle, are standing by to do whatever is needed."

"Thank you. Thank you both. Your support means the world to me, and I'm sure to Charlotte. Dex and I discussed this day and Charlotte's needs. We both felt the best way to help Charlotte in the short term is to keep her routine as stable as possible. That's what I'm going to do. She and I will stay busy making sure Dex's years of hard work building Calumet don't falter because he's gone. We need you and all of our partners to give Charlotte a purpose and make her granddaddy proud."

Julie hugged David and said, "Bless you. Dex was smart to find you."

David was relieved, but felt a foreboding he couldn't fully understand. The knowledge of Dex's warnings and Win Oakley's comments demanded time to think.

# CHAPTER 26

Musee lay in David's arms, resting her head on his chest, trying to calm her racing heart while listening to his booming rapidly in his chest.

"I need your help," he said.

Without moving, she said, "Sure."

"In the morning, Charlotte and I are going to fill the truck with produce for Wednesday's market. I'd like to have Charlotte tested by a psychological testing group so we can have a clear understanding of her mental capacity."

"Something wrong?"

"I don't know, but I have an uneasy feeling about things."

"Hold on," she said, sitting up. "One of my best customers at the store is a psychologist. I can call her and get a referral."

"Super. If you can, get an appointment for Friday, and if so, would you be willing to take her and kind of explain what is going on without her feeling put down about it?"

"Yes. Is it all right if I also make her an appointment with my gynecologist? Can you believe she has never seen one? She said Granny told her that periods are God's punishment for bad thoughts. Christ, she thinks her vagina has something to do with peeing. If I can get both appointments on Friday, would that work?"

"You bet. That'd be great. I need your help, and you'll be gone by Sunday. If you get the psychological testing set up, tell them we will want the results sent to us and a law firm in the city."

"Law firm?"

"Yeah, I have a friend at Mortimer and Castellani, one of the best firms in the country, if not the world. They are what Wall Street calls heavy hitters. My buddy owes me a big one. We'll see if he remembers. One other thing, please," he said, caressing her arm, but looking at her breasts. "While we're gone in the morning, will you go into Dex's office and look around for a safe? I haven't had time, but he said there is one. Didn't tell me where."

"That'll be fun." She kissed him on the cheek, stood up, and stretched, fully aware he was watching her naked body. "Need some beauty sleep. See you in the morning."

"Fooled me," he retorted.

Charlotte came down to breakfast in her regular khakis, loose fitting plaid shirt, and a ball cap. "Morning, you look like you're ready for work," David said.

"I am." She walked over to the stove and looked at the eggs David was stirring.

"Busy day today. We'll load up, and then I'll bring you back here. I've got to go to Win Oakley's office later. I didn't know Ellie Oakley was your godmother and Dex's first cousin. Y'all must have had a close friendship growing up."

"Huh?"

"Didn't Granny and Granddaddy have the Oakleys over on a regular basis?"

"No, I don't remember any times."

"Hmm. Hey, why don't you go get Musee. Tell her this is a working house, and we all get up early."

"I'll take her a cup of coffee." Charlotte went over to the pot and poured a cup. "Does she take sugar and milk?"

David had to think for a minute. "No milk, two level teaspoons of sugar." Charlotte put the sugar in, stirred it, and left the spoon in the cup. "Hey, David—"

"Hay is for horses," he responded.

"Did you know that if you leave a spoon in a cup of coffee and walk with it, you won't spill any?"

"Where did you hear that?"

"Granny told me."

"She was a smart woman."

"Real smart."

The van was loaded and ready by lunchtime. More importantly, each farmer-partner had let David know—not in so many words because that wasn't their way, but by their actions, and the actions of their spouses— that they wanted the status quo to continue, and, just as importantly, they'd indicated that if he needed assistance with Charlotte, their wives were ready to nurture her as one of their own. All David could think about during the loading was what kind of people command this much respect from their partners, neighbors, and community? He thought about the jungle on Wall Street where it was kill or be killed, dog eat dog, survival of the fittest, a place where respect was for the toughest, meanest, and most ruthless, not the kind, caring, and helpful people like Dex and Mary. Which was he? He wanted to be like Dex, but could he? He was still processing the fact that Dex was a killer when he was a teenager. What type of environment led kids to do that? David thought about the time Dex spoke quietly but menacingly to that customer who was rude to Charlie. Everyone within earshot knew a predator had spoken. Could David command that type of authority coming from his background? He didn't know, and he realized that a person can't fake it. He was confident he could be strong and firm, knowing what was right and wrong. All morning, way back in his subconscious, there was an alarm bell sounding, trying to get past the emotions of gratitude from and to Calumet's associates. He was ready for tomorrow; that was the key. Stability at the firm. Dex was always the businessman. He planned his death and funeral so it would have the least impact on the business. Smart, caring, but tough as nails. David was determined to be the same way.

*   *   *

"Come on, Charlotte. Let's go fix lunch for Musee. You girls are going to have the afternoon off. I've got to go into town. You think you can show Musee around, and teach her how to be a country girl?"

"She'll like being a country girl, won't she?"

"Musee, we're back," David called out.

"Be right there."

Musee walked into the kitchen with her laptop in her hand and glasses on. "How'd it go?"

"Good. We're really loaded for tomorrow." Charlotte answered.

"Great."

"How'd things go with you?" David asked, raising his eyebrows.

"So–so. I made two appointments, so that's good. I looked around and found what you needed. But there is a mini crisis at the store, which will evolve into a full-blown crisis if I'm not careful."

David looked concerned. "Anything I can do?"

"No, but tomorrow, I need to go into the store and try to dampen down the problem rather than be with y'all at the green market."

"Sure, eh, will you be coming back with us tomorrow evening?"

"I don't know. This is supposed to be my vacation, but in retailing, you really can't plan. Can I let you know tomorrow afternoon?"

"You're leaving us?" Charlotte asked, the fear evident in her voice.

Musee went over and hugged her. "If, for some reason, I must stay in the city tomorrow night, I'll be back here for the weekend, I promise. You don't have a cell phone, do you?"

"Granddaddy had a phone. I don't know how to use it."

"Well, young lady, this afternoon, we're going to go get you one, and I'm going to teach you how to FaceTime, so tomorrow night and Thursday, we can FaceTime whenever you want."

"What is head time?"

"Huh? No, FaceTime, not head time."

"What is face time?"

"It's when I call you on the phone, you answer, and we can talk and see each other. Not quite like being together, but better than not seeing each other."

"Oh, God," David feigned distress, "two young ladies with FaceTime on their cell phones. Life will never be the same."

"Don't pay attention to him, Charlotte. He's just jealous 'cause he's too ugly for anyone to want to FaceTime with him."

"Yeah," she giggled.

* * *

David sat at Dex's desk and made the first call. "Mortimer and Castellani, may I help you?"

"Brian O'Malley, please." David heard soothing music as he was transferred.

"Brian O'Malley's office."

"Good afternoon. This is David Wilson. May I speak to Mr. O'Malley, please?"

"May I tell him what this is in regard to?"

"Yes, tell him my name and that I have a new client for him." MC, as it was known on the Street, was the best, smartest, and most ruthless firm, and the most expensive.

"Where in the hell have you been?" a voice asked within seconds.

"O'Malley, no wonder you're not partner yet. Don't you know pleasant chit chat makes you more money than getting to the point?" David chided.

"Yes, I do, and I'm a senior associate, only having to work ninety hours a week instead of a hundred and twenty. I figure you don't have the money to pay for chit chat."

"I need your help. It's complicated. It has to do with an estate, trusts, businesses, and possibly a less than savory attorney/accountant."

"You want to tell me about it?"

"Not on the phone. I'd like to bring you a lot of papers, dump them in your struggling-to-make-partner lap, and let you tell me what needs to be done. Oh, yeah, just to further complicate things, it also involves custody of a special-needs adult."

"Jesus, Wilson, is there nothing simple about you? When do you want to be here?"

"How about five tomorrow afternoon? I'm going to have the special needs person with me. Is there a place she can sit so she doesn't hear what we're discussing?"

"Sure. How old is she?"

"Twenty-one."

"Okay, I'll block off an hour and a half for us. I'll get one of the young slavers, new associates to you, and let her spend time with the young lady. What's her name?"

"Charlotte Holmes."

"Got it. See you tomorrow, buddy."

David hung up. He thought back to that weekend at HBS, when the big, single question exam was coming up. Brian just did not grasp the concept of applying analysis to cases, which could lead to rational answers that weren't pie in the sky or illogical. David had worked out his own systematic way of assembling the facts and making sensible recommendations based on a logical decision tree, not hope and a prayer. Brian was having an anxiety attack, knowing he was going to fail. David went to Brian's room and spent all weekend helping him grasp David's system for responding to the cases and developing a solution. By ten that Sunday night, the light bulb in Brian's head turned on. "It's just like math," Brian had said. "You don't get it until you do. Then you can't understand why it seemed so hard."

Now, David thought, it's payback time.

David's next call let Win Oakley's secretary know that David would be bringing papers to his office. He grabbed his keys and headed to the bank to meet Marie Goodman.

*   *   *

"Are you girls going to play with those phones all night?"

"Maybe, right, Musee?" Charlotte was totally immersed in the technology of the phone and apps. "Musee, is this all phones will do?"

"You don't know half of it. I tell you what. Why don't we leave the dishes to David, and you and I go up to your room, and we'll go through the apps that come with the phone and get you some that I have on mine that will help you."

"Okay, that's awesome."

Charlotte walked out of the kitchen playing with her phone apps. Musee went over to David, gave him a full open mouth kiss, and whispered, "I'll do you in a while."

David finished the dishes and went to Dex's study. He extracted the contents of the bank box from the large, zippered canvas bag Marie Goodman had placed them in. The largest items were two ring binders. He opened the first one. There were plastic sleeves, each containing two deeds, one in the front and one in the back. The sleeves showed joint ownership of land by a corporation and an individual. David flipped through the binder and noticed that each deed was for a different corporation and individual ownership. The amount of land ranged from seven to fifteen acres. David recognized some of the individual names as farmer/producers Dex was currently doing business with. A couple of the deeds were stamped "cancelled," but those names were farmer-producers he had met and picked up from. He put aside the first binder and picked up the second. Half of the sleeves contained deeds and half were empty. He went back to the first binder, counted the deeds that were not cancelled, and then counted the deeds in the second binder. Twenty-five farms were owned jointly by twenty-five separate corporations and individuals. David sat back and thought about what he had in front of him. Obviously, Dex's obsession with risk was anal. That's not a bad way to be, he thought. Protect the downside and let the upside develop itself without micromanaging the outcome. He put the binders back in the canvas bag, along with Dex's will, the trust document, and the brokerage and bank statements. It dawned on him how different the bag was from the Italian leather briefcase he used to carry to work. In one of those moments that mark critical life education that most people go through, he realized that the trappings of success were not as important as actual success. Successful people focused on pleasing results, while failures focused on pleasing methods. He took the safe combination from the desk drawer and went over to the TV. Pushing it aside, he felt around the paneling on the wall. Pushing in slightly, a section of paneling sprang outward, and David removed it, exposing a large safe at least three feet by four feet. He tried the combination, and the safe didn't open. He tried the combination a second time, twisting the dial in the opposite direction. Again, the safe didn't open. He looked at the combination again, and then looked at the safe dial. He realized that the first number might be the times the dial should be turned. He tried the combination again and heard the tumbler click. Pulling on the door, he sat back and looked inside. There were papers, an envelope with his name on it, and another safe within the outer safe. David looked at the combination sheet. There wasn't another set of numbers on it. He opened the envelope with his name on it and found the combination for the inner safe. He opened the second door and gasped. It was stuffed full of vacuum shrink-wrapped cash. He pulled out one pack. On top of the money was a slip with the number twenty-five thousand. He pulled out another; the note said the same amount. He pulled out the other packs; each one had the same dollar amount on a slip of paper. He quickly counted the number of packs; sixty of them. A total of a million and a half.

David replaced all sixty packs, closed the inner safe, took all the papers to Dex's desk, and placed them in the canvas bag. He sat back in the chair. This is more than I can get my mind around in a hurry, David thought. The money spoke for itself. Dex was no unworldly farmer. A guy doesn't have a mill and a half in freedom money if he doesn't understand risks. Was this money from Dex's past life? David sat there with something about the money bothering him. He went back to the safe and opened it again. He felt around in the outer safe to make sure he had extracted all the papers. In the back of the safe, he felt something. He grabbed it and pulled. The sound of Velcro separating accompanied David finding a snub nose .22 revolver in his hand. He opened the inner safe again and took out three of the packs: one on top, one from the bottom, and one from the middle. The packs all contained hundred-dollar bills; the pack on top had bills with Secretary of the Treasury Gaither's name on them. The one from the middle had Secretary Sumner's name on them, and the ones from the bottom had Secretary Brady's name on the top bill. Either Dex had played with his money or he had been accumulating this stash for a long time. He thought for a few minutes and decided he wouldn't say anything about the money to Brian, at least not yet. Freedom money was personal to the person who had it.

David was wide awake at midnight, when Musee slipped under the sheet.

"You won't believe it, but Charlotte is a wiz with the phone."

"How difficult is it to use a phone?"

"I'm not talking about making a call, even FaceTime. She got that on the first explanation. She then, more or less on her own, went through each of the standard apps and figured out how to use them the way they're designed to be used. She went to the internet and figured that out. I let her handle my phone, and she wanted some of the apps I had loaded into hers, so I showed her how to get one from the app store, and then she went and got the rest herself. I thought she would never get to sleep; she was so excited. She even Face Timed me from one bed to the other. I think she's going to be okay until I get back. What about your afternoon? You find what you wanted?"

"Yeah, you can say that. I don't know if I told you, tomorrow after the market I'm meeting with an old HBS buddy, who's a big-time lawyer in the city. We'll be finished by six forty-five. You have time for a quick dinner?"

"Sure, I can take time. Where'd you like to go?"

"Where will you be?"

"At the store. Why don't we go to D B Bistro Moderne, sit in the bar area, and get something quick."

"Works for me."

"Then why don't you work on me."

# CHAPTER 27

"FaceTime me if he makes you work too hard," Musee said to Charlotte with a wink.

"He'll have to call you when I work him too hard," Charlotte said, winking back at her. Musee kissed her on the cheek and smiled at David.

"I'll meet you two at D B's at around six forty-five?" she said, looking at David.

"We'll be there."

Musee ran up the stairs to her apartment and changed into a business suit while calling for a black car from Dial 7. She grabbed her briefcase and went downstairs to meet the car.

Walking through the door of Raksin's, she was disappointed with her feelings about the store. She thought she would be excited to be back, even after a mini vacation of just two days. Her head moved from side to side, looking at the stock and signage, and noticing that some signs were not up to date. "Hi, Beth, how's it going?" she said to the sales associate in handbags. "Monica, how's Andrew's scouting coming along?" she said to the sales associate in sportswear. Throughout her walk to her office, the manager in her began to reappear, and the adrenaline and excitement of retailing started bubbling up through the uniqueness of David, Charlotte, and their life in the country.

"Hi, Hannah, good morning. How was the market? Anything interesting for Spring? The numbers I saw on the computer while I was gone seemed okay."

"They were terrible. So was the market time. I thought we had an agreement that you would be by my side when I went to market?"

"Look, I'm sorry, but there was a family emergency. As a matter of fact, I have to go back Friday for a few more days."

"Forget that. You're needed here. We're getting Holiday deliveries and have to develop the signage, and strategize how we're going to put the remaining Fall line on sale and mix in the new goods. You just can't take time off now. Maybe in January, but not now. That's all there is to it, Musee. Your primary responsibility—no, your primary obligation—is to this store. We're giving you a chance. Without Raksin's, you wouldn't have this opportunity."

"Whoa. Stop. What's going on? I've been gone for two days. You're the merchandise manager. I'm just your assistant. You're the one in charge, not me. This store operated without me for years, no decades, and you're saying it can't survive without me for one week? I don't think so." Musee dropped her briefcase on her desk, plopped into her seat, and looked straight at Hannah. Alarm bells were blaring in her head. *This is not logical*, she thought. *I had every task scheduled for this week done on Sunday morning before I left. She didn't have to do anything.* "Hannah, what's happening here? I had everything done Sunday before I left. We're not in peak season. Help me understand. Why the ranting? I didn't mean it the way it came out. Just, please, help me understand the urgency and crisis."

"Because you weren't here to go to market with me, I took Eve from sportswear."

"Eve? Evelyn Minsky, the junior sportswear buyer? What would she know about business wear and accessories?"

"It seems a lot. She was very helpful. She has a fresh perspective on business wear. You know, the latest trend in business casual. She worked in that area at her family stores scattered around South Carolina, before coming to New York."

"Really? How interesting." Musee was getting a sick feeling, with bile rising up to her throat. She sensed where this was going, but didn't want it to happen. Not now. She still needed this job. Student loans still had to be paid. The raise she got was going to her future. She needed to head this off. "Hannah, that's great that she has some ideas about business wear. Perhaps the three of us should have lunch today and talk about what y'all saw at the market." Musee smiled.

"Actually, I've got a lunch meeting with Carl from Stein & Company. They want to discuss our broadening their exposure in the stores. I'm going to press Carl for a bigger margin and first look at any end-of-season remainder off-price stuff."

"Shall I join you?" Musee said, while thinking about the shoddy merchandise Stein & Company created. Their one and only concern was making money now; they weren't interested in repeat business in the future. Musee felt her own demeanor change. This little episode was not because of her two days off. This appeared to be a fully thought-out coup. There is one way to confirm what's happening.

"Not necessary. I can handle Carl. I've worked with him before."

"Okay. Say, why don't I have lunch with Evelyn, Eve, as you call her, and she can fill me in on what y'all saw. I can go over the orders this morning. Do you have the paperwork?"

"That won't be necessary. She's having lunch with Uncle Hy ... some folks."

Calmly, Musee responded, "No problem. Well, I'd better get started on the orders. Do you have them?"

"Er, I forgot and left them at home. I was really bushed last night after reviewing them."

"Okay, I'll check the floor and make sure everything is moving smoothly." Musee started to leave but stopped and went back to her desk. She opened her briefcase and pulled out the sales reports she had printed while getting dressed, spreading them on her desk, and leaving her briefcase open. She started thinking of what she would need if she were to leave. It was apparent to her that she was going to be pushed out of her current position, and possibly made a buyer in junior sportswear. She vowed that was not going to happen. Her future, as far as she was concerned, was in business wear and accessories. She wasn't going to start over after learning the market and clientele, and then be pushed out a second time. Casually, she went through each of her desk drawers, taking out any items that could be useful later—her address book, promotional info from buying offices about this clearly defined market, personal notes from sales and operations people at various manufacturers. Every time she removed an item from her desk, she masked it with one of the sales printouts as she placed the item in her briefcase. When finished, she closed and locked the briefcase and placed it in the center of her desk with a slip of paper balanced against it in the back. If the case was disturbed, she'd know it. "I'm going to make the rounds on the floor. What time are you going to lunch, Hannah?"

"Today at eleven."

"Super, I'll be back before then." Walking the floor, Musee stopped and spoke to each sales associate and stock person. She caught up on the latest gossip and comments about what merchandise was easy to sell and which would likely be on the markdown rack at the end of the season. As she had always done, she took the most-likely-not-to-sell items and marked them down now, just past the crest of the season. She knew that these items were not terrible, but not a first or second choice for a customer, so she wanted to give the customers an incentive to figure out how the item would fit in their wardrobe. She put a few accessories close by the sales rack, ordered new signage, and spoke to the sales staff about this new opportunity. She looked at her watch, eleven forty-five, so she made her way back to the shared office. Hannah was gone, and Musee noticed her briefcase had been moved. Her spirits sagged with confirmation of what she suspected, while her anger rose as she thought about all the years she'd given to the store, and now this injustice is the result. Fairness was nonexistent. She unlocked the briefcase, found the spare thumb drive, and inserted it in her computer. Quickly, without trepidation, she transferred the corporate information of the suppliers she knew were the highest quality in all the areas in which she'd built her reputation. When finished, she placed the device in her briefcase and took it from her office. She placed it in a locker, where the sales associates stashed their outerwear, umbrellas, lunch, or anything not appropriate for the sales floor, and put the key in her pocket.

It was close to four when she got the call she knew was coming. "Musee, Mr. Raksin would like to see you on the sixth floor." Usually, it was an honor to be called to the executive offices. If a person was being fired, it was done in the stockroom on the floor where they worked, and then security would escort them out of the store. Being called to the sixth floor meant she wasn't going to be fired, at least not today. "Hi, Musee, he's expecting you. Go on in," Raksin's executive assistant said, when Musee walked into the executive suite.

"Thanks, Vera," Musee said, noticing that Vera had stopped looking at her and pretended to be busy on the computer, but she was not typing.

"Ms. O'Hara, thank you for coming up. How's your family emergency?"

"Calming down. Death in the family; you know how that goes. Funeral is Friday," she said, building a case for why she needed that day and Saturday off.

"Our condolences. When a member of the Raksin's family has sadness, we all have sadness. Please let your family know how sorry we are."

"Thank you, sir. I will. You wanted to see me?" Musee wasn't in the mood for his small talk and wanted to push the meeting to its inevitable conclusion—whatever that was.

"Yes, Ms. O'Hara. Hannah has told me what a great assistant you have been. She says you've been a big contributor to the division."

"Thank you, sir," Musee said. Are you kidding me, she thought. Musee knew Evelyn didn't know anything about business wear, and Raksin was going to find out the expensive way, if he was going to do what she thought he was about to do. She was seething inside as she smiled at him.

"I've been thinking of ways to reward you, Ms. O'Hara, and I've come up with a plan."

"Yes, sir. Thank you."

"I'm sure you're aware that senior management at Raksin's have employment contracts that stipulate their salaries, bonuses, and benefits." He paused and looked questioningly at Musee.

"Yes, sir. I'm aware." She didn't know where this was going, but her interest peaked. Senior management meant merchandise manager and up.

"Good. My plan is to treat you as a member of the senior management team and offer you an employment contract."

"As the assistant merchandise manager of the business wear division?"

"No. What I have in mind is to move you to junior sportswear and swimsuit buyer for the next year."

"I'm being demoted?"

"No, no, Ms. O'Hara. I want you to get experience in this division on the front line as a buyer. That would only be temporary. I expect the merchandise manager position to open up in a year. You would then naturally be the likeliest to assume that position. In the meantime, even though you will be a buyer, your salary will be increased to something comparable to the merchandise manager's salary, resulting in your getting a raise of seven hundred dollars a month."

Musee only heard part of what had been said. The clearest part was the seven hundred dollars a month increase. "I don't know what to say, Mr. Raksin. This is all happening so fast."

"I understand, and you have the distraction of the family emergency. I have here the employment agreement for your signature. If you want to sign it now, we can get rid of that formality and focus on your new position." He slid the contract in front of her and placed a pen alongside it.

Musee realized a trap was being set. "Mr. Raksin, this is all happening so fast. I'll tell you what. Let me take the agreement with me. I'll read it tonight and have it back on your desk in the morning."

"Ms. O'Hara, no need to delay. It's a standard agreement that we, in senior management, have all signed. Don't you want to join the ranks of senior management at Raksin's?"

"Mr. Raksin, I do. My dad, before he died, always told me to read anything before signing. I've always obeyed my father. You wouldn't want me to start disobeying him now, would you?"

"Of course not, Ms. O'Hara."

"I tell you what, Mr. Raksin. I've got a dinner appointment this evening. I'll be back in the store by seven thirty. I'll read the document at dinner, sign it, and return it to you by seven thirty. That's only three hours from now, so that shouldn't be a problem, should it?"

"Frankly, I'm disappointed in your lack of trust in me and the store, but that's fine."

"Mr. Raksin, it's not a matter of trust, just my upbringing. I know you wouldn't try to deceive me." Musee picked up the folder and held out her hand toward Raksin. "Thank you, sir, for this great opportunity."

Raksin stood and shook her hand. "I'll look forward to receiving the papers back at seven thirty, Ms. O'Hara. Enjoy your dinner. Is it with a supplier of the store?"

"Eh, no, sir. Someone I hope to convince to become an important supplier."

"Good luck, then."

Musee willed herself to think of Charlotte as she left the sixth floor and went back to her office. Hannah was there, so Musee detoured and went to the lockers, retrieved her briefcase, unlocked it, and placed the folder inside. She sent a text message to Hannah saying she would see her either at seven thirty tonight or in the morning. Walking out of the store, she called David, and told him she was headed to the Forty-second Street Library before meeting the two of them at DB at six forty-five.

David looked up from reviewing the contract Musee had given him. "You realize you can be fired for any reason, and if you left Raksin's employment, for any reason, you can't work in women's retailing in any form in the tri-state area, or on the internet selling to the tri-state area for two years?"

"Unreal, isn't it. If the sleaze had said I was going to get a two-hundred-dollar a month raise, I probably would have felt okay and signed on the spot without reading it. But he dangled a seven-hundred-dollar raise. I knew that was for more than a new job. It was a sign-away-your-career bonus. Nowhere in that agreement," she pointed to the papers, "does it say what grounds they would need for firing me. My bet is that I wouldn't have been the junior sportswear and swimsuit buyer for six months before I was canned. Boom, Musee O'Hara is toast in retailing."

"What's a sleaze?" Charlotte asked.

"A real greaseball," Musee said, putting her hand on Charlotte's.

"What's a greaseball?" Charlotte asked.

"A person who deliberately does something to hurt another person," David said, smiling at Charlotte.

"What are you going to do, Musee?" Charlotte asked, with genuine fear in her voice.

"I don't know. I need this job. Starting over in retailing is not an option. I'll figure something out. What blows me away is the lack of respect he has for me. He must think I'm some dumb bimbo without a brain in my head."

"What's a bimbo?"

"A female who doesn't think very well."

"Like me?"

Musee squeezed Charlotte's hand. "You're anything but a bimbo. Friday, you and I are going to prove it."

"I have an idea," David said. "I know where you can get a mentor/management position in a profitable business looking to expand. It's not the same kind of retailing you're used to, but it's looking to diversify. If you can come up with a business plan for what you want, the company could fund it."

"Seriously? Where?"

"Calumet Farms. You'll make the same salary you do now with potential bonuses as the business grows."

"You're making a real offer?"

"Sure am. The board's directors are sitting right here." He pointed to Charlotte and himself. "We can use a person of your caliber and experience to train the next generation." He nodded to Charlotte.

"Please, Musee, you can still sleep in my room. Please say yes."

"Yes," she said, smiling.

"Okay, let's go by Raksin's. Put a big X through each page. Write 'I resign effectively immediately.' Don't sign it, though. He'll know where it came from. Then let's go get some clothes from your place. We can arrange a mover to pack up everything and bring it up to the farm on his schedule."

# CHAPTER 28

"You know, all day today at the store, I felt like I was away from home, my real home. The place I belong. With the people I belong with. The people I feel are genuine, and, just as importantly, they love me. At least, I think they do. I'm pretty sure about Charlotte, but I'm not sure about anybody else."

"Do you doubt my love?"

"I don't doubt you love my body. You tend to prove that whenever you can, horny dog."

David turned onto his side and raised himself on his elbow. "Let me make this clear, because starting tomorrow, we'll be going full speed ahead, getting Charlotte tested and you on the path to your own business. I love you. I love every millimeter of your body, inside and out, but more than the obvious, I love your spunk, your brains, and your street smarts. I was led here to Calumet Farms by some guardian angel or higher power, and now I have a tremendous responsibility to Charlotte and to her granddaddy Dex, who entrusted her care to me, as well as the care of Calumet Farms. Don't ever think I don't want you by my side as my advisor, muse, partner, and lover. That's as clear as I can make it." He kissed her on the forehead.

"I L U 2," Musee said, snuggling up next to him. "I'm scared. My life has taken a sharp turn I didn't see coming."

"Well, you did what I was taught to do: open another door when one slams shut. The door you've opened leads to the end of the rainbow. Tell me about your internet fashion idea."

"You need to understand the background," Musee said, sitting up and pulling the sheet into her lap, covering her body entirely. "From the day girl babies are born, they're taught that their beauty and attractiveness to the male is the most important aspect of their lives. Think about the princess stories, the princess costumes you'll see just about every three- and four-year-old wearing. Think about the girl dolls. Have you ever seen any fat girl dolls? When little girls go to elementary school, they're dressed by their mothers to be "pretty' and attractive to the other children. When their bodies begin to develop in junior high, the stakes are upped. The girls are allowed by their parents to shorten their skirts and tighten their blouses. They become sensual walking advertisements at an age when they should be expanding their minds, but in a setting where they're supposed to entice the boys to notice them. In high school, it gets worse. A girl with brains realizes she'd better hide her interest in learning, or she won't be popular with the 'right' crowd. By college, they're in a highly competitive sexual environment where they learn that sex appeal translates into more social opportunities. So, what happens when they enter the business world? What have they been taught about getting ahead? What is their habit of dressing and body language? All their lives, they've used their attractiveness, their sensuality, to get ahead. Young women just do what they've been taught all their lives, and when they succeed in attracting their male co-workers, the males act the way their DNA is wired; they go for the bait.

"Okay, that's the background. The #ME TOO movement did more to lower the glass ceiling and thicken it than any misogynist Neanderthal could have ever hoped to do."

"No. Why do you say that?"

"Simple, think about it. Did any of those abused women stand up, tell those scum bags to stick it, and walk out with dignity? No, they wanted their jobs for a variety of reasons—family needs, climbing the ladder—you name it. I get it. But I can assure you, even down at middle management level, there won't be any more bonding sessions at the office, a bar, the golf course, or anywhere else. Even when only a few people are in a group, everyone has to be careful about using the words guys always use when they're getting to know each other. If a woman is there, the jokes and stories are cleaned up and meaningless. It's sad. Now, back to what I want to do.

"I want to create four different business outfits—skirt/pants, two blouse styles, and two jackets, traditional and Eisenhower. I want the basic garments to be available in four colors—maroon, navy, tan, and black. The blouse colors will be light blue, light pink, or white, and will be polished, wrinkle-free, cotton/silk blend. The suits will be wool/silk blend. The quality will be high, on the level of custom-tailored items. A career business woman between twenty-five and fifty, a new recruit or senior management, will be able to have these suits for years. They'll be classics. Every item can be mixed or matched. The look will be smart, professional, and feminine, but not sexy or sensual. In any meeting, the woman's mind will dominate, not her sensuality."

"Where's your differentiation from every other retailer?"

"I'm coming to that. The obvious question is just what you're asking. Why buy from us? When I first got to New York, the only job I could find in fashion was working for an older designer, Anna Duncan, who catered to a small but loyal group of professional women fighting their way to the top of their business. Anna didn't care about money. She felt she had a mission—give go-getting women pride in what they wear. Her life had been spent as a tailor and making patterns. Her clothes always had some special, unique, small signature telltale. You know, something that one woman would recognize on another, building a sense of sisterhood in whoever wore Anna's clothes. When she retired at eighty, she moved to Florida to be with her daughter. She sold me the copyrights on those wonderful and special patterns for ten dollars. She said, 'Musee, carry on helping women with the courage to climb the ladder of success. Make me proud.'"

Musee looked off into the room, her chin slightly quivering, but she took a deep breath and looked back at David.

"Do you still have them?"

"Of course. The challenge is translating the patterns I have on a USB into the latest CAD-CAM software. That takes special talent I don't have and can't afford."

"Do you know someone who does?"

"No, but I haven't looked. The cost would be way more than my resources, so I haven't looked."

"Okay, tomorrow you start looking for someone who can do the job. Find out the cost, and we'll figure out the best way to get the patterns usable for a private-label atelier like you want. Again, why the need for special business clothes? Don't women just wear what they want, rather than a 'uniform' or such?"

"Think about men. It doesn't matter if a guy is thin or fat, tall or short. All he has to do is put on a well-tailored suit, a nice tie, and he's accepted as a serious businessman. We want to bring that same perspective to business-women. Our suits will scream success and intelligence without crushing femininity. An overweight woman, a woman with a pooch, or a thin model can all look smart, intelligent, and feminine at the same time. Now for the golden egg. Every man wants something distinctive, and so does every woman, but in a good way. With men, it's the tie or watch. With women, accessories are the key. Scarfs, pins, jewelry, handbags, and belts are the way to say, 'I'm smart, intelligent, professional, and unique.' Most women don't know how to do this correctly. They just don't know how to package. I do.

That's been my success in my whole career. I want to sell them the basic suit options, and then sell them the entire package. I want them to come back each season or every other season and buy more accessories. My plan is to design and sell clothes with our own label. The customer will pay a slight premium to get the quality we give them. These are profitable but have a lower margin than accessories. While they will be fashionable, they won't go out of fashion. Initially, we'll have to use other people's accessories just taking the retailer's markup, which is respectable. But eventually, I want to have our own label on the accessories as well, not available anywhere except from us. We'll start with low- to moderately-priced accessories, and once established, move into the higher-priced level, where the markup is even higher."

"How are you going to scale the business? You can't do it all."

"One of my successes at Raksin's was to take the floor sales force and teach them how to see the way I see. They picked it up fast. I'm going to start with Charlotte, assuming you allow her to work with me rather than you at the green market. From there, I'll add the others for the call center, where all customer contact will be."

"Have a name for it yet?"

"Yep, GLF Fashions."

"Sounds interesting. What does GLF stand for?"

"Great Little Find."

"God, that's all exciting. Let's figure out what's needed and get going."

"Well, we've talked away our sex time. I've got to get back before Charlotte wakes up. It's a real turn-on when a guy is more interested in your mind than your body." She leaned over and kissed him on the cheek.

As David served breakfast, he said, "Okay, ladies, here's today's plan of action. Charlotte, remember, we have three cakes to bake before Saturday and only one oven. Do you think you and Musee can make at least two of them today?"

"Of course. We'll try for three. I need some ingredients."

"Musee, can you help Charlotte get whatever she needs?"

"Sure. Do we have wheels?"

"You've got the pickup. The keys are hanging by the door over there. Charlotte can tell you what farms have which ingredients. I'm taking the panel van on the regular pickup route this week. When the two of you have the first cake in the oven, how about taking a look at the barn. There's the farmhand apartment and the open area. You'll need a good electrician, and the internet company needs to take us up to the highest and most reliable speed. Oh, also ask the electrician to fix the box so he can install a big enough generator to keep it up and running when power is down. Come to think of it, get him to look for a generator that can service both the barn and the house."

"Whoa, slow down. What are you trying to do?" Musee asked.

"Charlotte needs an industrial kitchen to bake more than one cake at a time, so it seems to me that the kitchenette in the apartment should have enough space. The bedroom can serve as your office, and the rest of the space, depending on what you say, could be the beginning of your cutting floor and sewing area for your new internet business."

"You're serious, aren't you?"

"Serious as a heart attack."

"Who's having a heart attack?" Charlotte asked.

"He's just being silly," Musee said.

"Okay, ladies, we good? Tonight, we'll update each other on what happened today."

"All good," Musee said.

"This'll be fun," Charlotte chimed in.

✷ ✷ ✷

At dinner, the three of them took turns updating the others. Musee had helped Charlotte prepare some notes on what they accomplished, particularly the baking, and their decision to bake four cakes instead of just the three on order. Charlotte read her notes hesitantly, and, when finished, she looked up and beamed.

"Awesome, Charlotte. Really cool. Musee, how'd it go with you?"

"I looked over the whole space. It'll be great for a beginning. Besides a cutting table and sewing machines, though, we're going to need a stock room and a room for a mini call operation. The barn will be tight for all that. The electrician came out early, and I explained how much juice we'd need, and I asked him to determine what size generator we'd need for both the barn and the house. He said he'd get back to us by Monday with a quote. The internet guys say they can have us super-fast internet with a guaranteed 99.9% reliability whenever you say go."

"Go. If the electrician comes back with a reasonable quote, place the order. Push him for start and finish dates. Also, ask him for maintenance contracts for both the generator and electrical service. Don't let him do the minimum. Let's get excess capacity now for later."

"Got it. What about the putting up walls, taking out walls, etc.?"

"Marcel Hernandez goes to Pineville Baptist. I'll speak to him on Sunday at services. How many people are in your dream call center? Are you sure there will be enough room in the existing structure?"

"No, I'm not sure. Just eyeballing, it seems to be small and tight. Perhaps six to begin with in the call center, but that will only require three computers and phone sets because only two will likely be used regularly and one for backup. The staff can do other things when the phones aren't ringing. The challenge is that the lines need to be covered from six in the morning to midnight. Two people from six to ten in the morning, one from ten to three in the afternoon, and two from three to ten. Then just one till midnight."

"What about contracting a call center business?"

"That won't work. It takes a personal touch by trained females. I'll do the training and teach them how to sell."

"You teach the FAB?" Charlotte asked.

"FAB? What is FAB?"

"Features, advantages, benefits," she said. "Sell the benefits, not the features or advantages." She grinned, looked at David, and winked. "That's why I don't have to do dishes for the rest of my life." She giggled.

"Huh?" Musee looked from David to Charlotte and back to David.

"World's greatest saleswoman merged with the world's best fashion brain are an unstoppable pair. I can see it happening." David smiled at both.

"I got an idea," Charlotte said hesitantly.

"Shoot."

"Shoot who?"

"That means go ahead and tell us your idea," Musee said.

"Yeah, there's just the three of us in this big old house, right? We hardly ever use the living and dining rooms, and the kitchen has plenty of space. Why don't we put the new ovens in the kitchen and the computers and people in the living and dining rooms? That should be easy to do. If I'm baking, when the cakes are in the ovens, I can help cover the computers—if you show me how. Then the barn would have enough room, right?"

"Out of the mouth of babes ..." David said.

"That's not a good idea?"

"Charlotte, it's not just a good idea; it's a great idea. What he meant was that sometimes a fresh set of eyes can see solutions that experienced people overlook. You are a special gem, my dear. I'm so lucky to have you as a friend."

"Little sister," Charlotte corrected her.

"We're good. I'm beat. Come on, little sister. We have a long day tomorrow with the doctor and the advice giver."

# CHAPTER 29

Friday, after the market, David drove up to Musee's apartment shortly after six. The girls were waiting for him outside with another suitcase full of clothes and work papers Musee needed. On their way home, Charlotte was quiet and sat looking out the side window. David and Musee talked about the day at the market, and the fact David would have to get some resupply from the farmers on this week's schedule. Dropping Musee and Charlotte at the house, he said, "You ladies go ahead and eat some dinner. I'll get something when I return."

"I'll make you a plate of whatever we throw together," Musee said.

Inside, the two of them worked side by side, building a vegetable medley for dinner.

"You're mighty quiet, Charlotte. Anything you want to discuss?"

Charlotte just stared out the window toward the hill where her granny and granddaddy were buried. "Who is hey man?" she asked, tucking her head lower.

"Hey man? What man are you talking about?"

"You know, the doctor said I'm in touch with my hey man."

"Oh, you mean hymen, not hey man. That means you're a virgin, meaning that you've never had sex with a guy. Tonight before we go to sleep, I'll explain everything to you. It's complicated but, at the same time, not complicated. It's about joy, pleasure, and maybe creating a baby, so it's not something to be taken lightly, although, unfortunately, some girls learn about sex the wrong way. You'll learn the right way." Musee smiled and put some chopped onions in the pan with the potatoes.

"Why didn't Granny tell me about sex and these things? I know she loved me." Tears were rolling down Charlotte's face, while she continued to look down rather than at Musee. Musee dried her hands, turned Charlotte toward her, and pulled her into a hug.

Musee said softly, "Little sister, I don't know why Granny and Granddaddy sheltered you, but I'm sure part of it was because of what happened to your mom. I know without a doubt that they loved you with all their heart and soul. Think about it. Your granddaddy found David to take care of you after they'd both be gone, didn't he?" Charlotte nodded her head as it rested on Musee's shoulder.

"Having a big brother like David will make growing up easier and more fun," Musee said, stroking her hair.

"And he brought me a big sister."

"The three of us are a family."

★　★　★

"She wanted to know who her hey man was," Musee whispered in David's ear. "She now knows all about sex and how to pleasure herself and take the stress off if she doesn't have a boyfriend."

"Hey, man?"

"Hymen, she's a certified virgin. Some guy is going to be one of the luckiest guys on earth one day. You're one, too."

"How did the aptitude testing go?"

"Okay. I tried to explain to her that there were no right or wrong answers, to just say whatever came to mind after reading the questions. She finished each section ahead of time."

"You told them to send the results to Brian, right?"

"Yes, copies to both of you by email. David, I'll bet Charlotte does better than you or anyone else expects."

"Why do you say that?"

"Little things. You know that FAB sales technique? Why would she be able to learn, understand, and implement it so easily? How can she know how to make such a complicated cake from a recipe that's never been written down? How did she just flash on the idea to move the ovens and call center into the house instead of just leaving them in the barn? Maybe these things don't matter or show cognitive normalcy, but I think they do."

"Wouldn't that be great."

"Why did you want her tested?"

"Two reasons. First, I think you are closer to right than wrong for many of the same reasons. More importantly, do you remember Win Oakley's speech at Dex's funeral?"

"I remember he was a pompous fool."

"Remember that he said his wife was Dex's first cousin?"

"No, I didn't pick up on that. So what?"

"So, if that's true, she could petition the court for legal custody of the physical person and the financial affairs of a mentally challenged individual."

"Why? She's over twenty-one."

"Not mentally. If the court declares her mentally incompetent, as Mary and Dex told everyone, including Charlotte, her whole life, it doesn't matter how old she is."

"Jesus, that's scary. What can we do?"

"I wanted the testing to establish Charlotte's true mental capacity to make decisions. If she's below normal, I'll have to do something aggressive, maybe petition the court myself. I don't know. It's dicey. That's why I want Brian in on this."

"Okay, but we can't solve this tonight. There might not even be a problem, so ..." She slipped under the covers and stretched out, melding their bodies together as she kissed him passionately.

*　*　*

Musee pulled the covers of her bed up to her neck, completely relaxed and sedated. She stared at the ceiling, wondering how she'd become so lucky. From the other bed, she heard chuckling.

"Did you and David have fun?" The chuckle again.

"All right, young lady, you should be asleep. Tomorrow's a busy day."

A giggle.

# CHAPTER 30

"Afternoon, Your Honor. How are Isabel and the children?"

"She's fine, I guess. The last one left for college two months ago, and I think she is feeling the empty nest thing."

"Well, sir, it takes some getting used to, but it turns out pretty good. Travel, fun, romance—it all comes back. Give it time."

"More time to fish would be nice. That's for sure. What can I do for you, Win."

"Well, let me give you some background, Your Honor. You know Dex and Mary's grandchild is, what's the proper word, retarded."

"The polite term today is special needs."

"Sure, special needs. Anyway, you may or may not know, she's living in Dex's house with that young fella Dex had working for him. There's also another lady, about the fella's age or closer to Charlie's age, and the two of them aren't married, either. That's not right. My Ellie is Dex's first cousin and Charlie's only living relative. It seems to me that Mary and Dex would be happier to have Charlie living with family who could take care of her and not have her exposed to fornication and who knows what else. Why, with her impaired mental capacity, all kinds of things may be going on. Besides, she is Dex's heir, and her financial assets should be protected."

"What are you asking, Win?"

Win reached into his briefcase, pulled out a petition, and handed it to the judge. "Your Honor, I'm petitioning the court for custody of Charlie's physical person and financial affairs. As her only living relative, Ellie has standing in the eyes of the law."

"You have all your bases covered legally, Win?"

"Yes, Your Honor."

"You coming to court in the morning to file this formally?"

"Well, Your Honor, not exactly. You see, I'm not sure this guy David will be cooperative, so what I'm asking is for you to sign the petition Friday afternoon, give it to the sheriff to execute by picking up Charlie and delivering her to my house Friday evening. That way, she can be with Ellie for the weekend before that Wilson fella can do anything about it."

"That's true, Win, because I'm going fishing at my special place that even Bella doesn't know about, and I don't want to be disturbed. I'll sign the petition and put it on the docket for Monday morning court." He picked up the petition and started reading. After finishing, he picked up his pen, signed the petition, and hit the intercom.

"Sally, please come in here." He handed the petition to her and said, "Friday morning, give this to the sheriff to serve at five Friday afternoon."

"Thank you, Your Honor. You've done the right thing to protect an innocent young lady." Win rose, shook hands with the judge, and left. Outside in his car, he took a deep breath and smiled. His thoughts were on the money he would soon control and the ongoing fees he would enjoy through the years.

# CHAPTER 31

On Friday evening, David, Charlotte, and Musee were almost home after a long, busy day at the green market. Charlotte and Musee were working their phones, Charlotte texting girl questions, and Musee texting back the answers. What a day. What a week, so far. This was probably the best week we've had since Dex passed, David thought. Not only did they have a strong sales week, but the results of Charlotte's psychological tests came back. Her mental capacity was exactly average, not even leaning toward the low end of the scale, but in the middle. There was no chance anyone could judge her as being mentally incapable of making decisions for herself. The results showed that the decision-making capacity was normal, despite her development having been stunted. David looked over at Musee and Charlotte working their phones and knew Musee would take care of the stunted issue.

"I'll drop you girls off at the house, and y'all can relax and fix something for dinner. I'll go pick up some produce to fill in for tomorrow."

"I'll cook, Musee," Charlotte piped up.

"Okay by me," Musee responded.

David was almost at the gate before he realized it was open. His eyes followed the gravel drive up to the house, where he saw the front end of a car poking out from the side of the house. On the front, the car had a bulbar used by police forces around the country. Immediately, he stepped on the gas and went past the driveway.

"Hey, big guy, you passed the house," Musee said, looking over at David.

He drove on without speaking until he crested the hill. He turned into the neighbor's drive, backed up, and headed back to New York. He pulled onto the side of the road. "Musee, there is someone at the house. I think it's the police. If it is, then my fears about Win Oakley are true. Take out your and Charlotte's phones." Both of them did as told. "Okay, take the SIM cards out of them."

"They won't work," Musee protested, looking at him.

"Yes, you're right. But if you leave the SIM card in the phone, even if you turn it off, you can be located. We don't want that. Here's what we're going to do. I'm getting out here. I'll walk to the house and see what the police want. You go back to NYC. Park the van in its regular space at the green market. Then walk to your place. Don't take a cab or stop anywhere close to your apartment. Pick up something for the two of you to eat at a bodega on the way – not one close to your place. Once there, don't open the door for anybody. Unless I'm arrested, I'll be at—"

"Arrested? Are you serious?" Musee looked at him with wide eyes. Charlotte sat speechless, clinging to Musee's arm.

"I think they're coming to take Charlotte, and if I don't tell them where she is, they may arrest me."

"What are we going to do? Don't let them take me away." Charlotte pleaded, tears pooling in her eyes.

"Easy, Charlotte. Easy." David reached behind Musee and squeezed Charlotte's shoulder. "This is not unexpected. I've been speaking to someone who can straighten everything out. You stay with Musee, do as she says, and everything will be okay. Now, ladies, you know what to do?"

Musee was taking the SIM card from Charlotte's phone and putting it in a separate part of her wallet from where she'd put her own. "Phones disabled, put van in green market space, walk to bodega, not close to apartment, and then walk to apartment, lock the door, and pray until six thirty in the morning when you show up. Got it." Musee looked at David, who had his phone to his ear.

"Brian, it looks like Oakley has made his move. Really? Thank you. I'll be at the green market tomorrow unless I'm in jail. I'm counting on you." David clicked off his phone and opened the driver's door. "Musee, you have the law firm's emergency number, right?

Musee slid over under the wheel, looked at him, and said, "Yes. I love you."

"I love you, too," said Charlotte.

"I love both of you. Everything is going to be fine, I promise. The cavalry is on the way. Please be careful and smart. Get going." He shut the van door and waited until they were moving before starting to walk across the field to the house.

✶　✶　✶

"Evenin' sheriff, what brings you here?" David said, as he leaned against the police car.

"Evenin', Mr. Wilson. I've got a court order here to escort Miss Charlotte Holmes to her cousin's house. Is Ms. Holmes here?"

"No, sir, but she'll be here shortly. Why don't you come up on the porch? I'll get us some tea and a slice of that Granny cake Miss Holmes makes." David stepped back from the car door.

"That's mighty kind of you, Mr. Wilson."

"Sheriff, please just call me David. I'm not old enough to be a Mister yet." David walked to the porch and looked back at the sheriff coming behind him. "Have a seat, and I'll get the tea and cake."

David went to the kitchen, looked at his watch, and, at a deliberately slow pace, took out two plates, two forks, and poured tea into two glasses. He cut the sheriff a large piece of Granny cake and a normal one for himself. He hoped the sheriff would take his time eating. He needed ninety minutes for Musee and Charlotte to get to the safety of Musee's apartment. He handed the sheriff his tea and cake. As he sat down, he placed his phone on the table.

When the sheriff finished his second piece of cake, he looked at his watch. "Well, David, I've been here an hour. When did you say Miss Holmes was coming?"

Before David could answer, his phone vibrated. They both looked at the message. It was from Brian: *Got it. Activate AM.* David looked at the sheriff and smiled.

David was trying to stall for the full ninety minutes. Most of the time was already gone. "She should be here within the next half hour," David said, looking at his watch.

"You stalling me, David?" the sheriff asked, looking sideways at David. "You know, Dex was one of my best friends, if not the best. He helped me in ways people don't even know. He loved that granddaughter of his, was protective of her. Didn't want a repeat of the tragedy that fell upon his daughter."

"I'm not stalling you," David lied.

"My point, Mr. Wilson, is this. Dex was my friend. I aim to protect his granddaughter, so you need to understand that I have a job to do for the court and my friend. Don't go obstructing that job. We understand each other?"

'Yes, sir, sheriff. But let me ask you a question. If Dex's first cousin is Win Oakley's wife, how come he set up everything for me to take care of Charlotte? Why didn't Charlotte, when she was growing up, have regular family contact with Win's wife? Aren't those valid questions?"

The sheriff sat silent for a few minutes, rocking back and forth and staring out at his police car. Finally, he answered, "Mr. Wilson, those are fair questions. The problem is, as I see it, Judge Valenti signed a court order for me to pick up Charlie and take her to her cousin's. Like it or not. I'm going to do that. If the court order is wrong, you can take it up with the judge on Monday morning. Until then, I have a job to do, and I'm going to do it. Now, I'll only ask you once: Do you know where Miss Charlotte Holmes is?"

"Sheriff, all I know is she was due to be here," looking at his watch, "an hour and forty-five minutes ago. When she'll get here, I don't know. If she gets here, I don't know. If you feel I'm obstructing justice, I'll go with you to the police station, or you're welcome to wait here all night, if you wish."

"No, I'm not going to do that." The sheriff touched the microphone on his shoulder. "Missy, put out an APB for a white van with the name Calumet Farms on the sides. Include New York City in the alert area. Now, Mr. Wilson," the sheriff said, rising from his rocker, and reaching for his handcuffs, "please stand and put your hands behind your back."

"Really, sheriff? I'll come willingly."

"I know you would, but rules are rules. You can't imagine how many of my guests have said the same thing, and then changed their minds as they got close to the jail."

David did as the sheriff requested. Even though David had expected the possibility of arrest, he was unprepared for the reality of having metal restraints binding his hands behind his back, leaving him unable to do anything, even scratch his face when it itched. Trying to suppress his anxiety and fear, he thought about Dex. What would he do? Dex would quietly submit, particularly if it meant his plan of protecting Charlotte would unfold as he wanted. David realized that Brian was in charge now, and Brian would protect all of them. He started breathing deeply and slowly as the sheriff placed him in the back of the car.

* * *

Musee was scared, but she couldn't show Charlotte how petrified she was. Being a single female who survived the nightlife and hookup scenes in New York City hardened her on how quickly situations could spin out of control. She needed time to think, but Charlotte kept up constant chatter and asked a string of questions as they drove back to the city. Musee was certain they could put David's plan into action. Then it was a matter of waiting for him and his attorney to protect Charlotte. Her eyes darted from right to left to the side mirrors as they went down the Tappan Parkway, merged onto the Saw Mill Parkway, and then the Henry Hudson Parkway. She relaxed. They were in the city, and the van and two women wouldn't stand out. She was determined to keep Charlotte out of the clutches of the police and the judicial system.

At Eighty-fourth Street and Henry Hudson Parkway, Musee's adrenaline shot up as she noticed a police car along the side of the road. She looked in the truck's side  mirrors as they went by. A few seconds later, the police car pulled into traffic. The van was almost to the Seventy-ninth Street exit, and Musee took it, went around the circle, and up to Broadway. She didn't still see the police car behind her, so she turned right and headed south on Broadway. She felt lucky to have a straight shot to Union Square. She relaxed. Her luck turned. As the van passed Fifty-ninth Street, a police car was three cars back. How to protect Charlotte? Musee knew if Charlotte was in the van and the police stopped them, it would be worse than if Charlotte had been taken by a country sheriff. The NYC legal bureaucracy would swallow her up for weeks, if not months.

"Charlotte, let's have fun on this sister journey. I'm going to drop you off at Raksin's, you know, the store where I used to work. I want you to go to the third floor, ask for Stephanie, and tell her I want her to put together a career outfit for you and one for me. Doesn't that sound like fun?"

"Where will you be. I don't want us separated. I'm scared of getting lost."

"Little sister, you're not going to get lost. You'll be at the store trying on clothes while I park the van in its regular spot at Union Square. Then I'll come to the store, and you and I will walk to my apartment, which is only a few blocks away. Tomorrow morning, we'll put on our new clothes when David comes to get us. He'll be surprised."

"Yeah, he will. Why can't I go with you, and we walk back to the store together?"

Musee decided she needed to alert Charlotte without alarming her. "Little sister, there are a lot of policemen in NYC. It's possible they're looking for two gorgeous young ladies in a produce truck. If they see both of us, they may stop us and ask for identification. If they only see one, they probably won't pay any attention. I've noticed several police cars. By you going to the store, and me looking as ugly as I can, I can get the van parked and come back to the store. Make sense to you?"

"Yeah, big sister. I guess so."

"Okay, third floor, ask for Stephanie, and tell her what we want. Tell me what you're going to do."

"I'm going to the third floor, ask for Stephanie, and get her to put together a career outfit for me and you."

"Super! David is going to be really surprised when he sees his two best girls." Musee sighed. This might work, she thought. She saw the police car still behind her. She turned off Broadway at Thirty-seventh Street, went down to Ninth Avenue, and turned left and left again at Thirty-sixth Street. "Okay, little sister, see that grey building in the next block, the one with the pretty windows, and people coming out the door?"

"Yeah, Granddaddy used to bring me here at Christmas when I was little to look at the windows."

"Great. When I stop, hop out and go in the door quickly. I'll make sure you are in before I drive away." Charlotte grabbed her purse and put her hand on the door. "Charlotte, leave your purse here, and I'll bring it when I come. Less chance of losing it when you're trying on clothes. I love you, little sister." Musee reached over and squeezed Charlotte's hand.

"I love you too, big sister." Charlotte left the van and rushed into the store. Musee's eyes darted from the front, the two side streets, and the rear mirrors showing the traffic behind the van. No police cars were in sight. She leaned her head forward on her hands gripping the steering wheel.

"Thank you," she whispered to the world. At the corner, she turned right and headed back to Broadway and Union Square. She knew she had only a short time to park the van and get back to Raksin's before the store closed. She wondered how she would feel going back in there. Would Hannah still be there at this time of night? Doubtful. Would Mr. Raksin be there? Probably, but he wouldn't be on the third floor. Her eyes scanned the front, the side streets, and the rear mirrors. Almost there, and no police in sight. This is going to work. At the square, she parked the van in Calumet's regular space. Grabbing her and Charlotte's pocketbooks, she opened the van door and started stepping out. A hand grabbed her shoulder, pulled her out, and spun her around, pushing her up against the side of the van.

"Charlotte Holmes, you are under arrest."

Musee's shock and terror subsided somewhat, and she screamed, "I'm not Charlotte Holmes! Look in my pocketbook." The policewoman handed the two purses to her partner, who rifled through one, found a wallet, and opened it to see a card with the name and address of Charlotte Holmes.

"This says you're Charlotte Holmes."

"Wrong pocketbook. Look in the other one. My picture is on my driver's license confirming I'm Maureen O'Hara, a New York City resident." The officer opened the other purse, pulled out the wallet, looked at the license, then at Musee, then at the license, and then handed the wallet to the female officer.

"Where is Charlotte Holmes?" the officer demanded.

"I want to call my attorney," Musee responded, as she looked at her watch.

"Tell me where Ms. Holmes is, and you're free to go."

"I want to call my attorney."

The officer spoke into the microphone on her shoulder, explaining the situation. The response came back. "Bring her in." Musee looked at her watch again, realizing she only had an hour before the store closed.

"Turn around and put your hands behind your back." Musee did as she was told. The policewoman handcuffed her.

"I want to call my lawyer," she said again. Her desire to unload her frustration on the policewomen was kept in check by her concern for getting to Charlotte before Raksin's closed.

At the precinct, the officer took off the handcuffs and had her sit at a desk with another female officer. Musee asked over and over for the right to call her attorney, as she constantly checked her watch, seeing the time to Raksin's closing getting closer and closer. She had the emergency number that David emphasized was the only number to call if anything went wrong. She was panicking, thinking of Charlotte's fear if she wasn't there before the store closed. Why wouldn't they let her use the phone? Since she was not under arrest, the officer said she didn't need to be in a holding cell, nor did she have the right to a phone call. The corporal sitting next to her was friendly but professional. Musee willed herself to start crying. The officer asked her to calm down. Musee said she just wanted to call her attorney.

Shaking her head in disgust, the officer said, "What's the number?" Musee gave her the number, and the officer handed over the handset. After one ring, a female voice answered.

"Hi, this is Maureen O'Hara, and I'm at a police precinct. What? Hold on." Musee held the phone out and asked, "What precinct is this?"

"Nineteenth."

"The officer says the Nineteenth. No, no. I haven't said anything. Yes, thank you. Please hurry."

Forty minutes later, Musee and the young attorney rushed out of the police station. They jumped into a waiting car. Musee took the opportunity in the car to put in her SIM card and dial Stephanie—the store had been closed for thirty minutes.

"Steph? Musee. Is Charlotte with you?"

"No, where've you been. She was petrified."

"I can't explain now, but where was she the last time you saw her?"

"We dropped her at your apartment."

"Oh, thank God. Steph, I owe you one. I'll explain everything later."

Turning to the attorney, she said, "Charlotte is at my apartment. It's on Thirty-ninth Street, between Eighth and Ninth Avenues. Musee leaned back, closed her eyes, and thought about David. She quickly hit his speed dial number. No answer. She knew what that meant, or at least she thought she did. She pushed thoughts of David away; Charlotte was the issue. They still had to get some food. This time, they would stay together. She felt the bile rising in the back of her throat. How could she have thought separating would work? At least Charlotte is safe at the apartment. She realized that if she hadn't sent Charlotte into Raksin's, they'd both be in police custody.

As they pulled up to her apartment building, Musee took her keys from her bag when she realized there were no lights on. Taking the steps two at a time, she fumbled opening the door. She ran up the stairs, calling Charlotte's name. At her apartment, she unlocked the door and burst through, hitting the light switch as she went, calling for Charlotte. She felt nauseated as she realized Charlotte was not there. The attorney followed her into the apartment and assessed the situation.

"Easy, Musee. Just remain calm. Let's go ask the manager if he's seen her."

They went back to the first floor, and Musee banged on the manager's door. "Mr. Conrad, please open up."

The door opened, and the man looked at Musee. "Lower your voice. What can I do for you, Ms. O'Hara?"

"A friend of mine was dropped off here a little while ago. Did you let her in?"

"No, I did not."

"Oh my God, why not?"

"First, you hadn't given written permission to let her in, as the rules state. Second, she told me she was your little sister, and I know for a fact you don't have a sister in New York."

"Oh, God." Musee leaned against the wall to keep from falling.

The young attorney put her hand on Musee's shoulder and looked at the manager. "How long ago was she here?"

"About thirty minutes, tops. Is something wrong? Should I call the police?"

"No, sir. Nothing's wrong. Thank you for your help. If Ms. Holmes comes back, you have permission to let her into Ms. O'Hara's apartment, right, Musee?" the attorney said. Musee nodded. "Come on. Let's start looking for her."

The two women went back to the car. Once inside, the attorney asked, "I was the one who stayed with Charlotte while her guardian met with Brian. She didn't appear to be the type who would go to a bar, right?"

"Yes. Yes, she would not willingly go to a bar, but what if she were tricked into going with someone? She's so innocent, although I've tried to help her understand the real world. Oh God, what have I done?" Musee stared out the car window and started taking deep breaths to calm herself. "Let's try the Port Authority bus terminal. She might go to a place with lots of people around and a lot of light."

"Good idea. If she's not there, we can try Grand Central Station. Do you think she would go to Times Square?"

"No, I've warned her about places like that."

"Eddie, first the Port Authority Bus Terminal."

At the terminal, the two women split up and searched in vain. Back in the car, the attorney said, "Eddie, let's go to Grand Central Station, the Forty-second Street entrance." They searched every level.

Returning to the car, Musee tried David's phone again. It went straight to voicemail. She closed her eyes and sat for a few minutes, then said, "Let's go to the van. I'll get the van and start driving up and down the streets between Union Square and my apartment, blowing the horn. She may hear it and recognize the horn or see the van and flag me down."

"Really?"

"That's the only thing I can think of. It's better than doing what we're doing."

The black car pulled in behind the van. "Amanda, I can't thank you enough for everything you've done. There's no sense in you tying up your Friday night anymore."

"Musee, this is New York City. You can't drive and look at the same time. Brian's instructions to me were to make sure you and Charlotte were safe. If you're going to be riding around and blowing the horn, I can guarantee you'll need a lawyer again before the night is over." She turned to the driver. "Eddie, when we drive off, why don't you get some dinner. I'll call you when we need you."

"Yes, Ms. Harmon."

Charlotte entered Raksin's and was in awe of the sights before her. The cosmetic counters, the elegantly dressed sales professionals smiling and handing out flyers, the bright lights, and the styles and colors of the clothes. She spotted the elevators and went to the third floor.

"Hey, is Stephanie here," she said to the first person she saw upon leaving the elevator.

"Sure, I'll get her for you."

Moments later, Stephanie approached Charlotte. "May I help you?"

"Yeah, Musee asked me to come in and get you to select two outfits, one for me and one for her. I'm Charlotte, Musee's friend and little sister, sort of."

"Oh, yeah. You live up the country."

"Yeah, on a farm."

"Is Musee coming in?"

"She's parking the van."

"Okay, let's get started." Stephanie looked Charlotte over, not being able to get a good idea of her size due to her baggy boy-style clothes. "Let's try a four and go from there."

To Charlotte, the hour went by in what seemed like a few minutes. Suddenly, she realized the store was closing, and her fun vanished like a magician's coin. Stephanie asked. "When did Musee say she would be back? The store is closing in ten minutes. I'd better call her to see where is." Charlotte knew Musee was supposed to be back by now. Fighting back panic, Charlotte looked around the floor. They were turning off the lights.

"I don't know what happened to her. She was supposed to be back by now."

"Her phone doesn't even ring. Do you have someplace to go?"

"No. I guess I'll just have to wait outside for her," Charlotte said, her chin quivering.

"No, my boyfriend is picking me up. We'll drop you off at Musee's apartment. It's not far, just at Thirty-ninth Street." Charlotte's relief was visible.

"That's good. Thank you. What about these clothes?"

"I'll put them on the hold rack, and y'all can come in tomorrow and pay for them. Come on. Billy doesn't like to wait."

At Musee's, the three of them noticed that there were no lights on in her apartment. Billy said, "She's not here yet, but I'm sure she'll be home soon."

"Yeah, thanks for the ride." Charlotte went up the stoop and rang Musee's buzzer. There was no response. Looking at the list, she rang the manager's buzzer.

"Yeah, what do you want," came the reply.

"I'm a friend of Musee's. Can you let me in to wait for her?"

"Who are you?"

"I'm Charlotte Holmes, her little sister."

"Little sister? I happen to know that Musee doesn't have a sister in New York. Besides, she hasn't told me to let you or anyone else in. Go away before I call the cops."

The last response jolted Charlotte. The police wanted to take her away from David. She couldn't let that happen. She went to the lower step and sat down. She could wait here, she thought. But what if someone came along and grabbed her? She could go somewhere and wait for Musee, but where? If she left, how would Musee know where she was? She kept hugging herself, as the night air got cooler.

She got up and started walking to her left. At the end of the block, she saw the lights of the bars and restaurants. Hunger became her focus for a moment. She realized she didn't even have her pocketbook or any money. She didn't want to go into some restaurant, anyway. Musee would never find her there. She looked up at the street sign. If this is Ninth Avenue and Musee lives between Eighth and Ninth Avenue, then Eighth Avenue must be the other way, she thought. She turned around, stopped at Musee's, and sat down again. She realized that she had no identification at all. What if someone asked for proof of who she was? The urge to do something rather than nothing overwhelmed her. She got back up and walked to Eighth Avenue. More bars and restaurants. Hunger made her think about the green market and all the food there in the daytime. The van has the left-over fruits and vegetables, she thought. What do I do? A stab of fear gripped her. She could hear Musee saying every night, "Charlotte, you're a smart girl, as smart as anyone else. You've been sheltered, but you have good sense. Think through any situation, and trust your judgment about what to do. If you make a mistake, correct it."

She whispered, "Big sister, I believe you. I want to go to the van." She turned to her left and started walking. At the next block, she looked at the street sign and saw it said Fortieth Street. This is the wrong way, she thought. Turning around, she walked past her starting point to the next block, where the sign said Thirty-eighth Street. She stopped and closed her eyes, trying to remember the wide street Granddaddy used to turn onto from the street by the river. It was twice as wide as these streets and had a lot of lights, even in the daytime. She kept walking. Every time she passed a shadow close to the buildings, she moved toward the street side of the sidewalk.

A person came from between two parked cars and startled her. She moved back to the center of the sidewalk. She started to cry, but stopped herself. She thought of her grandfather's courage and confidence. Counting the streets down as she passed each one, she picked up her pace. At every new block, she looked up and down the street to see if she saw something familiar. Her fear grew as she walked. People stared at her. Was she doing what she should? Should she have waited at Musee's? She passed many couples and individuals hurrying along. Some ignored her; others looked at her and smiled. She didn't smile back and looked down if she saw someone looking at her. Musee told her, "Don't make eye contact with anyone, male or female."

What if she was wrong, and this wasn't the right way, she thought? She shoved her hands in her pants pockets as the outside cold began to mix with the fear-driven shiver inside. At Twenty-fifth Street, she looked up and saw bright lights two blocks ahead. She quickened her pace. At

Twenty-third Street, she looked right and left and saw the familiar stores and crowds of people. This was the street!

She stopped and thought about what side she would be looking at each morning when going to the green market. She realized it was the opposite side, and they would always travel to her left. She crossed over and started walking to her left. The sidewalks were crowded, and several people jostled her as she walked with her head down. She didn't notice the guy leaning against the drugstore window smoking a blunt. He noticed her. He recognized the signs of someone lost or homeless, constantly shoving their hands in their pockets and then taking them out and hugging their body. He leered at her and wet his cracked and sore-covered lips. Charlotte kept her head down and continued walking toward him. Stubbing out his blunt, he carefully put the roach in a small pouch. He moved away from the window on a path that intersected with hers. Charlotte knew she was on the right street, and the van and Musee were only a few blocks away. His thoughts were about the fun he and his friends would have later. He watched for his opportunity to grab her. She continued looking down and quickened her pace.

Suddenly, a hand raked across her breasts, startling her. Looking up, she was staring at a dirty face with a scraggly beard, broken teeth, and bad breath. A cruel smile stared back at her.

"Sorry, Missy, but I'm glad to see you. You looking to party? I've got some junk that will take you to the moon and a real party. Some friends of mine have a place nearby. Let's go have a party." By the time he had stopped talking, he had a firm grip on her upper arm and was pulling her toward a recessed area between buildings.

Charlotte remembered what her granddaddy always told her when she was young and would go across the green market. She took her free arm and waved it vigorously and hollered, "I'm coming, Granddaddy! Be right there." At the same time, she pulled her arm free. She quickly stepped into the middle of a group moving by, quickening her pace to put the group between the man and herself. She waved vigorously and called out again, "I'm coming, Granddaddy!" She did not look back. Her eyes searched for the next open store in case the man tried to grab her again.

It registered with her that she was scared but not terrified. Musee's voice kept looping through her mind. "Charlotte, you are smart. Trust your instincts in any situation." She kept looking at the stores, searching for the one where they always turned and headed to the green market. Finally, she spotted it up ahead. At the corner, she turned right and saw Union Square a few blocks ahead. She started to run, but slowed down at the next corner. She didn't want anyone to wonder why she was running and call the police. As she crossed Eighteenth Street, she saw the back of the van parked in its regular place.

Musee is here! Her anxiety subsided, anxious to tell Musee how she made it by herself all the way from the apartment. Trying to open the van's door, she found it locked. Fear exploded through her body, and she started crying. Leaning against the cold van, the cool air and her tiredness caused her to close her eyes. She felt herself slipping into sleep. She sprang awake, remembering the spare key. Going to the front of the van, she ran her fingers through the grill row by row until she found the latch. The hood sprang open, and she reached down to the battery shelf, just like her granddaddy had shown her, and found the magnetic box with a spare key. She shut the hood, opened the door, and climbed into the van, locking the door behind her. Crawling over the front bench seat, she pulled her pillow out from behind it, stacked up some empty boxes. and lay down. She was asleep in minutes.

*   *   *

Musee and Amanda walked to the van's passenger door and unlocked it. As they climbed in, Charlotte called out, "Musee, you're here!"

Both women jumped and let out involuntary screams. Musee said, "Charlotte, it's you!" and burst into tears as the two reached over the seat and hugged. "I love you," they said in unison.

"How did you get here?"

Charlotte gave a vivid description of her journey from Musee's to the van. Musee, listening intently, noted a change in Charlotte's tone and voice. Her speech was no longer that of an insecure person. She spoke with a confidence Musee hadn't heard before. After a moment, Charlotte noticed Amanda and said, "Hey, don't I know you?"

"Hey, Charlotte, we met at the law firm a few weeks ago."

"You were so nice. I'm glad you're here. Why are you here?"

Musee answered, "I let you out at the store because I saw police cars following us. The police detained me when I parked the van. Amanda came and got me free, and she's been helping me look for you."

"This has been an awesome evening, don't you think?" Charlotte asked.

"That's an understatement. Amanda, can we hitch a ride with you back to my apartment?"

"Sure, lock up, and Eddie can take us."

"Who's Eddie?" Charlotte asked.

"He works part time for the law firm. He's our driver."

Finally, in the apartment, Musee started crying and shaking. Charlotte went to her and hugged her. "Don't cry, big sister. We're here together."

"I know. I know. I just thought something bad had happened to you. I'm all right."

"David will be here in the morning, but we won't have enough to sell unless he brings more produce."

"Little sister, David might not be here in the morning. I can't get him to answer his phone. The sheriff may have arrested him."

"If David's not here early, we need to go to the market and set up, or else we could lose our regular spot. There's not much there, but maybe he'll come by lunchtime."

Musee looked at Charlotte and marveled at a new, self-assured Charlotte emerging from the smothered child she and David knew. Won't he be surprised, she thought.

# CHAPTER 32

The sky was blue, bluer than he had ever seen it. Sal Valenti cast again. The only sounds were the gurgle of the stream, the chirping birds in the trees, and the rustling of the leaves left on the trees. Not another soul was around. The judge stood knee deep in the cold water, patiently casting at the spots where he believed the fish were holding in a patch of calm water just on the downstream side of some boulders. Suddenly, a trout leaped and took his fly! A heartbeat skipped, and the judge entered the ecstasy phase of his life: He and a fish were having a battle of wits. Only one would win, although both would survive to compete again. This was heaven to Sal, totally focused on playing the fish. Letting the fish run more than he used to when he was young, he enjoyed the flow of energy coursing through the rod. Some people say fishermen take up fly fishing when they're tired of catching fish. Not me, Sal thought. Fly fishing was like being a judge. A judge had to be at the top of his game, not just knowing the law, but knowing people, when they were honest but couldn't prove it, and those who were dishonest and trying to hide it. In fly fishing, you had to know the river, the places where trout like to hang out, what they're interested in eating that day, and how to allow a fish to wear itself out but still have enough energy to recover when released. Being a judge and a fly fisherman gave him immense pleasure. He slowly brought the fish in. "Come to me, baby, come easy, so you can swim another day," he said aloud to the fish. As it came closer, he reached over his shoulder, brought his net around, and gently lifted the fish from the water. A beautiful two-pound rainbow. Gingerly taking the fish from the net, he used his pliers to unhook it. He placed the fish back in the water, loosened his grip, and let the fish swim off when it was ready.

"Well done, Your Honor," Brian O'Malley said. "Greetings from Kurt Hudson." Judge Valenti almost fell into the stream.

"Boy, don't you know not to sneak up on old people. You can scare them to death."

"My apologies, Judge. I didn't want to disturb a masterful catch and release. It was like a movie they made a few years back." Judge Valenti looked at the young man standing on the bank. He had on pac shoes, tin cloth pants, a wool plaid shirt, and a tin cloth cap. Looked like something straight out of one of those catalogs. Even without him dropping the name of his former law school roommate and best friend, the judge knew he was a lawyer. Instead of a fly rod, he was carrying a folio. A leather folio. An expensive leather folio. He was not here for fishing or talking. Something big was going on.

"You have a name, son?"

"Brian O'Malley, sir. I'm a senior associate at Mortimer and Castellani."

"So that's how you know Kurt. He your slave master?"

"Well, I wouldn't want him to think I said that."

"No, you wouldn't. Okay, so what's the issue?"

"Your Honor, you signed a court order remanding Charlotte Holmes to the physical and financial custody of Win and Ellie Oakley. That petition was based on fraudulent information deliberately concocted by Win and Ellie Oakley. All the proof of this fraud is attached to this petition, a copy of which is at your office. Kurt ... Mr. Hudson will appear at the hearing Monday morning and aggressively defend against Mr. Oakley's petition. He will also make sure regional and local media are aware of this injustice and covering the proceedings."

Judge Valenti waded back to shore and placed his rod against a sapling growing near the stream. He went over and sat on a boulder in front of Brian.

"Kurt won't do that to me. He knows it, and so do I. Can you raise him on your phone? I left mine in my truck."

"He knew you would say that, so he suggested a better solution. I have with me a petition for your signature that negates the fraudulent petition and instructs the sheriff to stop seeking Miss Charlotte Holmes, and assist me in having Win Oakley relinquish all legal and accounting records concerning Dex, Mary, and Charlotte Holmes. If he does that, Mr. Hudson, on behalf of Miss Holmes, will not file charges and have him arrested for fraud. This whole issue will never have happened."

"I bet you have a pen with you, don't you, son." Sal held out his hand.

"Yes, sir." Brian opened his folio, took out two copies of the petition, placed them on top of the folio, and took a pen from his shirt pocket.

"I've always made a practice of reading everything before I sign it, so have a seat over there on that boulder, unless you want to try your hand at fly fishing, while I look over this petition." Brian walked over to the boulder and sat down. He pulled out his cell phone and activated the GPS app, locking in the position.

Five minutes later, Judge Valenti signed both copies of the petition, stood up, and handed the folio, papers, and pen back to Brian. "Tell Kurt I appreciate his concern for me and my court. I owe him. Tell him that. Just don't tell him where you found me. You understand?"

"Yes, sir."

"Now, there are fish in this stream waiting to avoid my flies. Have a good day, Mr. O'Malley."

*   *   *

Two hours later, Brian was standing at the front door of Win Oakley's home ringing his doorbell. Gone were the pac shoes, plaid shirt, and tin cloth pants and cap. In their place was a tailored black pin stripe suit, white shirt, red tie, and black wingtips. He carried his folio with him. He rang the doorbell again and again. Finally, an overweight man in a bathrobe flung the door open and said, "Who the hell are you? Do you know what time it is?"

"Yes," Brian said, looking at his Apple watch. "It's nine thirty Saturday morning. As to who I am, frankly, I'm your worst enemy. My name is Brian O'Malley. I'm a senior associate at Mortimer & Castellini, and I'm here representing Miss Charlotte Holmes. You filed a fraudulent petition with Judge Valenti regarding Miss Holmes. I have presented Judge Valenti proof of your fraud—"

"You're full o' crap. Judge Valenti is out of town."

"Yes, he's fly fishing at his favorite fishing spot exactly forty minutes north of here. Would you like the GPS co-ordinates or just look at his signature on this new petition dismissing all the claims you have on Miss Holmes's physical and financial custody?"

"Look here, you little dunce. You don't know anything about my wife's family kinship with Charlotte Holmes, nor anything Dex Holmes asked me to do for her."

"Actually, Mr. Oakley, I do. I have proof from Lincolnton, Illinois, that your wife has no blood relationship with Miss Holmes. Now, here's what you're going to do. You and I are going to your office. You're going to give me all copies of any records you have regarding Dex Holmes, any of his companies, Miss Holmes, and any digital copies of those records. Further, you will allow me to access your computer records so I can irrevocably wipe your hard drive clean of any Holmes family records."

"And if I don't?"

"Look over my shoulder across the street." Brian did the same and then looked back at Win. "If I give the signal, the sheriff will come over here and arrest you for fraud. You will be disbarred, and your accounting license will be permanently revoked. Frankly, Mr. Oakley, I hope you refuse." Brian smiled.

Oakley looked from Brian to the sheriff, who touched his hat, and back to Brian. He visibly sighed and said, "Let me get dressed."

"No, sir, come as you are. We're going to have this wrapped up in thirty minutes, or Mr. Hudson intends to take matters in hand. There will be no consideration for you, if that happens."

David, who was released by the sheriff when Brian returned to Pineville with the new petition, was on his way to Union Square green market in the second van with additional produce. He saw Musee had called several times, returned her calls, and was relieved to know that the two of them were well and at the market with what little produce they had. His phone vibrated, and he cut his eyes to see: DONE. He smiled and silently thanked Fil, Dex, Mary, and all the guardian angels looking out for this family of three.

# CHAPTER 33

"Where's Charlotte?" David asked as he set a pitcher of tea and a plate of cookies on the porch table. He eased into Dex's rocker, comfortable with the worn pattern. Musee sat in a new rocker, not exactly like the ones David and Charlotte used. The child rocker was relegated to the barn for future use.

"She said she wanted to go talk to Granny. She still loves them as much as ever. I can't understand what they did. It was cruel."

"They loved her with all their hearts and souls. I don't think they ever thought about anything other than shielding Charlotte from the risks that killed her mother. They went with their gut feelings, entirely out of love. There's no do-overs in bringing up a kid. They were wrong, but you can't really fault them."

"Yeah."

"You sound like Charlotte when she was Charlie."

"Yeah, yes, sir."

"Speaking of yeah, when are we getting married? It's been weeks since I asked and you accepted."

"Who said I accepted?"

"It was a package deal. You couldn't come here without accepting my marriage proposal. It was one sentence, not two, so you're hooked."

"Since when did you go to law school?"

"I didn't, but I've got a real bulldog for a lawyer." David reached over and started to caress her cheek. "I love you. I'm serious, Musee, whenever you're ready."

She took his hand and kissed it. "I'm ready, but Charlotte's not. She still needs a big sister. Every night when we're getting ready for bed, she still has a ton of questions. When we get in our beds, I answer her questions and give her more info. I can almost see and hear the gears in her brain turning and absorbing what I say. After we get married, I'll be in our bedroom getting ready for bed. If that's too soon, she'd still be in her room with all these questions and no big sister to answer. Do you understand?" Musee took two of his fingers and slipped them into her mouth. She ran her tongue around them and looked at him.

"Jesus, stop that," David said, but he didn't pull his hand away. "I already have a hard on." She took his fingers out of her mouth and wiped them on her shirt against her breast.

"Marcel gave me the quote for reconfiguring the barn and the house. I gave him the go-ahead. He said it'll take seven weeks from start to finish," Musee said, after taking a deep breath to calm herself. "It'll cost money, but we need a good software engineer, and a baker for the cakes since we're starting to sell a good number. That reminds me, can Marcel and the electrician start by wiring the house kitchen for three ovens, even before starting on the barn? We need those ovens."

"Sure, I'll call him in the morning and give him the oven details and tell him to prioritize that part," David responded.

"Great."

"What else besides the software engineer?"

"A baker or someone who can be trained as a baker. Someone who can work with Charlotte and learn how to make the cakes. David, you know me. I don't have a snobby bone in my body, so what I'm about to say is said out of kindness."

"What?"

"The best sales associates I found were those who weren't real smart and knew it. They were good people, without exception, and proud to be sales associates, so they worked hard to be as good as they could. We don't need people who see these jobs as stepping stones to bigger and better."

"Where are you going with this?"

"I'd like to go to the voc-tech school and the high school. Talk to the counselors, get them to refer me to some of their C students. Young people who work hard but know that they're not going to be scientists or literary stars. We need a cutter and a seamstress to start. If we have seven weeks until the barn is ready, I can have the two of them trained in that time. Charlotte can train the baker, with my help if necessary, but I don't think it will be."

"Okay, see what you can find. You may have to go to the internet to find the software engineer."

"Well, what I'm thinking is starting in a cloud store, a firm that can help build the web site and has the ability to securely handle Apple Pay, PayPal, other fintech payment systems, and credit cards. The engineer can work with the site to customize it for us, so they must be bright, open, and speak the language, drawing on the knowledge of the cloud and other site engineers. I'd like it to be a woman if that's okay with you."

"Find what you want. I trust you. This is your baby, so run with it."

# CHAPTER 34

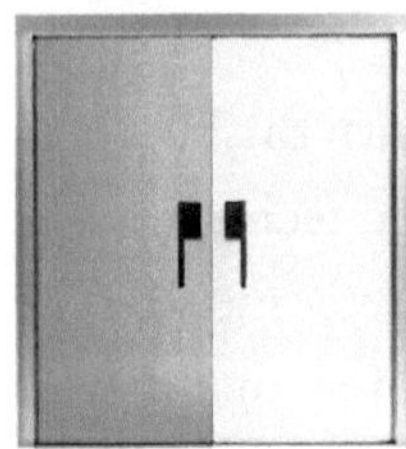

David was at the sink finishing the dinner dishes, looking up the hill toward the graves, having a conversation with Dex in his thoughts.

"I want to trade you," Musee said, looking from Charlotte to David.

"Huh?"

"I want to trade you," Musee repeated. She and Charlotte sat at the kitchen table, both nursing cups of hot tea as David did the dishes.

He turned, dried his hands, and responded, "I didn't know I was bad enough to be traded."

"Not you, silly," Charlotte piped up, grinning from ear to ear. David knew something was up from the look on her face.

"Okay, you two. What's up?"

"I've found two potential employees, if you like 'em. One, Andy Strickland, is at the voc-tech school learning mechanics, but wants to work outside. The other, Sam Oglesby, is also at the voc-tech and has a knack for CAD-CAM, which is a skill we'll need in the cutting area. I figure he could also begin as the baker. The new ovens are being delivered tomorrow and will be operational the next day. Our cake-making capacity will be at least fifty per week, if we do ten per day."

"Okay, I get it, so what's the trade?"

"I figure Andy, who wants to work outside, would be super working with you at the green market." David realized what Musee was getting around to and worried that Charlotte would take his response the wrong way, no matter what he said.

"But I have Charlotte here as my green market partner," he said, trying to box Musee in.

"Yeah, but she's what I want. I get Charlotte, and you get Andy, the mechanic that wants to work outside."

"Well, the last time I heard, they had outlawed slavery. So," he turned to Charlotte, "what do you want, young lady?" Charlotte's grin disappeared, realizing she had to choose between the two of them. David immediately understood her dilemma and said, "I guess big sisters always want to be with little sisters, and little sisters always want to be with big sisters. Poor old big brothers have to settle for other guys who burp, chew tobacco, and look scruffy, instead of beautiful, sweet, and kind."

"Is that yes?" Musee interjected, grabbing Charlotte's hand.

"Yeah, yes, sir," David said, winking at Charlotte, who was grinning again. "Seriously, Musee, what's the plan?"

"The cake production ramps up, with you being able to take as many orders as you can get. We're also thinking about sending half cakes with you to the city for restaurants to try. We'll get their acceptance first so you're not wasting time and cake."

"What's the story on the fashion business?"

"Three more weeks till the barn is finished. Sam, the CAD-CAM guy, starts next Monday and will be ready for his first computer cutting on some sample fabric in two weeks. I don't have a seamstress yet, but I have two interviews scheduled. RFPs—requests for proposals—are going out today to cloud companies and web designers. My challenge is finding a software engineer. I've interviewed two—a guy and a girl—and

I'm not happy with either. I've put some feelers out on the internet, so maybe I'll hear something soon."

"What's Plan B?"

"Outsourcing to a freelancer. That's not very efficient, though."

"Startups are classic for inefficiencies. The object is to get up and running, not to save money, Ms. CEO. You have good instincts, and now, the best assistant CEO in New York State." He smiled over at Charlotte. "So, when does this trade happen?"

"Andy will be here at six in the morning to go to market with you." Musee blew him a kiss. "Now, we bakers and entrepreneurs have a long day ahead of us that we need to plan for, so we're going to get ready for bed and girl talk."

It was an hour after midnight when Musee slid under the covers of David's bed. She helped him understand that she was results oriented as well as skilled at pleasing methods.

# CHAPTER 35

Charlotte was in the kitchen baking cakes when she spotted a strange man going into the barn. A few minutes later, he came out and stood in the side yard looking around for someone. She put down the mixer, dried her hands on the dish towel she kept on her shoulder when working in the kitchen, and stepped out onto the porch. She raised her voice so he could hear her and said, "May I help you?"

The guy looked over to the porch, smiled, and started walking over to her. "Good morning, I'm looking for Ms. O'Hara."

"Who are you?"

"I'm Sam, Sam Oglesby. Who are you?"

"I'm Charlotte. Musee—Ms. O'Hara—had to go in to town. Was she expecting you?"

"No, I'm supposed to start working Monday, but I thought I'd come by and see if I could look around and get an understanding of where I'll be working. She said I would be using a CAD-CAM computer and baking. I figured this way I could be useful Monday from the start."

"You're the guy from the voc-tech school Musee told me about?"

Sam flushed with embarrassment, looked down, and, still grinning, said, "That's me."

"Do you always grin?"

Sam stopped grinning and said, "Yes, ma'am. There's enough sadness in the world without me adding to it. Besides, my momma always told me people were prettier or handsomer when they had a grin on their faces, so I want to be handsomer."

"I'm not a ma'am. We're about the same age. Call me Charlotte and I'll call you Sam. I'm the baker you're going to help make cakes. So come on in, and I'll start teaching you how to make a Granny cake. Have you ever baked before?"

"I used to help my momma do all kinds of baking around all the holidays, when she would bake enough for the family and all their friends. Her pies were to die for. At least, that's what all the neighbors said."

"Did you get too old to help her bake?"

Sam stopped looking at Charlotte, looked down, and then away up the hill. "She passed three years ago just before I graduated from high school."

Charlotte blushed, reached to touch his hand, but quickly pulled her hand back and said, "I'm sorry for your loss. I understand how you feel. My granny died four years ago and my granddaddy died just a few months ago. They raised me, and I miss them too."

"Where are your parents?"

"My mother died when I was born, and I never had a father."

"I'm sorry for your loss."

In the kitchen, Sam saw Charlotte had all the dry ingredients for one cake in small glass bowls lined up in the order she put them in the mixer. The wet ingredients were separate on the other side of the mixer. Even though she'd never used a recipe before David wrote it down, she was precise about how much of each ingredient went into each cake.

Sam listened as Charlotte explained her process and exclaimed, "Wow, you have a super system!" Charlotte beamed and grinned. "Now, you're grinning a lot," Sam said.

An hour later, Musee walked into the kitchen and saw Sam with an apron on. "Sam, what are you doing here? You're not supposed to start until Monday."

"Yes, ma'am, I know. I came by today to sort of get the lay of the land, and Charlotte put me to work."

"We have two cakes in the oven and are starting to assemble the ingredients for a third," Charlotte said, wiping her hands on the towel on her shoulder.

"Good. Don't let me stop you. Sam, when the two of you break for lunch, come find me, and we can get your employee paperwork done. Monday you can spend the day learning the CAD-CAM cutting software."

When Musee left, Sam said timidly to Charlotte, "Charlotte, have you thought about getting a large bowl where you can thoroughly mix the dry ingredients for several cakes at once? That would cut down on the prep time for each cake."

Charlotte looked at Sam and started to respond. "Sam, I do it ..." when she quickly realized that his idea was a good one. She wondered why she hadn't thought of it herself. "That's an interesting idea. Look in the bottom cabinets over there, and see if there's a bowl we can use."

Sam found one that was big enough to hold all the ingredients for several cakes. "Okay, I'll use these measured ingredients while you figure out how many cakes can be made from the ingredients you put in that bowl."

When the third cake was in the oven, Sam had determined that the dry ingredients for five cakes could be mixed in the larger bowl. Charlotte lined up the wet ingredients that could not be premixed. She realized that cake production going forward would be faster. By the end of the day, they had eight cakes for market the next day, four of which were presold, three would be available for sale, and one for samples. She was proud of the day's accomplishments. She also knew she had to go talk to Granny about Sam.

After Sam left and Charlotte returned from talking to Granny, she sat in the kitchen drinking a glass of tea, trying to process her feelings. Sam was a big help, he was nice, and he wasn't a showoff. She was afraid she wasn't going to act right around him, and he wouldn't like her. She longed to talk to Musee about what to do. Lost in her thoughts, she didn't hear Musee come into the kitchen.

"I love it when you bake," Musee said, taking a deep sniff. "The house smells so good." She looked down at Charlotte, who had a puzzled look on her face. "What's the matter, Charlotte? Was there a problem working with Sam?"

"It was okay, I guess."

"You guess? You want to explain that to me while I get a glass of tea?"

"He's baked before with his mother, and he's a know-it-all."

"Really?"

"His ideas were good ones, though. It sped up the baking process without hurting the cakes."

"That's a good thing, right?"

"I guess so."

"Anything else about him you want to talk about?"

"Not right now, maybe tonight."

"Great idea. David called and said he was going to restock the truck before coming home, so let's you and me put dinner together."

# CHAPTER 36

David and Andy were breaking down the tent after a highly successful day at the green market. They had sold twenty cakes, all special orders, and delivered six more halves to restaurants. The onions, potatoes, winter squash, apples, and pears they had during these cold days were well received by the hardy souls scouring the green market for something good and fresh.

"Andy, would you mind finishing packing up? Hurley said he had a special vintage Long Island Merlot. I want to get a bottle for Musee."

"Not a problem, David."

David was pleased; nothing was a problem for Andy. In the four months he'd been with David, he'd learned a great deal about their partner relationships, packing the van, setting up, and smiling at customers. He believed that Andy had enough experience and commitment to handle the Union Square market. Now it was time to find a helper for Andy. David was convinced Andy could handle the green market operation. Musee was up and running with the fashion business, the cake operation was a success, and he had added two more farmer/partners. More than anything else, David was mulling over the potential for a fresh green market on Calumet's roadside. Start small, just as Dex taught him. Let the business grow with sweat equity and word of mouth.

"Andy, here, I got two bottles of the special merlot. One is for you and your girl. How 'bout you drive. I've got an idea I'd like to run past you."

"Sure."

*   *   *

"What are you doing here at this hour?" David said as he came through the kitchen door with the bottle of wine under his elbow and carrying a box of produce for tonight's meal. "You usually don't leave the barn before eight." He looked past her and saw two weekend bags sitting in the hall. "Going somewhere?"

"Yes, we are. Tonight is special. Put the veggies in the fridge. You won't be cooking tonight. What's with the bottle of wine?"

"Why am I not cooking? The wine is for the three of us to have with our fresh veggies and those pork chops I brought home last night. This is a special vintage Long Island merlot. Hurley—you know him, he's got the tent two places over—he was able to buy several bottles from the winery as a favor for supplying the owner with herbs for her party. He says it's really special."

"Great. Charlotte and Sam can have it for their special night."

"Huh?"

"It's complicated. Charlotte is upstairs getting dressed. She and Sam have a date tonight."

"Date? Am I missing something?"

"Remember, Sam Oglesby doubles as a baker in the early morning and our computer fabric cutter the rest of the day?"

"Sure, he and Andy started at the same time. I thought you said he and Charlotte were competitive in everything. I'm sorta surprised he's still around."

"They were, and he's still here. From the beginning, they were competitive, but clicked with respect for each other's ideas. Sam helped her with baking and scaling up their output. He then started showing her how the CAD-CAM works and how precisely it can cut layers of fabric, virtually eliminating waste and downtime. On his first day, he showed her how to mix the dry ingredients for multiple cakes, increasing production dramatically. Next thing I know, I'd lost a lunch partner—they ate together, either in the kitchen when they were baking or at the computer in the cutting area. Didn't I mention this?"

"First I've heard of it."

"Since the first day, they had ear-to-ear grins on their faces every day. Not only that, but you'd think they were drunk all the time. Accidently, and I use the word loosely, bumping into each other. Well, with some coaxing from me, he finally got up the courage to ask her out on a date. Tonight is date night."

"The beginning of a long courtship, I hope."

"You sound like a dad or her big brother. They've had a four-month courtship, going through all of the phases. Remember, they've spent six days a week together, eight to ten hours a day, for four months. Yeah, and don't forget—they're over twenty-one. If it works out, I figure her Hey Man's days are numbered."

"Jesus, he's not going to get it in the back seat of his car, is he? I can't believe this. Is she ready for something as complicated as sex and love?"

"She's ready, and they're not going to 'get it' in the backseat of his truck. They're going to Momma Stella's for a romantic Italian meal. Then they're going to the movies. I forgot the title, but it's a rom-com. Finally, they're coming back here for some alone time and this great Long Island merlot." She pointed to the bottle on the counter. "Then nature will handle it from there. They're both ready, even if it's the blind leading the blind."

"He's never gotten any?"

"I don't know for sure, but I'd bet on it."

"Oh boy, what a night! He ought to go buy a lottery ticket, 'cause he's about to be the luckiest guy on Earth."

"I beg your pardon. You are going to be the luckiest guy on Earth tonight." She put her arms around his neck and pressed her pubic bone into his groin.

"You're right," he said, kissing her neck. "Are we going to just hide in our room?"

"No, that's what the bags are for. I've booked us a cabin at the state park for the evening. Those are our clothes for church in the morning." She nodded toward the bags.

"Let me go up and get my other shoes."

"No can do. Charlotte would fall to pieces if she saw you right now. No little girl wants her father or big brother looking on while she's getting ready to go from being a girl to a woman. You can get the shoes in the morning when we come pick them up for church."

"Sam's going to church with us?"

"David, my dear, if I'm right, Sam is going to be your brother-in-law, or whatever, in short order, so get used to it. He's really a nice guy."

"Yeah, but shouldn't he come ask for her hand while I'm cleaning my gun, so he gets the message to treat her right?"

"Somehow, I get the sense he's like Charlotte—developmentally stunted to the point of being free from all the crap and self-absorption that afflict most of us at that age. He's kind, gentle, and clearly adores the ground Charlotte walks on."

"Okay, Ms. CEO, what's the plan?"

"We're in cabin six at the state park. You take the bags and head over there. At lunch, I took the picnic basket over with some cheeses, a French baguette baked in our own ovens, ham, and slices of Granny cake. The ham and cheese are in the fridge, so remind me when I get there to take them out. We're going to have a twilight picnic by the lake. The moon is full tonight, and we're going to watch it come up over the trees."

"You think of everything."

Musee put her head on his chest. "We can't let our ventures get in the way of being the focus of each other's life. We've got to balance better. I never dreamed I could love somebody as fiercely as I love you. That's wonderful and scary at the same time. Sometimes I get shaky thinking about what life would be like without you. Our time together has to be as important as any other time."

"It is," David said, kissing her hair. "What we have accomplished in the time we've been together is stunning. This'll be a fun evening. What time will you be there?"

"Sam's picking Charlotte up in thirty minutes, so I should be there in forty. Now go and let me give her last-minute coaching for the big event of her short life."

# CHAPTER 37

The four of them sat around the kitchen table. Sam had given Charlotte his deceased mother's engagement ring three weeks before. Pastor Tom was expected in thirty minutes to discuss the wedding plans. Charlotte sat with her hand in Sam's. She looked from Musee to David and said, "Sam and I have two requests about the wedding." She looked at Sam, and he nodded in agreement.

"First, we'd like to make it a double wedding, with the two of you getting married in the same ceremony, assuming you know each other well enough to get married." Charlotte giggled, looking at Musee, who blushed and looked at David. David raised his eyebrows and opened his mouth wide.

"Little sisters are not supposed to tell big brothers when to get married."

"They are," she retorted, "if her big brother and sister are too blind to see that they couldn't live without each other."

"I'll have you know, I asked your big sister to marry me well over a year ago. She just won't say yes."

Charlotte looked at Musee. "Is that so?"

Musee smiled and touched Charlotte's cheek. "You weren't ready for me to marry this guy. Now you are, so I'll finally give him an answer. NO!"

"What?" David said. Charlotte, not knowing if she was joking, just sat there.

"Just kidding, just kidding." Musee looked at David. "Yes, I'll marry you."

They burst into raucous laughter. Musee leaned over and gave David a peck on the cheek. Charlotte leaned her head against Sam's and smiled.

"What's your second request?"

"Actually, it's longer-term. You said before that you and Musee would move out of this house when Sam and I got married. I'd like to make another proposal. You two stay in this house and let's build Sam and me a house on the hill, just across the gravel road from Granny, Granddaddy, and Edith. That's a special place for me, and I'd like to spend the rest of my life close to Granny and Granddaddy. I want them to see their great grandchildren when they're born. What Sam and I want," she looked at Sam and then at David and Musee, "is a small place now, two bedrooms, a great room, and a big kitchen like we have here. As our kids come along, we can add to the house. The most important thing is for the kitchen, great room, and our bedroom to have windows that look across the road to where they are." Charlotte looked at David with glistening eyes. "We'd like to set the date for the wedding when the house is ready, if you agree."

"Charlotte, you and Sam call Marcel in the morning. Get together with him, and tell him what you want. Show him where you want it. Tell him it needs to be high priority to get it done, the right way and fast, in that order."

"What about costs?" Charlotte asked.

"Get it done right, just the way you want it, and fast. The costs will be right; that's the kind of guy he is. You two decide on the details and layout you want for your home. You'll be there for the rest of your lives, so do it right from the beginning. Don't forget about a generator. I think I hear Pastor Tom's car pulling up outside."

"Before we go, David, there is one other thing. Do you think we could have this kitchen table in our kitchen?" Charlotte asked sheepishly.

"You bet you can," David replied softly. "Anything you want from here is yours for your new home."

# CHAPTER 38

Just like in the old house, the kitchen was the largest room in Charlotte and Sam's home. The two kitchens were almost identical—wide pine-board floor, a double window above the sink, looking out through the wide front porch running the length of the house and across to the three graves, yards of counter space, with cabinets and drawers below and cabinets above. Sitting on the counter among the various kitchen jars and utensils was the bottle for Mary's fresh flowers. Instead of the paper flower Charlotte bought years ago were fresh flowers from Charlotte's cutting garden between the front porch and the gravel road.

Small talk updating everyone about the agricultural businesses—the Union Square market, the baking business, the steady but disciplined growth of farmer-partners, and the fresh produce stand out by the paved highway—had been the focus throughout dinner. David turned to Musee and asked, "Musee, you're awfully quiet tonight. Something on your mind you want to talk about?"

"I'm uneasy. Sam pulled a trial balance and cash flow statement today, and GLF is still bleeding money at an unacceptable rate. I can't allow this endeavor to be a burden on the other businesses."

"What's the problem, revenue or cost structure?"

"The cost structure was put in place to handle more revenue than we're generating. Even so, the costs are not out of line. We have to stay slightly ahead of the revenue to keep from disappointing customers who place orders. We have good people and the headcount is right, don't you think, Charlotte?"

"I agree with Musee. We're a bit different from most retailers because we don't have a peak season. We sell to women who want to look professional, and their boyfriends, spouses, or significant others don't think of them in those terms. We also sell quality that doesn't wear out fast, so our customers don't fill up a closet with clothes that go out of style. That's good for them, but challenging for GLF's sales. Revenue is our weak point—how to increase revenue."

"That's how I see it, too," Musee said.

"What are you doing to get more professional women to give GLF a try?"

Musee responded, "Social media as well as print media don't seem all that effective."

"LinkedIn is the best advertising," Charlotte chimed in, who was sitting away from the table, her hands rubbing her ever-expanding belly. "The second best are certain web sites where bloggers and podcast influencers have a good following of professional women. Something else I want to say—when Granddaddy was just starting to take me to Union Square, he'd tell me stories about when he and Granny first started the business. He said a business takes five years—no matter what business, or profession, for that matter—to get firmly established and succeed. He said the most important step a person can take during those first five years is just to make sure their business survives. Time, he said, was worth as much as money getting established. So we have three years to go. David, can we make it at the rate we're losing money," she asked, looking at David.

David reached over and put his hand over Musee's. "We're blessed. As we were just saying, the agri and bakery businesses are smoking. The farm stand is picking up volume. We have as much time as we need to get GLF established. What I'm confident about is that you three make a strong team and will find the right formula for success."

"Musee, don't you still have your customer list from Raksin's?" Sam asked.

"Sure, a third of them are GLF customers now."

Charlotte looked at Sam. "Sam, of the four categories in GLF, which have lower profit margins, and which have the highest?"

"The skirt/pants category turns the least profit; next are the jacket styles. The most profitable line is accessories, and second is blouses."

Charlotte turned to Musee and said, "Okay, Musee, what about trying two new approaches. First, every name on your Raksin's list, those who have found us and those who haven't, why don't we give them an incentive: If they buy a jacket and a blouse, we'll give them pants or a skirt for free. When they call in, the style consultant on the phone can suggest accessories for them to buy. Using the new computer imaging so they can see the outfit and how the accessory makes it 'pop' should seal the sale. We can reduce our non-LinkedIn ad budget to cover a lot of the give-away costs. Second, let's select some bloggers and podcaster women who have a high profile with professional women's issues and reward them for their professionalism with an entire outfit from GLF, the clothier of professional women."

Sam looked around the table. "While we're brainstorming, I have an idea that's been rattling around in my brain. It's not unusual for somebody to have a store or company suggest to their significant other what they might want for Christmas or a birthday. Let's suggest to our customers and all new customers that, if we have their birthday and the contact for their spouse or special friend, we'll alert them about that special item the customer would want." With a grin, he added, "Call it the 'Eddie the Elf' program."

The four burst out laughing. "From the mouths of babes...." Musee said, "come brilliant ideas. I could write a personal note to each person, telling them how important they are to the cause of professionalism in the workplace. We can get our publicist to develop stories unique to the specific towns where they're located for insertion into the local print and broadcast media."

"Outstanding ideas, Charlotte and Sam."

# Epilogue

"Granny Charlotte, why do we all go to Uncle David and Aunt Musee's for dinner on Saturday night?" three-year-old Mary asked.

"A long time ago, when your Uncle David joined your great great granddaddy and me in our business, the three of us started a tradition of having a meal together at the end of the week to discuss the business and anything else we thought was interesting."

"And that's my great granddaddy across the gravel road?"

"He's your great great—two greats—granddaddy. He and Granny Mary started all of what we have around us, and your Uncle David, Aunt Musee, Granddaddy Sam, and I built it into what we have now. One day, you might live in this house with your mommy and daddy when Uncle David, Aunt Musee, Granddaddy Sam, and I are across the gravel road. Then you can come talk to me like I do with Granddaddy Dex and Granny Mary, the person you're named after."

"Please don't go anywhere, Granny. I still need to talk to you now."

# Book Club Questions

1. David's world completely collapsed in a week. Do you know someone who has experienced a sudden negative event that irrevocably changed their life? How do you think such a situation should be handled?

2. David believed he needed the right time and atmosphere in which to tell Meg of his firing. Should he have told her right away? Would it have made a difference in her reaction?

3. David's life, from his teen years until Fil's death, was influenced by a mentor. Was someone in your life a mentor or guardian angel to you? What was their impact, and was it lasting?

4. Meg took David's firing as a threat to her future. Was she justified in taking that position? Were there other influences? Do you think many marriages are fragile?

5. Mary and Dex were devastated by what happened to their daughter. Is it possible to justify their decision to shelter Charlie (Charlotte) from the real world? Was there another alternative?

6. Dex overpaid David one time early in their relationship. Do

you think he did so deliberately as a test of David's honesty?

7.  David taught Charlie (Charlotte) the Features, Advantages, and Benefit method of selling. Have you ever heard of the FAB method? Does it make sense to you?

8.   Musee worked diligently to be the best department manager at Raksin's. When the merchandise manager's job became available, it went to the store owner's niece instead of to Musee. Did Musee handle her work disappointment correctly? Would you have done it differently?

9.  Dex made David an offer to join Calumet Farms and learn the business. What do you think was the primary reason David took the offer? Given what he knew at the time the offer was made, would you have taken it?

10. Disappointed about not hearing from David after he said he would call, Musee was confronted with an opportunity to meet and date a successful, good-looking guy who could possibly enhance her career path. Did she make the right decision to cancel the dinner with Jack Ballentine and the CEO of his company?

11. Tim Roy, one of the best farmers at Calumet, wanted to leave the partnership. Do you think David's approach to handling Tim Roy was correct? Would you have handled it differently?

12. Sherm and Meg don't seem to have the same focus. Do you think they will stay together? How would you handle the relationship if you were Meg?

13. Dex never told David he was dying until it became obvious. Do you think Dex handled his physical crisis correctly? Why?

# Acknowledgments

I should start by thanking the vendors and management of the Union Square Green Market. If you've never been, it is worth visiting the next time you are in New York. Bring money, the products sold are great. There are some B/W photos of this market on my website www. uniquereads.com. See for yourself this interesting happening every Monday, Wednesday, Friday, and Saturday.

Developmental editing (Scribendi.com) and proof reading (Proofreaders.com) were handled by two fine services. Any mistakes still in the manuscript are mine.

Glen Edelstein of hudsonvalleybookdesign.com masterfully developed the cover and interior design of the book.

Sheree Adams, my assistant for all digital things, answered my frantic requests with calm professional retrieval of what I needed.

This is a work of fiction. Elio's is a real restaurant that is superb. If you're in New York, you should make a point of going there. It's on Second Avenue between 84th and 85th.

The scenes described on the High Line were real back before the developers and tourists changed that wonderful place. Actually, that's the point about New York. The city constantly changes, and mostly that's a good thing.

Finally, Judy, my wife, muse, motivator, and best critic reads drafts, discusses clarity, and overall keeps me on course to finish my projects. Life would be empty without her.